SUNDAY NIGHT I stared at myself in the mirror. The transformation was amazing. A little concealer under the eyes, Jolie's favorite berry stain on my cheeks, golden highlights around my face, compliments of Trent, and a tiny bit of cleavage. I looked like a new version of myself. A happier, prettier, more confident version. Maybe I no longer had to be the orphaned girl that everyone pitied, the zombie girl whose face was splashed across the covers of *People* and the regional papers because her mother left her a mysterious apology. Maybe this was my chance to try on a new life.

lipstick
apology

lipstick

JENNIFER JABALEY

apology

razOr
bill

Lipstick Apology

RAZORBILL

Published by the Penguin Group
Penguin Young Readers Group
345 Hudson Street, New York, New York 10014, U.S.A.
Penguin Group (USA) Inc., 375 Hudson Street, New York, New York 10014, U.S.A.
Penguin Group (Canada), 90 Eglinton Avenue East, Suite 700, Toronto, Ontario,
Canada M4P 2Y3 (a division of Pearson Penguin Canada Inc.)
Penguin Books Ltd, 80 Strand, London WC2R 0RL, England
Penguin Ireland, 25 St Stephen's Green, Dublin 2, Ireland (a division of Penguin Books Ltd)
Penguin Group (Australia), 250 Camberwell Road, Camberwell, Victoria 3124, Australia
(a division of Pearson Australia Group Pty Ltd)
Penguin Books India Pvt Ltd, 11 Community Centre, Panchsheel Park, New Delhi – 110 017, India
Penguin Group (NZ), 67 Apollo Drive, Rosedale, North Shore 0632, New Zealand
(a division of Pearson New Zealand Ltd.)

Penguin Books (South Africa) (Pty) Ltd, 24 Sturdee Avenue, Rosebank, Johannesburg 2196,
South Africa

Penguin Books Ltd, Registered Offices: 80 Strand, London WC2R 0RL, England

10 9 8 7 6 5 4

Library of Congress Cataloging-in-Publication Data

Jabaley, Jennifer.
Lipstick apology / by Jennifer Jabaley.
p. cm.

Summary: After her parents' sudden death, sixteen-year-old Emily leaves Pennsylvania for her
aunt's New York City apartment, private school, and disconcerting new relationships, all the while
puzzling over her mother's mysterious apology to her.

ISBN: 9781595142313
[1. Grief—Fiction. 2. Moving, Household—Fiction. 3. Aunts—Fiction. 4. Dating (Social customs)—
Fiction. 5. Schools—Fiction. 6. Orphans—Fiction. 7. New York (N.Y.)—Fiction. I. Title

PZ7.J127 Lip 2009
[Fic] 22
2008039716
Printed in the United States of America

FOR MY FAMILY

prologue

STEVE MCCAFFITY JUST UNDRESSED ME with his eyes.

Okay, maybe I'm still clothed, but we definitely made eye contact. Well, actually, he might have only glanced at the tiny chocolate stain on my V-neck—so it *was* noticeable.

I decided to level with myself. It was actually quite possible that Steve McCaffity didn't even know that I existed.

I stared at him, lounging on my living room couch in a T-shirt that revealed his impressive biceps, looking like he owned the place. I stood in the doorway trying to muster the courage to approach the guy who hadn't yet realized that we were destined to be together. I glanced back at my best friend, Georgia, who was standing in the kitchen, monitoring the party activity. A couple of hours ago Georgia had decided we should shut off the overheads and drape Christmas lights from the cabinets for a better atmosphere. I'd been skeptical—Christmas lights in early June? Wasn't this supposed to be a summer-themed party since the school year had just ended?

Either way, the red and green flickering lights danced on

the faces of people I barely knew. I felt a twinge of guilt letting the popular crowd invade our kitchen—my mom's favorite room—just to have a chance to talk to Steve.

Georgia raised her eyebrows at me, her dark curly ponytail bobbing. *Emily*, she mouthed, *go talk to him!*

I shook my head and scampered back toward her. "He doesn't even know my name."

"Wimp," Georgia said. "Look at him, he's watching you!" She gestured across the crowd toward Steve. Jeez, there were like fifty kids in my living room, and the party had only gotten started an hour ago! Just went to show how little else was going on in our quaint Pennsylvania suburb on a warm night in June. I saw Steve, still on the couch. He *was* looking at me, but his face was all scrunched up.

"He's just trying to figure out how he knows you," Georgia said in an encouraging voice as she nudged me forward. "This is just like on *Rhapsody in Rio* when Gabriela asked Fernando for a new mop and Fernando scrunched up his face and asked, *Who are you, you gorgeous thing?* And Gabriela said, *I'm your maid. I've worked here every day for a year.* And Fernando said, *How have I failed to notice this creature of beauty until now?* And they fell madly in love."

One thing about Georgia: she was addicted to soaps, psychics, and all things melodramatic.

Steve's face *was* all twisted, and I thought just maybe there was a chance he was finally seeing me and opening his heart to the possibilities. But then he pulled a lime wedge out of his mouth and tossed it on the floor. I stared down at the lime. *How could he do that in my home?* I surveyed the room: the soft, tan couch with plaid throw pillows, the circular ring on the wooden coffee table where Dad's mug perpetually sat, the sun-distressed leather recliner. To me, all these things signified a home, a place to relax and be myself, but as the ancient wine stain on the rug jumped into focus, I wondered if to others, the room appeared shabby. I suddenly felt uncomfortable in my own house.

When I looked over again, Steve was kissing Lexi Bollins—like, on the mouth. *This is so typical of my life,* I thought. *Things go from bad to worse.*

I tore through the kitchen, grabbed a box of donuts, and bolted to the solitude of our basement. I sat on Mom's stool and stared at her oil painting of our huge, backyard weeping willow tree. Touching the drying paint, I had an overwhelming urge to call my parents. Not to confess about the party, but just to hear their voices. I reached for my cell phone, then remembered my cotton skirt didn't have pockets. Oh, well, they were probably still in flight, hovering somewhere over the West Coast.

"Oh my God! Release your grip on the Entemann's!" Georgia yelled as she came downstairs. "No time to sulk!"

"Do you ever feel like you just fade into the background?" I asked, taking another bite of the chocolate donut. "And it's not just Steve—nobody ever notices me." I pointed upstairs. "They don't even know whose house they're in."

Georgia sighed and sat on a stack of art books. "You just need to take more chances—be a little more visible."

"But how?"

"How?" she asked more to herself. "I know! I'll call Sister Ginger!" She patted the butt of her tight jeans, then gave up and said, "Give me your cell."

I shook my head. "It's upstairs charging. But I'm not taking advice from a crazy psychic."

Georgia disappeared upstairs. I looked over at a water-color portrait Mom had painted of me. Even with her artistic ability I still looked bland. I had apple cheeks that my mom swore were high cheekbones but really just made my face look chubby. A round face on a toothpick body. I had blond hair, but not blond enough. I had blue eyes, but not blue enough. It was like I needed one more stroke of color.

"Okay," Georgia said, coming back downstairs. "The good news is it was *not* an international call." She held out the house cordless phone. "Riley Goodwin used your landline to call her boyfriend." She looked down at the screen. "Seventy-two minutes ago. It's a 404 area code. Any guesses?" She shrugged, then dialed a number by heart. "Yes, Sister Ginger?"

I heard Georgia say my name and birthday as I reached out and touched Mom's paintbrush, still coated with phthalo green paint.

Georgia grabbed my arm, her eyebrows raised to her hairline. "Sister Ginger says tonight you will be noticed in a BIG WAY." She tossed the phone to the ground.

"I'm not listening to that crazy psychic. Last time you wound up with orange hair!"

Georgia examined a strand of her dark curls. "Come on, be adventurous," she begged.

My stomach clenched at the thought. I nervously reached up to adjust my glasses. Georgia motioned to my face. "Emily, stop. You're wearing your contacts."

"Right," I said, taking my index finger off the bridge of my nose. Whenever I was nervous, my finger reflexively went to the spot where it had pushed sliding glasses back into place for eight years—that was half my life! It was a hard habit to break. "Okay," I said, taking a deep breath. "Let's go get noticed."

Back in the living room, Tanner Montgomery switched off my CD and started hooking up his own iPod to the computer. Immediately loud bass shook the floors and rattled the family photo frames on the mantel.

I tried to pretend I recognized the song and yelled, "Good choice!" But no one heard me. I had a better idea.

"What are you doing?" Georgia was frantic.

"I'm going to dance on the counter. Get noticed," I explained as I pulled myself onto its cool surface.

"I *do not* think that's what Sister Ginger had in mind!" Georgia put her hands on her hips and huffed. "Well, at least take your shoes off; your mom will notice scuff marks!"

I leaned down toward her. "I'm not taking my shoes off and displaying my abnormalities to the whole school!"

She shook her head disapprovingly. "God, you're so obsessed with your toes!"

"What's wrong with your toes?" a girl from my gym class asked while pulling herself onto the kitchen counter to join me.

"Her second toe curls over the third," Georgia said, demonstrating with her fingers.

"Gross," gym girl screamed.

"Georgia!" I exploded.

Just then the front door swung open and two shaky Jimmy Choos stepped onto the floor. My aunt Jolie took a couple more steps into the foyer and stood there frozen. Her makeup was smudged and her hair winged back behind her as if blowing in an unseen wind.

"Jolie?" I asked, stunned. Why was Aunt Jolie here?

Aunt Jolie was a celebrity makeup artist. She was always polished to perfection. Always.

Jolie lived in Manhattan. She wouldn't make the two-hour trip unless my parents asked her to check up on me while they were away. And they'd only left for San Francisco this afternoon!

Jolie weaved her way through the maze of people toward the kitchen, a weird, somewhat dazed look in her clear green eyes.

I eased myself off the counter. "What are you doing here, Jolie? How did you get here?"

"I borrowed Trent's car," Jolie said, speaking of her business partner and hairstylist to the stars, Trent Mason. She ran her fingers through her knotty blond hair. "It's a convertible. I couldn't figure out how to get the, uh." She stared at me for a second. "The, uh. The top up."

Something was seriously wrong with this picture. "Um, did Mom ask you to check up on me, because that's supremely lame."

"Your mom didn't ask me to come," Jolie said, her face still expressionless. "I've been trying to call you."

A breeze blew through the open door and I got goose bumps on my arms.

"I was in a cab," Jolie continued. Was she blinking back tears? "And I saw the news." She looked up at the five girls dancing on the counter as if suddenly noticing the ongoing party. "Oh my God," she whispered. "You don't know."

"What? What don't I know?" My back stiffened.

Jolie turned toward Georgia. "You've got ten minutes to get everyone out of this house."

Georgia's eyes bulged. She scrambled into the living room.

Without another word, Jolie took my hand and pulled me up the stairs away from the chaos. She opened my bedroom door and motioned for me to sit on the bed.

"What is going on?" I asked, releasing my hand from her grip.

"Emily." Her voice shook. "Emily, I. They. The news. Your parents. I saw." She gulped, tears sliding down her face. "I'm so sorry, baby. I'm so sorry."

I was in a cab and I saw the news. Your parents. Her words didn't make any sense, but they made my spine tingle and my mouth go dry. I grabbed the remote control off the nightstand, my heart pounding wildly in my chest. The back of my neck felt liquid-hot. I clicked the power button and found a news channel, my fingers fumbling on the remote. And there, scrawling across the bottom of the TV screen in ticker tape, was the answer. The words Jolie couldn't say.

SkyAmerica Flight #565 bound for San Francisco has crashed into a field in Provo, Utah. The jet, transporting 245 passengers, left Philadelphia airport at 5:00 p.m. earlier today. It appears the pilot was attempting an emergency landing at the Provo Municipal Airport when things went awry. The cause of the crash, at this time, is unknown. Emergency medical help and the local police force are at the scene of the crash. At this time, no survivors have been found.

I stood there, remote in my hand, and stared at the screen. *No survivors have been found.*

I grabbed my cell phone off the charger. Twenty-six missed calls. I scrolled through, seeing unrecognizable numbers, my stomach clenching as I saw on the caller ID list *Provo, UT.*

Nothing made sense. I dropped the cell phone on the floor somewhere and then sank down to the carpet, resting my head against the yellow bedspread. Jolie sat next to me, wrapping her arm around my waist as the barrage of news stories flashed endlessly on the screen.

The house quieted and eventually, the noise from the street quieted, leaving just the sound of the cherry blossom branches tapping against my window screen in the warm June breeze. I watched the red electric numbers slowly change on my alarm clock from 10:35 p.m. up and up to 11:43 p..m, just me and Jolie sitting on my bedroom floor, holding each other, silently staring at the TV. When my lids got heavy, I let them fall, sinking into a restless sleep.

A cramp in my neck woke me several hours later. Jolie was still pressed up against my shoulder, her head leaning on the edge of the bed, but her eyes were red-rimmed and open. The TV was still on. We stared at each other, uncertain what to do. Should I get up and take a shower? Should Jolie make some phone calls? Should we go downstairs and eat breakfast? But neither of us moved. Suddenly, the news anchor's voice seemed to rise an octave, catching our attention.

Who is Emily? she asked. Words scrolled across the top of the screen in bold capital letters: WHO IS EMILY?

My mouth was parched. My throat ached with an intense pain I'd never felt before.

The camera zoomed in on the news anchor. She was standing next to a fireman who was holding a large mangled piece of plastic in his hands.

We're here among the wreckage from Flight 565, which made a crash landing earlier this evening. As the emergency medical help searched for any survivors and crews combed the rubble for the black box, there's been an interesting find . . . The camera zoomed in on the plastic slab in the fireman's char-covered hands.

I breathed in, out, in again. This was not happening. I saw coral lipstick. God-awful, unforgettable, coral lipstick. We begged my mother to stop wearing that lipstick.

This is a tray table, the news anchor explained. *Written across this tray table in what appears to be lipstick is the desperate plea of a passenger who perhaps knew she would not make it off this flight . . .*

The camera zoomed in even closer on the coral lipstick writing. It was smudged, but, unbelievably, the message was still clear. It read: EMILY PLEASE FORGIVE ME.

chapter one

"EMILY, WE'RE HERE!"

"You're sitting there like a human-size packet of Sweet'n Low." I stared at Jolie as she parked the Lexus.

She propped her Versace sunglasses on top of her blond hair and looked at me, a horrible fake smile plastered on her face. "What, babe?"

I gestured to her neatly pressed white pants and bubble-gum-colored silk halter. "You're all pink and artificially sweet."

Her smile faltered. "I'm just trying to make this easier on you."

"Don't bother." I rebuckled my seat belt. "I'm not going in there." I nodded toward the sixteen-story glass and aluminum tower across the street. The early September sun bounced off the reflective building, shining more light than I had seen all summer. Well, except for the paparazzi flashbulbs that captured my grief-stricken hideousness and shared it with the tabloid reading world.

I shook my head and pushed my sunglasses closer to my eyes. "I can't do this. I can't go in there." I gestured with my chin across the street toward the entrance to her apartment. "Where's the front lawn? The driveway? That thing doesn't even have a stoop. It just has . . . rotating doors. And a doorman!" I reached over and tried to restart the car, but Jolie grabbed my hand.

"I can't live in *New York City*." I concentrated on not hyper-ventilating. "I need to go back to Pennsylvania, where things are normal. People live in houses with NORMAL DOORS! What do you say we just hook a U-ie and head back home. I need to go home."

"Honey," Jolie said in that sugary voice again. "This *is* your home now."

I looked at the contemporary building with its hard edges. It was even more formal than my father's engineering firm in Philadelphia. Just behind us a parking spot feud was erupting between a Mercedes and an Escalade. Across the busy street, bikers sped along a harsh, wide river, the Hudson.

"Can't you just let me finish high school with Georgia in Pennsylvania?" I begged, knowing I'd be terrified to enter those halls again, but anything seemed better than this loud, unfa-miliar place. "It's only a couple years before I go off to college. I need her. We were going to be on the prom committee this year," I said, my voice breaking slightly. I knew it sounded stupid, that I was rambling.

Jolie gripped the steering wheel. "My job is here, Emily. My apartment is here. My life is here."

I wanted to say, *What about my life?* But that was the point, wasn't it. I didn't have a life anymore. Life as I had always known it was over.

I was silent as we retrieved our bags from the trunk.

We walked through the cold lobby and onto an elevator, which dinged several times, then spit us back out. Jolie walked at lightning speed down a long, doorless and windowless corridor and swung open the door at its end. "Welcome home," she said.

I remembered my mom telling me that Jolie's apartment was amazing. Her makeup line, Jolie Jane Cosmetics, had really taken off, especially amongst the celebrities, allowing Jolie to live like her pampered clientele. As I stared into the immense apartment, I thought, *Man, she must sell a lot of lipstick.*

The living room had soaring ceilings and an entire glass wall of windows that framed the Hudson River. A white leather couch and chair surrounded a plasma TV. There was a scattering of photographs: Jolie and a man standing in front of the Eiffel Tower. Jolie and a different man skiing. Jolie and a group of women singing into a microphone, cocktail glasses in their hands. Stacks of fashion and celebrity magazines filled baskets next to the fireplace, and a few wilting plants hung near the windows.

I followed Jolie down a hallway as she rambled about asking Trent to fix the bedroom for me. She opened the door and sighed.

"Jeez," Jolie said, looking at the pink and purple bedspread covered with dragonflies and ladybugs. "Trent is obviously under the impression that you're nine years old."

The room was long and rectangular with a cold, dark wood floor and wall panels of elaborate moldings. The room was even nicer than the one in the Hilton we'd stayed at two summers ago. I dropped my duffel bag by the bed.

"Jolie," I said, recognizing the cream upholstered headboard from photos, "is this *your* bedroom?"

"Nah," she said, "it's your room now. I had Trent move my stuff into the office."

My throat constricted. "You didn't have to do that."

She ignored me. "Don't worry." She tapped the bedspread. "This pink nightmare will be gone by tomorrow."

We heard a quick knock at the front door followed by shuffling feet.

I had seen pictures of Jolie's best friend, Trent, and had heard countless stories of his escapades, but I could honestly say that nothing prepared me for our first actual encounter. He was tall and sculpted, dressed head to toe in black, with spiky hair and kind, gray eyes. He paused at the bedroom door, and for a second, pain—or maybe pity—flickered over his face like a shadow when he looked at me. Then his eyes slowly moved upward and he whispered, "Virgin." He inched toward me, hands outstretched, aimed at my head. "Vir-gin."

Jolie smacked him on the arm. "Leave her alone!"

Oh my God. My face flamed with humiliation.

"Never processed." He inched closer. "Never colored."

Huh?

He inched closer. "Never flat-ironed. Oh my God, do you not even blow-dry?" His voice was shrill.

He was about to caress my head when Jolie pushed him

away. "Don't molest my niece's hair!" She turned to me. "Ignore him; he's over-caffeinated."

Trent backed away, mocked insult, and sat down on the bed. "It's just so rare. You practically have to find an infant to get virgin hair around here."

Jolie rolled her eyes. "Emily, this nutcase is Trent. Unfortunately, you'll be seeing a lot of him."

Trent stared at me again with his warm, gray eyes and shook his head as he pushed my half grown-out bangs out of my face. "Listen, honey. Trent doesn't do trauma. Trend doesn't do *sad*. Trent does hair. So when you need me," he announced, standing up, "you'll tell me, right, Goldilocks?"

Jolie sighed. "Okay, that's enough out of you. Let's let Emily unpack and relax."

They walked out. And that, right there, summed up the vast difference between Jolie and my mother. My mother would never have left me alone.

THE ROOM LOOKED SO BARREN. There were no knick-knacks or photos on top of the dresser. The bookshelves just had a few artfully placed faux books with names of the classics printed on the front. The walls were empty. At first I thought Trent might have taken down decorations to allow me to put up my own things, but I didn't see any nail holes. I sat on the rectangular Persian rug and unzipped my duffel bag. It felt odd, like I was unpacking at a hotel. I glanced up at the vast beige walls and hoped that when the movers brought the rest of my things, it would feel more like home.

A few minutes later I heard laughter and followed the

voices down the hall. The door was open, so I peered in. This room was slightly smaller than my bedroom but much more cluttered. A glass-shelved rolling cart was filled with black jars emblazed with a gold *JJ* logo. There was a full-length framed mirror in the corner. Atop a kidney-shaped desk was a pile of mail. Propped up behind the stack of envelopes was a document with a boldfaced heading that read: LEGAL GUARDIANSHIP. In all the empty slots my full name had been typed.

Jolie and Trent were sitting on a small twin bed. They looked up at me.

"Jolie, seriously, I don't need the room with the big bed. I can sleep in here," I said.

"The sad truth is," Trent said, "your auntie, here, doesn't need the big bed either. As of late, her makeup brushes get more action than she does, if you get my drift."

Eeeewww. I wanted to plug my ears. I knew Jolie's history was what my mom called serial dating. But I hadn't heard of any love interests since her arrival in Pennsylvania three months ago.

"Trent." Jolie sounded exasperated. "Can we please not analyze my life right now?"

Trent looked at me and mouthed, *Touchy!* He got up and we followed him into the living room. The setting sun was casting a soft spotlight through the floor-to-ceiling windows. Maybe it was the three weeks of reporters camped out back in Pennsylvania, clicking cameras through our windows, but suddenly I felt like I was standing in a glass box—exposed to the world.

"So," I said. "You don't have any blinds?"

"Blinds?" Trent said like one would say *cancer* or *cellulite.* "On these windows?"

Jolie looked at me, her eyes reading my unease. She walked over to the wall, pressed a button, and shades moved down, hiding the wall of glass.

"I'm starving," Trent said, walking into the enormous L-shaped kitchen. "Look at these sparkling black countertops," Trent said to me. "So pristine. And that's not a reflection of your aunt's excellent housekeeping skills. No, no, it's due to the fact that the only thing that's ever been made in here is a small grease fire. And mad passionate love, maybe, if the mood was right."

"TRENT!" Jolie yelled.

"Sorry." Trent giggled. "Basically her kitchen is more like a closet for takeout menus and a coffeepot."

"I can cook," Jolie said, a little too defensively, and then started to laugh because we all knew that was untrue. "Well, I definitely want to learn. But for tonight, how's Chinese?"

My eyes drifted to the corner of the kitchen. There was a familiar cotton apron hanging from a hook on the wall. I walked toward it confirming my suspicion. It was my mother's. It was a retro-style apron that tied around the waist and had a border of white lace. I remembered the Christmas that Mom hinted she wanted that apron by leaving the catalog propped open for weeks. But Dad missed the hint and bought her a pearl necklace instead. Mom cried Christmas morning and my dad and I laughed that any woman would prefer an apron over pearls.

Needless to say, Dad ordered the apron the next day. And now, for some reason, it was hanging in Jolie's kitchen.

Jolie read my mind. "Your mom gave me this apron after last year's Fourth of July barbecue. Remember when everyone was teasing me because I put heavy cream in the French onion dip instead of *sour cream*?"

"Good Lord," Trent mocked.

"Well, afterward your mom handed me her apron and said maybe it would bring me luck in the kitchen." Jolie gazed at the silver reflections from the refrigerator.

I reached out and touched the scratchy fabric of the apron, running my finger over a stain near the bottom. I suddenly needed to be alone. I excused myself and raced down the long corridor to my new bedroom. I braced myself against the windowpane and looked out at the million-dollar view—the maze of streets, the flutter of activity, and the vast waters of the Hudson River. Staring at the ripple of waves made me miss the serene, quiet Delaware River. Just a few miles from my old home a rickety, one-lane bridge marked where Washington had crossed the Delaware. The grassy banks with the trees arching over the water right near the bridge had always been my own private haven. But now this new river stretched on for miles, bordered not by trees but tall, gray buildings. And with its raging currents splashing below me, echoing my racing mind, it offered me no peace.

Where am I? I thought. *How did I get here?* For the last three months I sat on our tan couch in a hazy blur watching *E! True Hollywood Story*. Georgia had hovered over me with talk of Ouija board and John Edward's *Crossing Over* marathons as options to contact my mother and crack the code of her mystery apology. She'd sit next to me—for hours at a time—and rattle off plans: plans for the prom committee, for which colleges we'd apply to, where to go back-to-school shopping. She'd tried to keep me updated on the gossip about our other friends from school, but it had been hard to focus on any of that. The world seemed so fuzzy. She'd tried to get me to put on a bathing suit and leave the house, even buying me a pair of funky sandals that hid my toes. But when I refused, she finally went on without me. It was like the world for everyone else was still turning, but for me, it had stopped.

Jolie had carted me off to shrink appointments and bought me books about grief. But all the voodoo and psychobabble in the world couldn't help me understand my mother's final words. Those words raced through my head for three months. Three endless summer months. And then we left. I was dragged from the only home I knew with no parents and no answers. And I still didn't know what she meant.

I leaned my head against the enormous cold windowpane and in the distance the Hudson flowed on, utterly indifferent.

chapter two

"EMILY," JOLIE SAID. "I think school will be good for you, and you've already missed the first week."

"Can't I just have a few more weeks to adjust? This is a big city..."

"Well, you wouldn't know," Jolie said, pulling the cashmere afghan off my legs. "You haven't left the apartment."

"We've only been here for a few days!" I grabbed the cover back.

Jolie sat down on the edge of the shiny glass coffee table. "Look, we're not doing this again. This hermit thing. You need to get out. Being back in school, around kids your own age, will help you..." She looked at the ceiling as if struggling to pick her words. "Help you move on. Obviously we need to try something different—the grief counselors were no help."

"They were all wack jobs," I said.

"They were *all* wack jobs?" Jolie challenged me.

"Uh, YEAH. Dr. Manchester wore a *bow tie* and kept pushing freaky back-to-nature retreats. Dr. Rogers was a Jimmy Buffett wannabe sailor who insisted on calling his boat *his little dinghy*. Like, *Sometimes the water splashes my little dinghy.* And Dr. Frix was totally sports-obsessed. He needs to be a coach, not a shrink. If I had to hear, *Tackle the issue,* or, *Rise to the challenge,* one more time, I'd scream. It's all just a big waste of time and money."

Jolie threw her hands up in the air. "Okay, no more shrinks, no more counselors. But you *have* to go to school." She crossed her legs. "I was thinking it's been a while since you've . . . *cleaned up*, so I've planned a weekend of fun and pampering. A real makeover to get you ready for your new school."

"You think it'll take a whole weekend to make me over? Do I really look that bad?" I was trying to be funny, but Jolie's lips puckered up like she was trying not to comment.

"Okay," I mumbled. "Make me presentable for school on Monday." What did it matter, anyway?

THE NEXT MORNING Jolie stood in my bedroom doorway with her hands on her tiny hips, looking tan and cheerful. "Today's going to be so much fun!" She beamed. "First we're going to Cornelia Day Spa for some much-needed pampering. I booked us this new ninety-minute algae body treatment that everyone keeps raving about."

"Ninety minutes? Doesn't that seem a bit . . . excessive?"

"Trust me. By the time we walk out of there, we'll be as smooth as a baby's butt." She giggled and took a sip of her Starbucks. I wondered how long she'd been up. "Then I thought we'd finish up with some quick pedicures."

Pedicures?? As in someone touching my crooked toes?? I started to sweat.

"After the spa, we're going bra and underwear shopping!" She said this as if I just won a fabulous game show grand prize.

"Okay!" I faked enthusiasm. This was going to be a total disaster.

Jolie started for the hall, then spun around. "Oh! And I thought tomorrow I could help you with some makeup tricks and Trent could give you highlights. If you want them, I mean."

I looked down at the ends of my dark blond hair. "Yeah, sure."

"Awesome! We'll leave in ten minutes. Just wear spa attire." She left.

I frantically dialed Georgia. "She's making me display my deformed feet for the world to mock me!"

"Huh?"

"PEDICURES! She won't let me back out. She called me a HERMIT!"

"Okay, relax," Georgia said. "First of all, they always shove this Styrofoam contraption between your toes, which will make them look less crooked. It's not so bad. Think of Josie Leonard." Josie Leonard was a girl in our class with a nub for her left index finger—some accident with a sharp knife. "Josie came back from camp with a smoking hot boyfriend—I saw them at the Coldstone Creamery on Thursday. If he could overlook the nubby finger, a random pedicurist can definitely ignore your weird toes."

I hung up feeling slightly less panicked and wondered exactly what *spa attire* meant. I decided on a pair of faded black yoga pants and a red T-shirt. I grabbed my Nikes and walked into the living room. Jolie was sitting on the floor tying her shoes. She was dressed in low-rider navy spandex pants and a fitted striped tank top that flaunted her toned arms. She looked straight out of an American Apparel ad.

Jolie grabbed her Starbucks cup and we walked into the hall. As we rode the elevator down, I stared at my ragged reflection in the mirrored doors. My long hair, which usually lightened in the summer, was dull and shapeless. My skin was ashy pale and my eyes looked almost black in the fluorescent light. I looked like a horror movie version of myself. I tucked some flyaway hairs behind my ear and convinced myself I could survive this day. It's not like Jolie knew that I would much prefer a chick flick and nachos. Mom would know. Georgia would know. I needed to find a way to make things normal again. But how?

We walked a few blocks down tree-lined Perry Street, then turned onto Bleecker Street. The sidewalks were filled with Saturday morning shoppers carrying sleek handbags with impressive logos. The storefronts had large, glass display windows and signs hanging from wrought iron posts. Jolie stopped in front of Cynthia Rowley and gazed at the faceless mannequin sporting a flirty blue dress with metallic T-strap heels. She started walking again, her head craned toward a boutique shoe store display of towering strappy heels.

"A lot of people assume I'm a Park Avenue kind of girl," Jolie said, tossing her coffee cup in the trash. *"An uptown girl,"* she sang. "But I love the West Village. It's the perfect escape from the flash and glitz." She gestured toward the boutiques. "Everything is nicely balanced here—not so . . . fantastical. I feel like I belong. And I know you will too."

We stopped at a light and I nodded absently while trying to decipher if the price tag on the cotton kimono pajamas in the children's store window really did say $160.

"Now when you go to school," Jolie continued, "you'll continue for another few blocks, then turn left at the pizza place."

I knew full well that I could never retrace our path without a map. "Oh, sure." I faked confidence as we crossed a cobblestone square. We made a few more turns and arrived at the spa.

"Welcome," a breathy woman dressed in white purred from behind a glass desk. "Welcome to our center for beauty synergy." She smiled at Jolie. "Ah. Miss Jane, nice to see you again. I see you've scheduled two body harmonies and two signature pedicures. Wonderful selections." She tapped on the keyboard, then peered over her rhinestone glasses. "With tax that brings your total to seven oh-five."

Seven hundred and five . . . DOLLARS?

Without a note of hesitation, Jolie opened her wallet and slapped a platinum credit card on the desk.

I remembered a few years ago when Mom decided to throw a surprise birthday party for Dad. She went all out buying thick slabs of filet mignon, imported cheeses, and vintage wines. When the bills came in, Dad bellowed, *Six hundred dollars at Costco? What? Did they slaughter and butcher the cows while you waited? You must REALLY love me,* he'd joked, his anger passing over as he pulled my mom into a big embrace. And that was six hundred dollars—and it fed a whole party. I wondered what Dad would think about Jolie spending seven hundred and five dollars to *primp before school?*

"Thank you, Miss Jane," the breathy lady said. "You both

may proceed to the women's locker room, where your aestheticians will greet you and discuss your skin care goals."

Goals? How about a goal of getting out of here?

We walked into the locker room and were greeted by two women identically dressed in white button-down smocks. A petite woman took my elbow and steered me toward a bench at the far end of the room. Jolie and a redhead disappeared around a hall lined with trickling fountains, giggling and talking about some guy named Sven.

My heart started to flutter. Where was Jolie going? I couldn't do this alone. All this spa stuff was foreign to me. The closest I'd ever come to a spa was when Coach Callihan massaged a charley horse in my calf during tennis semifinals last year.

"My name is Ming," the woman said. She reached over, opened a locker, and placed its contents on the bench in front of me. "We provide robes, slippers, and wraps. Please undress and I'll return momentarily to begin your procedures."

Procedures? Why did this sound like I was getting a gallbladder removal or something equally horrific? I stared at the bundle of garments and my head started to spin. *Do I wear the robe or the wrap? Or somehow both? What am I doing here? I don't belong at this fancy place in the middle of this city with its billions of people. I just want to go back to Pennsylvania, curl up on the couch, and watch the E! channel for another three months.* I wasn't ready for this. I wasn't ready for anything. Not for school, not for spas—nothing.

Aside from the drive to New York, I hadn't been *outside*. At all. Not since the day after the accident, when I ingested six double-chocolate donuts, propelled myself off the sofa, and decided to confront the paparazzi. I had walked out my front door, my hair sticking up in points like the Statue of Liberty, smears of chocolate icing on my lips. Squinting into the flashing cameras, I told the reporters, "My mother's last words are a mystery to me."

Three days later, Georgia had bounded through the door with a copy of *People*. I was on the cover clad in my heart-pattern pajamas, with no bra on (who knew an A cup could sag?) and no signs of airbrushing. One look at that sad display and I had buried my head in the pillows and didn't set foot on the front porch again for three months.

How was it that Jolie thought my first venture back into society should be at a fancy spa? There was too much exposure, too much vulnerability.

I was half naked, bent over with my head in my hands when Ming returned to find me in full-on panic mode, taking deep breaths.

I felt her cool fingers on my shoulder and looked up, dazed. Ming's angular face softened. She helped me ease out of my top and wrapped the robe around me. Then, as fast as her kindness came, it was gone and she was back to business. She turned and walked toward the door. She paused and said, "Are you coming?"

After ninety minutes of being poked at, scrubbed, scalded, wrapped, and soaked, Jolie and I were finally reunited in the Pedicure Parlor, where we were seated on an elevated bench.

"Take off your shoes, please," the nail technician said to me.

Jolie plunked her feet into the tiled sink filled with sudsy water.

"Um." I panicked. "My feet are a little . . ."

"We see it all," the technician snapped, and reached for my slippers. In a flash, my feet were plunged into the water. I let the bubble suds foam up and hide my toes.

Jolie looked over at me, her face serious. "You know, after almost two hours of meditation, I've had an epiphany."

Here it comes, I thought. *The sermon about life and death, family and moving on, accepting new roles and new directions . . .* I inhaled slowly.

She began. "I think there comes a time in every woman's life when miniskirts are no longer an option." She pulled her robe up slightly and observed her thighs. "I like my legs. But still, a woman at a certain age can't get away with creeping hemlines."

I looked at her. "Trent?"

She nodded, grinning at me and rolling her eyes. It was possibly the first *real* smile I'd seen on her all summer. "He busted me yesterday for that blue outfit—he told me I was one pin curl away from looking like Blanche from *The Golden Girls*— you know, not dressing age appropriately."

"Blanche is like *double* your age," I said.

"Yeah, but the point is I'm not sixteen anymore."

"Sixteen sucks," I said.

Jolie smirked. "So, have you picked a color yet for your toes? Because the new night neutral from Chanel is really hot right now."

I thought about how Jolie's life revolved around fashion trends and makeup and how she just assumed I would be comfortable with that too. "Okay," I said. "That color is fine."

The technician came back, dried off my feet, and placed them on a towel. *Did she just smirk?* I clenched my fists. She pulled out two pink spongy toe dividers and began to wrestle the contraption between my toes. *She definitely laughed. I will kill Jolie,* I thought. But Jolie was oblivious, reading *Vogue.*

After no success, the technician used scissors to cut off one of the dividers and just let my two toes stay curled into each other. My face was flaming for pretty much the entire procedure.

When our polish was dry, we took a cab uptown. Boutique awnings fluttered along Lexington Avenue. As we pulled up in front of a store with silky nighties hanging on display and I felt the tacky nail polish stick to my socks, I knew this was round two of the day of mortification.

Jolie opened the glass door and a *ding-ding* announced our arrival. A silver-haired woman dressed in a peach suit scuffled over.

"We have an appointment for Emily to be fitted for some bras." Jolie nodded toward me.

Appointment? Who ever heard of making an appointment for bras?

"Well," the peach suit lady said. "I'm your fit special-ist, and," she pointed to a gold-plated name tag, "my name is Emily too." She reached up for the tape measure that hung around her neck and ushered me into a fancy dressing room decked out with velvet chairs and a large framed mirror. Jolie went off to browse.

Emily Too closed the door and turned to me. "So, what did you have in mind, honey?" After a moment of awkward silence, she asked, "Were you looking to . . . enhance?"

I tugged at the front of my red T-shirt, unable to meet her eyes. I could feel the heat rising in my cheeks. "Um, sure," I said, panicking, knowing once she put that tape measure to work, she'd see there wasn't much to work with, let alone enhance.

She gently lifted my arms and expertly wrapped the tape measure around my rib cage, then chest.

"Not much calculation required, ha ha," I said nervously.

The lady winked at me kindly and clicked her tongue. "Be right back, hon."

Moments later she returned with an armload of bras. She arranged them neatly on a rack and said, "Take your time, dear. Call me if you need help."

I selected a bra and against all odds, it did, somehow, defy nature and give me just a smidge of cleavage. I glanced down at the price tag. Not possible. The price of sandblasting your kneecaps was nothing compared to the amazing price of cleavage.

I sat down on the plush velvet armchair, staring at myself in the mirror. Everything was artificial, like I had literally put on someone else's life. But as I sat there wearing nothing but a butter-soft, overpriced yellow bra, the realization dawned on me. This *was* my life now.

There was a knock on my dressing room door. "Em?" Jolie's anxious voice asked from the hall. "Do you need help? Am I supposed to come in?" She tried the locked doorknob without success. Two seconds later, Jolie squatted down and crawled under the mahogany door.

I grabbed my shirt and covered my chest. "Jolie! What are you doing?" I shrieked.

"I don't know!" She put her hands up to her face. "I DON'T KNOW! Do I come in and help you with the bras? Do I give you some privacy? I have no *freaking* clue!" She started running her fingers through her beautiful hair with a manic gesture.

I didn't know what to say, so I sat back down on the oversized chair.

Jolie took out her cell phone and pointed to it. "I just hit my speed dial to ask Jill what to do, then it hits me—SHE'S NOT HERE! I feel like someone just amputated my right arm. Then I think about you, and how she's your mother. Your *mother*. And your *father*—gone." She climbed up into the velvet chair next to me and I awkwardly put my arm around her.

"It'll be okay." I patted her head as she wept softly and wondered why the world felt fuzzy.

An arm reached under the door and extended a box of Kleenex without a word. Jolie reached over and took it.

I'm not sure how long we stayed in that fitting room, but when we finally emerged and made our way to the front desk, the sun was setting, casting long shadows through the front glass windows.

Jolie extended the yellow bra. "We'll take this one." She dabbed at her nose with a crumpled tissue. "Um, you know what? Just give us seven more of the same style in a variety of colors. With matching underwear."

After paying, Jolie hailed a cab and we hopped in, each of us staring out the greasy window into the now-darkening sky.

• • •

SUNDAY NIGHT I stared at myself in the mirror. The transformation was amazing. A little concealer under the eyes, Jolie's
favorite berry stain on my cheeks, golden highlights around my
face, compliments of Trent, and a tiny bit of cleavage. I looked
like a new version of myself. A happier, prettier, more confident version. Maybe I no longer had to be the orphaned girl
that everyone pitied, the zombie girl whose face was splashed
across the covers of *People* and the regional papers because
her mother left her a mysterious apology. Maybe this was my
chance to try on a new life.

chapter three

"I CAN'T GO TO SCHOOL TODAY," I called from the bathroom.

Jolie popped her head in. "Why? You look great. You did your makeup just like I showed you."

I turned my head to the side to give her a view of the festering zit on my chin.

"Oh," Jolie said. "Wait a sec." She returned a moment later with a tube in her hand. She squirted white cream on her finger and started toward my chin.

I pushed her finger away and grabbed the tube from her. "This is hemorrhoid cream!" I yelled.

"Just be still," she said, dabbing it on my enormous zit. "This stuff is amazing. It decreases the swelling and reduces the redness. By the time you get to school, no one will even notice it." She recapped the tube. "I have a team of scientists working on anti-blemish creams and nothing works as well as good old Preparation H."

Jolie smoothed the sleeve of my polo. "What do you need? Pencils? Erasers?"

"It's not first grade, Jolie."

"Right, okay. I'm going to walk with you to school today so you don't get lost."

I imagined that first impression. "No! I mean, no thanks, Jolie. I can figure it out."

"I'm just worried," Jolie said. "The West Village doesn't follow the grid system—it can be humbling even to a seasoned New Yorker."

Grid system? Whatever—I had to do this alone. "I Map-Quested it. I'll be okay." I walked out of the apartment and tried to convince myself of just that. When it came to navigational skills, though, I had none. I almost smiled to myself, recalling the time Georgia and I tried to take the train into Philly to see a movie without telling our parents, and we ended up on the outbound line instead.

Now as I walked on the narrow, cobblestone street, people whizzed by, staring at me, I was sure. I tried to blend in and look casual, whipping out my cell phone and pretending to text, but when the crowd stopped at the corner of 6th Avenue, I smacked into someone's back.

"Sorry," I mumbled, and shoved my phone away. I crossed the street. When I started seeing purple NYU flags blowing in the breeze, I fluffed my newly styled hair. Maybe people would mistake me for a college student.

I finally saw a red brick building with a green sign that read: *The Darlington School.* I stood around the corner, several yards from the large glass doors, with my heart beating crazily as kids filed through without a second glance in my direction.

What if everyone recognizes me from the news coverage? What if they all take pity on the hideous, grief-stricken girl whose mother left her a creepy message? I whipped out a compact mirror to reassure myself that my new looks were still intact. Maybe that would be enough to disguise me.

I approached the double doors and walked into the lobby. The ceiling soared three stories above. I never considered my old school dull, but everything here seemed to sparkle like someone had squirted Windex over every surface. My heart fluttered in my chest. I walked up to the tall mahogany desk.

The secretary greeted me with an overzealous smile. "We've been expecting you!" She handed me my schedule and said she'd show me around.

Darlington seemed too posh to be a school, with its mahogany-lined walls, glistening clean lockers, and a fireplace in the cafeteria. As I walked into homeroom, my teacher, Mr. Woods, stood up and announced, "Class, this is Emily Carson; please give her a warm welcome."

The students smiled and clapped.

Did they really just clap? I wondered what exactly Jolie had said to the school administrators. I found an empty seat and everyone resumed their conversations.

An olive-skinned boy with dark curly hair turned around. "Hey," he said in a husky voice.

"Hi," I said.

"First day?" he asked.

"What, you mean they don't clap like that every day?" I asked sarcastically.

"Right," he said, his cheeks reddening. "Obviously."

I worried that I sounded like a jerk, so I smiled and asked, "What's your first class?"

He leaned over and glanced at my schedule. He smelled oddly sweet. "Oh, hey," he said. "I have first-period history too. Meyers. He's boring as hell. I'll walk you there. You're in my sixth-period chem class too."

"Cool," I said. The bell rang and we walked together toward the door.

"What's your name?" I asked.

"Anthony."

"I'm Emily," I said as we walked through the crowded hallway.

He nodded. "Right—the clapping." He smiled.

I am such an idiot.

We rounded a corner. "Emily from Pennsylvania," Anthony said.

I spun my head around. "How did you know that?" I asked. My heart raced as I recalled the never-ending news broadcasts.

Anthony looked wide-eyed and caught off guard. He held a door open and ushered me into a seat next to him. "They told us," he whispered.

"What?" I said, a little too loudly, and my new history teacher looked up from his desk. He hobbled over and dumped a book and some photocopied papers onto my desk. "Miss Carson, I presume?" He panted.

I nodded, feeling all eyes turn toward me.

Anthony scribbled something on a piece of paper, then slid

a note onto my desk. *I knew you were from PA because they told us about you last week, before you came.*

Who's they? I scrawled, and handed it back.

Principal, VP, you know, the admin.

Why?

They wanted us to be sensitive to your situation.

I was boiling. Why couldn't everyone just leave me alone? *What IS my situation????*

I waited to see what he would write. *Your parents died . . . Your face was splashed across the news . . . Your mother's creepy mystery message . . .*

He scribbled and passed me the paper. *You have a tremendous body odor situation.*

I giggled.

Mr. Meyers looked over at me, surprisingly pleased. "Thank you, Miss Carson, at least someone is paying attention to my jokes."

Anthony burst out laughing.

Mr. Meyers smirked. "Don't be a kiss-up, Mr. Rucelli."

My next three classes were uneventful. Then I was forced to face the most crucial element of my new school transition: the lunchroom. One wrong squat toward a seat in a geographically undesirable location could forever land me with an invisible badge of unpopularity. I didn't want to sit in the corner with the unknowns again.

I opened the cafeteria door and walked toward the food line near the mantel, which I discovered was *not* in fact a working fireplace, merely a decorative piece. The choices were overwhelming. No mystery meat and frozen pizza—this was actual *food*. Fresh wraps, sandwiches on rustic focaccia bread with goat cheese oozing out the sides, fruit bowls, croissants, organic-looking pasta salads. Even the potato chips were kettle-cooked. I decided on some good comfort food and got a bowl of clam chowder. I grabbed a Diet Coke and began my seat search. It was difficult to know where to sit because with everyone in the same uniform green shirts, it was impossible to decipher cliques on first viewing.

The lunchroom didn't have long lunchroom tables like I was accustomed to. Instead, there were café-style circular tables made from more of that mahogany wood. It was a much more intimate setting and therefore all the more intimidating. I scanned around hoping to find Anthony, the only person I had really talked to. But I didn't see him.

"Hey," I heard someone call out.

I turned around and saw two girls sitting at a table, waterfalls of shiny hair cascading down their backs. The blond was fair-skinned with ocean blue eyes and invisible blond eyebrows that made her eyes seem exaggerated and wide. Despite her look of perpetual surprise, it was her popping eyes that gave her a unique, alluring look. She had a spray of freckles across her nose and was very petite, almost frail. She waved at me. "Come here."

I walked over to the table and the two girls motioned for me to sit.

The brunette was taller than the blond, with an angular, sculpted face. She seemed athletic and toned, which next to the daintiness of the blond made her seem almost big. But I guessed she couldn't be more than a size four. She twirled her mini diamond earrings.

"You're new here?" the blond asked.

"I'm Emily," I said.

They nodded as if this was no surprise.

"I'm Andi," said the blond.

"I'm Lindsey," the brunette said. "So how's your first day going?"

"Oh my God!" Andi interrupted, her bright blue eyes widening. "Did they not tell you about the soup?" She grabbed at her chest like she was in pain. "I know soup is supposed to be healthy and all, but it is a total fact that the cream of chowder from this kitchen has twenty-eight grams of fat. TWENTY-EIGHT! Can you believe that? They might as well shove a Whopper in a blender and call it a light snack."

I stared at my bowl of soup, obviously the wrong choice. I looked over at their salads with small cups of dressing on the side. I was hungry, but I felt strangely obligated not to eat the soup.

Andi held out her tube of hand lotion. "Want some?"

I shook my head no.

"It's weird, but I noticed my hands get so dry after a shoot." Andi rubbed the lotion over her hands.

"Shoot?" I asked.

Andi looked down at her hands. "Yeah, I did this little Guess shoot over the weekend. I don't model that much anymore, though, too busy."

I thought I saw Lindsey roll her eyes.

"Andi used to be an American Girl model. Like four years ago," Lindsey informed me. Andi punched her in the arm. "What? It's true! So how do you like it here so far?" Lindsey asked, turning back to me.

"It's okay," I said. "It's an adjustment."

Lindsey leaned in, her dark hair falling around her face. She whispered, "How are you handling everything?"

Andi gasped, her hand flying up to her mouth.

"I know we're not supposed to say anything—" Lindsey said quickly.

Andi cut her off. "It was totally forbidden."

"That's insane," I said. "Why is it forbidden to ask me a question? That's so messed up."

Andi answered with a deep impersonating voice. "You've been badgered enough. Here at Darlington, we will show you the respect you deserve."

I was thinking that maybe that was a decent point when Lindsey said, "It's such a load of crap. I wouldn't be surprised if down the road, we read a big article in the paper about how Darlington handled such a sticky situation with grace and dignity. The administration will use this for publicity, which totally goes against everything they're preaching."

So I was no longer a national headline, but a "sticky situation." I stared at my soup and played with the strand of pearls around my neck.

"That's such a pretty necklace," Lindsey said, releasing her finger from her square diamond earring and pointing to the pearls. "Where did you get it?"

I took a deep breath and willed myself to loosen my grip on the necklace. "These were my mom's."

Lindsey cocked her head, her brown hair falling over her cheek. "They're beautiful."

"Thanks," I mumbled, looking down again at my soup.

Andi dipped a carrot stick in dressing. "So, have you met any guys of interest?"

"Well," I said, "there was this really sweet guy I met this morning."

They leaned in with anticipation.

"His name is Anthony," I said.

Andi's brow furrowed with confusion. "Do we have an Anthony in our class?" she asked, tucking a blond strand behind her ear.

"Dark, curly hair?" I said.

Lindsey nodded. "Anthony Rucelli."

Andi crinkled her blond eyebrows like she still wasn't sure. "Wait, is that the guy who eats lunch in the *library* every day?" She nodded to herself. "That's right. I know who you're talking about. Aidan sat next to him in trig and he texts his *mother* like fifty times a day. And he chews his pencils. Whatever." She sliced her hand through the air as if dismissing the thought of him.

"He seemed nice," I said. I felt like I made some kind of mistake, like with the soup.

"He may be nice," Andi said. "But he's never at any parties, and at school he just kind of fades into the background." She stood up with determination. I noticed her take on the school uniform included a cute khaki skirt rather than pants and that her hunter green top with tiny detail on the cap sleeves was unbuttoned at the bottom like she'd just thrown it on one second ago. She really did look like a Guess model. I felt a little awed just to be in her presence. "Come on, after everything you've been through, you deserve to meet *the real guys*."

We walked across the room toward a table near the patio doors. As we crossed the cafeteria, Andi's hand flew left and right, like a flight attendant pointing out the exit doors.

"That's Walker Montgomery—his dad works at NBC studios. Travis Martin—his parents are the defense attorney team from that huge murder-dismember-mob case last year. Helena Lender—as in the bagel. Lucas Bailey—his dad runs a hedge fund downtown—incredibly rich."

We stopped in front of the patio doors. "And these," Andi did the flight attendant hands again, "are the guys." She looked around. "Where's Owen?" she asked no one in particular.

Two guys sat at the table, casually joking and eating burgers. Both had perfect faces with shiny white teeth.

Note to self: Get some Crest Whitestrips.

The guy with shaggy brown hair jumped up and pecked Andi on the cheek.

Andi turned to me. "Emily, this is my boyfriend, Aidan."

He nodded. "Hey." He pushed his hair away from his eyes.

Lindsey put her hand on my shoulder. "This is Emily's first day."

The lanky guy stood up, reached over for a few napkins, and balled them up. He flexed his wrist and shot the napkin wad halfway across the room into the garbage can.

"Swish," Aidan said, giving the beanpole a high five.

"That's Ethan," Andi said. "Our resident basketball star. He's being recruited by every college in the country. Even the NBA has contacted him."

Ethan did an exaggerated bow before sitting back down.

Then, out of the blue, like flowers stirring in the breeze, all heads in the cafeteria turned. Through the doors walked a guy. And even in this room of flawlessness, he transcended perfection. It wasn't his short, blond hair, or his intense, jade green eyes. It was some imperceptible quality that made all eyes just linger and swoon. As he breezed through the lunchroom toward us, my breath caught.

Andi's flight attendant hand shot out toward Mr. Perfect. "This is Owen."

O-wen. Even his name had a singsong quality that made me breathy.

He smiled at me, and *crash boom*—it was like someone pressed two paddles to my chest and shocked the life back into me.

"Hi," I squeaked out.

"Hi," Owen said, holding his gaze a little longer than necessary.

The electricity coursed through my veins with rapid fire. There was no doubt in my mind that if I reached out and touched him, just the slightest contact, there would be a spark.

Owen pulled out a wooden lunchroom chair and motioned for me to sit down. "So," he said. "Where are you from?"

"Cut the crap," Lindsey interjected, sitting down next to me. "She knows that we know about her situation."

"I'm so sorry about your parents," Owen said, resting his hand lightly on my knee.

Spark, spark, spark. I looked down for steam coming off my khakis. His forearms were tan and muscular, and I wondered if maybe he played tennis like me.

"So," Owen continued. "Tell me how, after such a tragedy, do you look so amazing?"

Oh my God. Thank you, Jolie, for the body massage and cleavage-enhancing bra. Thank you, Trent, for the highlights and layers.

I was still struggling to respond when Aidan released his grip on Andi and made a motion with his hand.

Owen looked at the time on his cell phone. "Gotta go. See ya." He smiled at me. As he followed Aidan and Ethan, the sun from the big bay windows cast a pale glow on his short golden hair.

The rest of the day, I floated on clouds. Owen thought I looked amazing. Owen, the most perfect, beautiful guy I'd ever met, thought *I* looked amazing. Who cared if everyone was being nice to me just because the principal instructed them to?

For the first time since my move to New York, the constant visions of airplanes and tray tables were replaced by a thirty-second conversation with a hot boy.

chapter four

"SO, HOW WAS YOUR FIRST DAY?" Jolie chirped as she came through the apartment door later that night.

"It was," I looked up from my homework and thought for a minute, "different."

Jolie nodded as if that was exactly what she expected me to say.

Trent barged in right behind her, juggling several Thai food cartons. He set the boxes down on the oval table on the far side of the kitchen bar.

"Do you live in this building too?" I asked. He always seemed to be two minutes away.

"Oh, honey. I'm rich, but not this rich." Trent winked.

Jolie sat down at the table. "He lives in a brownstone a few blocks away."

"Right near where the *Sex and the City* tour bus stops. My home may not be as posh, but it's trendy." He pulled out a chair and sat down. "How was your first day? What'd I miss?"

"Nothing, I just said it was different." I walked toward the steaming food.

"Oh, no," Trent moaned. "Different, like all the guys have tattoos that say MOM and insist on teaching you how to hock a loogie?"

Jolie rolled her eyes and mouthed, *His college years*, under her breath.

Trent snarled toward Jolie. "Don't dismiss my awful, damaging experiences."

I smiled.

Jolie opened a carton of pad Thai. "That was twenty years ago; will you let it go?"

Trent quivered. "I still have nightmares about my freshman roommate, Bobby Joe, and his obsession with tractors."

Jolie rolled her eyes, then opened the plastic silverware from the wrappings.

I set the paper plates out. "No tattoos and no loogies," I said. "Just . . . different."

Jolie raised her eyebrows at me.

It was so hard to pinpoint. Darlington seemed like a whole other universe. At my old high school our girls didn't carry Prada bags and have modeling jobs on the side. Our lunchroom didn't have a fireplace and Starbucks Frappuccinos in glass bottles. No one knew parental employment histories or compared whose apartment had the best view of the river.

I looked at Jolie and Trent's eager eyes and decided to narrow my focus to something they could relate to: appearances. "They all looked effortless," I said, scooping up some rice.

"But Em," Jolie said, setting her spoon of tom ka ga back in her bowl. "Look at you. You look effortless too."

"It took a whole TEAM of people to make me look this way," I protested.

"Life is about teamwork," Trent said, slurping up a rice noodle.

"Yeah, okay, but today was my first day. I was aiming high, trying to make a good impression. These people just showed up on an ordinary day looking . . . perfect."

Blank stares.

"You mean I have to do this EVERY DAY?"

"It's all about maintenance, sweetheart." Trent reached for a summer roll. "Like, when a chestnut brown comes in waving a picture of Gwyneth Paltrow, I say platinum blond is all about commitment. Either you do it religiously, or you don't venture there in the first place."

I sighed and looked out the window toward the river.

"Did you meet anyone nice?" Jolie asked, looking anxious, like she was afraid I'd say I was shoved into my locker or tripped in the hall.

I tried to act relaxed. I didn't want her to be more stressed about my transition than I already was. "I met two girls, Andi and Lindsey," I said casually. "And I met some guys: Aidan, Ethan and Owen." I felt myself get a little flustered remembering Owen's deep green eyes. "It's so weird, I mean, all the boys' names start with vowels. It's like a big vowel cluster," I blabbered.

"*Your* name starts with a vowel," Jolie said, her forehead crinkled in a look of suspicion.

"You're blushing," Trent said, pointing his fork at me. "Why are you blushing?"

"I'm not blushing; it's just, um, the food's a little spicy." I fanned myself with a napkin.

"You talk about some boys and suddenly you're all giddy." Trent's eyes narrowed on me. "Spill."

"Well, there was this one guy . . ." I confessed.

Trent's ears perked up. "Do tell," he said.

"His name is Owen . . ."

"Owen is a hot-boy name," Trent interjected.

I bit my lip.

"Knew it," Trent said, shaking his head.

"Yes, he's . . ." I sighed.

"Stop swooning," Trent said, "and describe."

"Tall, athletic, blondish hair with really green eyes and this amazing smile . . . But it's more than just that," I said. "It's like, I don't know, he's just—I can't put my finger on it. He has this magnetism. Like he just lights up a room and everyone wants to be near him."

Trent held up his hand to stop me. "No, honey, sorry," he said. "Stay away."

"Away? Why?" I asked.

"I can smell his charm from here and that charisma means one thing. PLAYER. PLAY-ER. You know what Stevie Nicks says: *Thunder only happens when it's raining. Players only love you when they're playing.* You're too innocent; he'll have you swinging from the rafters in a matter of weeks."

"Emily would not be *swinging from the rafters*," Jolie said.

"Trust me," Trent continued, "he's *dangerous*."

"Really?" I asked, and wondered if it could be true.

"PLAY-ER. Ask Jolie," Trent said, pointing to Jolie, who

was cracking open a fortune cookie. "She has plenty of experience with PLAYERS, don't ya?"

"Trent," Jolie said with exasperation. "This is my *niece*. We're not at The Odeon discussing *my love life.*" She collected our paper plates and headed into the kitchen.

"Come on," Trent teased Jolie. "Maybe Emily can learn from *all* your mistakes. Tell us about Leo. Ooh, or what about, who was that financial guy? Parker! Or how about Honey Buns? Tell us about *Honey Buns!*"

"Trent!" Jolie stomped around the bar into the main part of the kitchen. I didn't know if she was upset with Trent for bringing up all her failed relationships or whether she was just uneasy discussing my crush.

Trent waved his hand through the air. *Touchy*, he mouthed behind her back.

I smiled and collected my books. "I'm going to my room to finish my homework."

Every year, after the first day of school, my parents and I would sit around and make predictions: Which class would be the hardest? Which teacher would become my favorite? It felt strange that with Jolie and Trent we discussed none of this, only boys.

I looked out my bedroom window. A red light flickered on the dark water. I looked up and saw an airplane flying. Maybe it was descending toward Newark Airport or maybe it was an optical illusion from the waves, but either way, to me the plane looked like it was going down. I turned away from that dreadful river, the haunting image making my heart thump. I collapsed on my bed and started talking.

Hi, Mom and Dad. It's me, Emily, I whispered. *I'm sure you know that, but I just wanted to clarify in case you're, like, getting vibes from elsewhere. Anyway, I miss you guys. I miss you guys so much. You don't even know what it's like. It's like a whole different life now. I know I'll make new friends, but everyone seems so different here. I miss my old school. I miss our house. I miss real dinners with metal utensils. Mom, I really wish I understood what your apology meant. What were you sorry about? You were the perfect mother. You never did a single thing wrong. The only thing I hate you for is being gone.* At this my voice choked up, and I couldn't keep my whisper rant going.

But I wanted to know they heard me. "Mom, Dad, move something!" I demanded. I searched my room for any evidence of their presence. I pointed to a picture frame. "If you can hear me, move this frame! Come on, you've seen *Ghost*!" But the frame remained immobile.

I flopped my head back down on the bed, the soft fibers of the new cream-colored comforter (Jolie had gotten rid of the pink one already) caressing my cheek.

I felt the familiar tingly sensation I'd felt all summer. Like my body was full of pins and needles, and pretty soon I knew it would be impossible to move my body at all. I'd be paralyzed, like I'd been for months, unable to get up from the couch for hours, even days.

I rolled over quickly and picked up my cell and looked at all the missed calls from Georgia. I decided not to call her. It was too late anyway.

I thought about my day. Meeting Owen was the first time in three months that I didn't think about the accident or the

mystery apology. But then Trent told me that Owen was probably just insincere and going to break my heart. And Jolie didn't
disagree.

And maybe they were right.

Then again, what heart did I have left to be broken?

chapter five

EVERYTHING BECOMES MORE CHAOTIC, I jotted into my notebook before glancing back up at the blackboard.

"It's the second law of thermodynamics," Mrs. Klein explained. "The universe becomes more disorderly. This law doesn't come from complicated theory and equations; it comes from human experience. An ice cube melts in a warm room. Air in tires will blow out if the tire is punctured. Energy disperses from being localized to becoming more widely spread out. This is a powerful aid to help us understand why the world works as it does."

I sat, mesmerized by this concept. Maybe my life in Pennsylvania was too contained. Maybe my family was "too perfect" and this crazy law of thermodynamics forced an explosion into my natural course of events, propelling me into this world of chaos and uncertainty.

"Is that okay?"

I whipped around. "Huh?"

Anthony was staring at me. "Do you want to be my lab partner?" he repeated.

"Oh, sure." I followed him to the side lab bench. Mrs. Klein had covered the board with chemistry equations and calculations while I was daydreaming.

"You do realize that you'll be shackled to me for the rest of the semester." He ran his fingers through his dark curly hair. He laughed at my blank face. "So this is how it's going to be, huh? I'll be the only one paying attention."

"Sorry," I said. "Brain fart."

He pushed over his notes. "Well, let me know when your mind is done breaking wind, because apparently a lab write-up is due every week," Anthony said. "And then a final report with all our calculations and findings is due at the end of the semester. And we need to, like, pick a topic." He twirled his number-two pencil in his hand, and I noticed the pencil had bite marks on it.

The classroom door swung open, and everyone turned their attention to the front of the room. A new girl walked in. She handed a slip of paper to the teacher and adjusted her weight awkwardly from leg to leg.

Mrs. Klein scanned the sheet and said to no one in particular, "Transfer student." Mrs. Klein looked up and said, "Class, this is Carly Stroud. She transferred from a school in Connecticut."

I had been at Darlington for a couple weeks now and was starting to feel a little less like a fish out of water. It was now almost the end of September, and I wondered briefly why Carly had just transferred, a month into junior year.

Carly looked innocent, doe-eyed, and hopeful as she yanked her too-tight green shirt down to cover her midriff better. I cringed. Even in my old school filled with imperfection, she wouldn't stand much chance. She was clearly trying too hard, wearing a uniform that was probably several sizes too small. The worst things about this new girl standing in the front of the room, worse than being a little chubby, worse than her mousy brown hair and lack of makeup, were her huge plastic tortoise shell glasses with diamonds on the sides.

There was no applause for Carly. No school-wide request for a "warm welcome."

The teacher continued, "Let's see, you'll need a partner." As she scanned the room, Mrs. Klein's eyes fell on a group of three, nestled in the corner.

"Ethan," Mrs. Klein said, "I'd like you to pair up with Carly." Then she turned her eyes to the new girl. "Stay after class and I'll bring you up to speed on the project."

I recognized Ethan as the beanpole basketball star from the lunchroom.

As Mrs. Klein pointed her finger at Ethan, he collected his things slowly, reluctantly, and I saw him exchange an unmistakable expression with his buddies. He was not happy about this switch. With his books in his hand, Ethan dragged himself toward Carly, his basketball pendant bouncing on his chest with every long stride.

I looked toward Carly. As she stood there, witnessing his lack of enthusiasm, she had to know she was unwanted. I willed her to look toward me so I could smile. But her head slumped down, fixated on her shoes.

I shook my head and turned back to Anthony, who was

already at work. Whoa. "I've got to be honest," I said, watching him jot down notes. "Science has never been my strongest subject."

"Not a wiz kid, huh?" Anthony asked. "So what's your specialty, then?"

"Well, I don't know, maybe English. I like to read. You actually *like* chemistry? Or are you just showing off?" I asked.

"Yeah." He raised his eyebrow at me. "Actually, I do. I like that there's only one answer, and if you do the calculations and follow the instructions, you will eventually find what you're looking for." He thought for a second. "Really, it's a lot like baking."

"And you bake?" I asked, surprised.

"Yeah. I guess I've just always been around it. My mom owns a bakery," he said.

"Really?"

"Yup, CornerShop Bakery. Just around the corner! And by corner I mean it's nine stops from here on the F line."

"And you help her out?"

"All the time," he said as he lined the test tubes into a row, and pointed for me to hand him a cup and a club-shaped thing.

"What do you mean, *all the time*?" I handed him the items.

"I do the morning shift," Anthony said. "Mortar and pestle," he said, holding up the cup and club, then laughed at my face. "They're for grinding."

"Oh." I scooped some of the white compound into the cup. Anthony started to crush it with the club.

"Anyway, I go in before school and prepare the breakfast stuff—pastries, bread." He smiled and his teeth looked white against his slightly olive skin. "I do a great croissant."

Mrs. Klein walked by, glancing over our shoulders. Anthony looked up and said, "Forty-seven."

"Excellent." Mrs. Klein nodded and walked on. Apparently he had worked some equation while simultaneously grinding our compound, organizing the glassware, and recalling his morning bakery inventory.

"You go in *before* school?" I asked, shocked.

"Right," he said. "I get there about five."

"Five?" I half screamed. "A.M.?"

He laughed. "I only stay until quarter to seven," he said. He scooped up the white material and gingerly added it to a test tube. Then he took a label, wrote our names on it, and stuck it to the test tube. "Have you ever had a job?" he asked.

"Of course."

"Oh," he said, "because most of the people at this school have never had a job."

"Hmm," I said, thinking how everyone back home did something to earn extra cash, even if it was shoveling snow. "Well, when I was fourteen, I got a job vacuuming at a nursing home." I smiled, shaking my head. "It was a riot because every day when I'd get up to the eighth floor, the Alzheimer's ward, there was this man, Mr. Wilson, and he thought I was his dead wife, Lucy. Well, apparently there was a past incident with another woman. When he saw me, he would grab my elbow and scream, 'Forgive me, Lucy. Oh, *PLEASE* forgive me.'"

Suddenly, I froze. *Please forgive me.* Those were my mother's final words. Was it a common dying plea? I wondered how many people spent their lives harboring feelings of guilt until in their final moments, it expelled out of them like a ruptured balloon?

"Earth to Emily," Anthony said, waving a Sharpie at me. "Another brain fart?"

I tried to smile as the bell rang.

We gathered our things and filed out the door. I walked slowly in hopes of talking with the new girl, Carly, but her conversation with Mrs. Klein seemed to go on forever.

So I just walked on alone.

A FEW DAYS LATER AT LUNCH I set my salad down beside Lindsey and Andi, who had become my lunchtime regulars. I couldn't believe my luck. Not only to escape the whole lunchroom debacle, but to be instantly catapulted to the highest tier of social standings. I couldn't stop analyzing the situation—two new students in one week. Somehow I wound up sitting with Darlington royalty and Carly was stuck by herself, eating in the corner with a romance novel. Why? And was Anthony really eating in the library?

Here's the truth: I was never this popular at my old school. I wasn't like a geek or a loser or anything, but I never wore the homecoming crown either. Georgia and I used to say we were just on the fringes of top-rank popularity. I was lucky because my varsity tennis doubles partner, Lacey, was a total elite and sometimes she'd invite me to parties. Though once, freshman year, when I went to a Halloween party at Lacey's house, this guy Jordan from my Spanish class asked me what school I went to. But maybe he didn't recognize me because of my costume.

So I couldn't exactly wrap my head around why in the course of one week I'd been launched into Darlington's high-society lunch crowd. Sure, my once-dishwater blond hair now sparkled with golden honey streaks. And Trent taught me how to scrunch my hair to give it soft waves. My eyes, once a bland navy blue, now with an application of Jolie's Brandywine shadow, looked the color of a clear sky at dusk. And my mandatory hunter green polo and khakis blended so I didn't have to worry if I was in outdated jeans. But I really didn't think I was that far off the mark previously. My only conclusion was that for some reason my story—my brief national newscast and the mystery surrounding it—had something to do with everyone's eagerness to befriend me.

Andi waved hi to me as I sat down. Oh, well. It was better than eating lunch in the corner with a romance novel.

"Honestly," Lindsey said to Andi, "why would they want to leave New York at Christmastime?" Lindsey turned to me, her chocolate eyes dark and sad. "My stupid parents are making me go to Aspen for Christmas," she said, tucking her brown hair behind her ears.

"But Christmas is over two months away," I said, pouring dressing over my salad. Ugh. I didn't want to think about what the holidays would be like this year. I was so used to Mom turning our house into a Yuletide extravaganza and Jolie didn't even own a tablecloth.

Lindsey waved a celery stalk in the air. "My mother is just too lazy to put up the decorations. That's what this trip is really about." Her voice was filled with disgust.

Andi looked at her in surprise. "Can't you just hire someone to decorate? That's what we do every year." She dipped her fork into the salad dressing and smelled it. "I don't think this is low-fat ranch. Look at it. It's too creamy."

"You hire someone to decorate?" I asked. "Doesn't that take away all the fun?"

They looked at me like I was an adorable puppy who'd just walked in off the street.

"Christmas has always been my favorite time of year. My mom and I decorated the whole house and Dad was always on hot chocolate duty."

"Oh," Andi interrupted, eyes wide, "Did he spike the cocoa? Last year when I was shooting for American Eagle's winter sweater line, Aidan brought me hot chocolate and it was totally spiked."

"No," I said surprised, "it's just hot chocolate. But Mom served it in reindeer mugs. And every year we laughed at all the ornaments I made when I was young."

"You have homemade ornaments?" Andi asked with genuine shock.

I was debating whether to attempt an explanation of the egg carton variety ornaments from kindergarten when Lindsey spoke.

"That is *so* nice. I mean, your parents actually want to spend time with you." Lindsey seemed wistful.

They *did*, I thought, and reached up to touch the strand of pearls around my neck.

"I cannot believe how selfish I'm being," Lindsey said. "This will be your first holiday without your parents, and I'm complaining about a trip. I am so sorry." She put her arm around me. "We need to make a vow that we'll make this a really special Christmas for Emily."

"Definitely," Andi said, "It'll be an American Girl special. All wholesome and cheery." She gave a megawatt smile and shrugged one shoulder. Now that I thought about it, she *did* look vaguely familiar.

Lindsey rolled her eyes. Then she turned to me and said, "Well, at least now I can tell my parents that I can't go to Aspen because I have to stay and help a friend through a crisis."

To hear Lindsey announce our friendship took me a little by surprise. I was happy, of course, but deep inside at the sound of the word *friend*, I ached for Georgia. She understood home-made ornaments and knew that hot chocolate was only topped with marshmallows. With Lindsey and Andi, somehow I felt like a younger sibling tagging along, innocent and clueless.

Lindsey and Andi were talking more about holiday plans when I spotted the other new girl, Carly, enter the cafeteria. She held a tray table in front of herself like a shield. I wanted to flag her over, ask her to sit with us and rescue her like I was rescued on my first day. But I didn't think I had earned that authority yet.

As I watched her find an empty table in the corner, I caught a glimpse of Owen and a few of the guys walking toward our table. My heart started to race.

"Hey," Owen said, his eyes crinkling in the corners as he smiled. "Next weekend. My house. Team and Squad."

"Awesome," Andi said flirtatiously, twirling her blond hair around her finger.

"It'll be great," Owen said, smiling right at me. "I can't wait to see you there." His green eyes fixed on mine, sending lightning bolts down my spine.

I chickened out and looked away. I had no idea what they were talking about and felt too self-conscious to ask, but thankfully Lindsey rescued me.

"Team and Squad is a Darlington ritual. Every year there's a huge party the week before homecoming, and all the guys wear football uniforms and all the girls wear cheerleading outfits," Lindsey said. "It started years ago, and just the actual football players and cheerleaders would dress up. But then one year, a couple of people showed up dressed in random uniforms— not even Darlington colors. I think it actually was a joke, but it started this whole big tradition where everyone gets dressed up, and each year the costumes get more crazy."

"It's always the biggest party of the year," Andi said. She turned to Aidan and smiled. "Last year," Andi continued, "Aidan's dad called in a favor and hooked me up with a vintage Dallas Cowboys cheerleader uniform."

All the guys nodded and smiled.

"You looked hot," Aidan said. "Are you going to wear that again?"

"I don't double dip." Andi flung her blond hair over her shoulder. "I think Lindsey and I are going to prowl some costume shops."

"And Emily, you can come too," Lindsey added.

"Thanks," I said, then dared to look up at Owen. *Say something! Think of something! Anything!*

He smiled.

"So," I said pointing at Owen's varsity jacket, "are you a football player?"

Owen looked down at his green and gold jacket. "No, actually, this is for swimming. Our meets are on Wednesdays," he said, leaning down toward me. "You should come watch us."

I was quite certain the temperature inside the lunchroom jumped twenty degrees because suddenly, I was a sweaty mess. I wanted to scream: *When? Where? What time?*

"So the party's at my house," Owen continued. "Can't wait to see what you wear. Extra credit if you bring pom-poms." He gave a devilish grin.

Then all the guys turned and walked away.

My heart pounded. *Extra credit for pom-poms?* I didn't even know what that meant.

"Oh my God." Andi's blue eyes popped. "Owen is totally into you."

"No," I said, my face flaming. "You think?"

"I'll ask Aidan if Owen has mentioned you," Andi suggested.

"Oh, no, don't do that," I said. *Don't be that obvious.*

Lindsey smiled. "You *so* want to know if he likes you."

"No, no, really," I protested, looking down.

Andi contemplated this for a minute. "Wait," she said, pointing at me with her nail file. "Do you have a boyfriend in Pennsylvania?"

"I never thought of that!" Lindsey said. "You could be totally in love."

I panicked. How could I tell these girls that aside from a few double dates to the bowling alley and one short-lived relation-ship in the ninth grade, I was totally inexperienced? Then it occurred to me that they didn't *have* to know my exact history. My mind raced and the words just sort of fell out of my mouth. "Well, *in love*?" I hesitated. "Not exactly . . ."

"What do you mean *not exactly*?" Lindsey whispered, and inched closer.

"There was this guy, Steve McCaffity . . ." I started.

They held their breath.

"We were pretty into each other." The words just sounded good.

They nodded, unblinking and eager.

"But then it was over," I said, waving my hand casually.

"What happened?" Andi asked. "Did he cheat? Was he a jerk? Did you catch him with a friend?"

"No," I said, concocting a story. "He, um, Steve was just really busy." I spiraled away from a little white lie to the full-blown pathological kind. "He was the varsity quarterback, and I just felt like I was always second best to football."

I could see their growing admiration, but I couldn't quite pinpoint if it was because he was a popular athlete or that I had the courage to demand my importance.

"Wow," Lindsey said. "A breakup *and* losing your parents. You poor thing."

"So," Andi said, "was he there for you—after the accident—even though you broke up with him?"

"Well," I said, gazing out the patio doors toward the school terrace. "It wasn't exactly an easy breakup. He didn't take it well." This was getting ridiculous.

Lindsey and Andi looked intrigued.

"So," Andi said, smiling in her natural flirtatious way. "A girl with a past."

I faked a yawn. "It's a really long story. I'll tell you everything another time." And with that, I picked up my bag, waved goodbye, and headed to my next class, leaving them with their mouths slightly open, an expression of surprise written all over their faces.

I've told lies before, of course. *Yes, Dad, I took the garbage out,* or, *No, Georgia, I didn't forget to* TiVo Rhapsody in Rio. But this lie tasted different. It left a cool minty feeling coursing through my veins that made me feel energized. But why? Why couldn't I just look Andi and Lindsey in the eye and tell them, No, I didn't have a boyfriend?

It was just too addictive being the new me.

When I got home from school, I called Georgia in the safety of my room.

"Hey," Georgia answered on the first ring. "I was totally just thinking about you."

"Really?" I asked.

"Yeah," she said. "I've been dying to tell you what happened in history today." Georgia went on to explain in elaborate detail how Mr. Peterson's lesson had sweeping parallels to last season's *Rhapsody in Rio* cliff-hanger where the Rodrigues family plotted revenge against the Santos family.

I listened silently.

"What's wrong?" Georgia asked.

I didn't know what to say. I missed my parents, I missed Georgia, I even missed Mr. Peterson's stupid history class. But

I didn't say that. Instead I said, "I don't fit in. I mean, I do fit in, but that's the problem. I fit in because Jolie makes my zits go away with hemorrhoid cream, and Trent gave me highlights, and I have an interesting story to tell. But if any of these people met me four months ago, he wouldn't give me the time of day."

"Who's he?" Georgia asked.

"I meant *they*."

"You said *he*."

There was silence.

"Okay," Georgia said. "I'm not even going into why you're using hemorrhoid cream, but I detect a Freudian slip, and I want to know who HE is."

"Well," I said, "there is this guy, Owen. He's tall and has these amazing green eyes and his skin is golden . . ."

"Sounds like he goes tanning. I mean, come on, it's almost October."

"Shut up!" I said. "Seriously, his eyes, they're like emerald green."

"Colored contacts?"

"Quit it! I'm serious. He's beautiful. And he actually seems interested in me."

"And why is that so hard to believe?"

"Because the girls here are beautiful and I'm just afraid he's only interested because I'm *the new girl*. In a few weeks I'll be like old stale bread and then I'll have no one."

It was quiet for a second on the other end, then Georgia spoke. "Em, you just lost your parents. It was a major shock and I think it's normal to be afraid you're going to lose everything, to feel alone. But you don't have to worry, because I'm always here. Besides, stale bread makes the best pudding. Just channeling my grandma for a sec."

"I know, I know," I said, maybe a little too sharply. "But Georgia, I need friends *here*. I need to start over. I don't want to be *Emily of the accident* anymore. And Andi and Lindsey seem to like me, but G, these girls are *flawless*. And they're super-rich."

"That doesn't make them especially interesting," Georgia said with a subtle bite.

I sighed.

"Come on, Em. We didn't bond talking about eyeliners and designer clothes. Maybe these girls aren't the kind of friends you need."

"We met when we were six," I snapped. "It was different."

"Okay," Georgia said softly.

We hung up, and for the first time ever I felt like Georgia just didn't understand. Everything had changed.

Everything had changed forever.

chapter six

"SO WHEN IS HE COMING?" Jolie asked. It was a brisk evening in early October and she was wrapping a luscious black cashmere scarf around her neck while looking at me with worry in her eyes.

"Fifteen minutes," I said, putting my chemistry lab book on the kitchen table. "Anthony's totally going to regret asking me to be his partner when he realizes how useless I am at this stuff." I thought about how that comment would have irritated my mom because she always preached the power of positive thinking. But Jolie just laughed.

"I remember chemistry. Ugh!" Jolie shuddered as she grabbed her keys. "You'll be okay? I don't have to go." She paused in the hallway, guilt flashing across her pretty face.

"Just go," I said. "You haven't been to a party in like five days!" I teased.

Jolie smiled and touched my cheek. Her dangly earrings sparkled. She looked so pretty when she was going out, it made me feel even worse that my presence had deprived her of that for so long. "I won't be out late. Call if you need anything." As

Jolie opened the door, she collided with Anthony, a white bakery box in his hand.

"Anthony?" Jolie asked.

"Yup," he answered.

"What'd you bring me?" Jolie asked, nodding toward the box.

"Donuts," he said, unraveling the string and opening up the box.

"I like you already," Jolie said, scooping up a Boston cream. "The chemistry queen is awaiting your arrival." She waved goodbye, then left.

Anthony walked in. "Was that your aunt?" But without waiting for a reply, he stepped into the living room and said, "Wow, nice place." He went over to the window. "Great view."

I walked over toward him and followed his gaze. Looking through the oversized windows made you feel like you were in a bird's nest amid the copper and rust leaves, observing the Hudson River Park bike paths and piers. I could see the appeal to others, but for me, the Hudson was a constant reminder that I was no longer in Pennsylvania. The water was rough and impersonal here, with barges passing slowly through all hours of the night and day. At home the river was lush and relaxing; here it was lined on both sides by concrete, and the impersonal skyline of New Jersey stared back from the other side.

"The only view I have," Anthony said, "is into Mr. and Mrs. Delafonte's apartment. And believe me, you don't want your eyes to wander there."

"Why?" I asked.

"Well, first, Mr. Delafonte's not too shy with a knife and

fork, if you know what I mean. So, he's pushing three hundred. And he has a habit of walking around in his briefs."

"Eeeew!" I said.

"I know," Anthony said, "and on one really unfortunate occasion, I witnessed him flailing his arms and legs around while watching a kick-boxing video."

"Oh, get that man some blinds!" I said, letting out a big belly laugh.

"Good God," Anthony said in response to my outburst.

I recalled one night when my mom and I were watching *Saturday Night Live* and I let out a hearty laugh. A strange, almost nostalgic look passed over her face. *That laugh,* she had said, *out of someone as tiny as you. I'm surprised you don't break a rib.*

"I know," I said to Anthony. "I laugh like a man."

"A man?" he teased. "Sounds more like a flock of geese just flew by, honking and snorting."

I let myself laugh again, realizing it had been too long since I was amused. "Come on, let's tackle this lab report."

We sat down at the kitchen table and I grabbed two donuts, shoving them in my mouth.

"You eat like a man, too!" Anthony teased.

"I don't *always* eat this way. Just when I'm stressed."

"Don't be stressed," he said. "It's not that hard. I'll help you."

I dusted off my hands and pulled out my notebook. I opened it up to the first page, which had one calculation printed in pencil at the top of the page. I had worked for over an hour on that problem, but now it seemed inadequate, filling up only two lines on the page.

Anthony tried to suppress a smile, but the corners of his mouth quivered. He opened his canvas backpack, pulled out the beaker containing our mystery compound, and placed it next to his lab book and chewed-up pencils on the table. He reached again into the bag.

"Oh," he said. "I almost forgot." He pulled out a smaller white pastry box and placed it in front of me. "This is my specialty. It's the best." He smiled and pointed his finger at me. "Only when we finish this lab will I let you sample my masterpiece."

I shouldn't have opened it. But even if I hadn't, the smell would have given it away. Subtle lemon. I lifted the lid. A rectangle slice of lemon pound cake with a smear of sugar glaze on the top. Just like my mother's. My mother's lemon pound cake was like a secret bond between us. She knew one slice could jostle me out of any funk.

"What's wrong? Are you really that bad at chemistry?" Anthony joked. "Emily?" he said. "Seriously, you look like you've seen a ghost."

"I'm sorry," I said. "Forget it." I shook my head and reached for a pencil.

He opened the lab book and flipped through a few pages. "Allright, so the compound we began with had a molecular weight of . . ." His words sounded far away like they were in a tunnel. He put his pencil down and waved his hand. "Hello? Hey, are you okay?"

"My mom . . ." I said, clutching my pencil until my knuckles turned white.

He nodded, waiting.

"My mom . . . she was a lemon pound cake junkie." I pointed to the white box.

"Oh," he said softly. "I'm sorry." He put his hand on the box, almost as if he was trying to cover it up.

"You didn't know," I said. I was quiet for a beat. "It's just that I finally started to make progress in my life, but all these little memories keep creeping in. And then I remember that my parents are gone, and my mom had some big mystery secret that I still don't understand, and I feel sad all over again." *Do not cry! Do not cry!*

Anthony had a crease between his eyebrows that made him look confused.

"You saw, right?" I asked, blinking rapidly. "About my mom, and her message on the tray table?"

He bit his lip. "Uh-huh," he said. "Yes." His crease grew deeper, and his eyebrows came so close together they almost touched. "Are you saying that you never figured out why your mom was apologizing?"

I shook my head and looked down at my two lines of calculations.

"Did you look?" he asked. "For an answer, did you look?"

It felt slightly accusatory. I sat up a little straighter. I thought back to the three months I spent lying horizontal on the couch, ingesting carbs and channel surfing.

"Oh," he said.

"Oh—what?" I asked, looking back up at him and seeing his brown eyes filled with, what? Pity? "WHAT?" I said again more aggressively.

"Never mind," Anthony said, picking up his calculator.

I grabbed the Casio out of his hand and smacked it down on the table. "No," I said. "Tell me what you're thinking."

There were fifteen seconds of silence.

Anthony looked me square in the eyes. "Well, if it was me and my mom left me an unexplained apology, I would ransack everything until I got an answer. Did you search the house? Rummage through drawers and closets? I mean, did you even Google her? It just seems like maybe you don't want to know the answer."

"*Google her?!!!* And what do you think it would say? *Jill Carson, PTA superstar!*" I felt all my blood rushing to my face. "What makes you think you know anything about me, or my mom, or her stupid apology?" My voice was shaky but loud. "In the three months since my parents died," I smacked down his calculator three times for emphasis, "I've had to pack up all my things, say goodbye to all my friends, move to a new place, start a new school, and try to make new friends. OH! And squeeze in shrink visits Jolie made me go to because in addition to everything else, I'm trying to get over the fact that my parents are DEAD!" I threw his calculator across the room and slammed my hands down on the table. It didn't really hurt, but I burst out crying.

Anthony reached over and grabbed my hands. He looked at them, but since there was no obvious injury other than a red splotch, he awkwardly dropped them and sat back in his chair. "I'm sorry," he said. "I'm such a jerk. I should mind my own business."

My face was hot and wet. I felt exhausted, and my lungs burned like I had just climbed a mountain.

Anthony sat next to me, patiently, as if waiting to dispel another outburst.

We weren't touching in any physical way, but in my state of emotional breakdown, I felt this unexpected connection to him. Not like the electric sparks that fired between Owen and me, but something smaller and less intense. Like an electric blanket slowly heating up and enveloping me in a haze of warmth. It was comfort. I felt comfort.

In a move very uncharacteristic of me, I leaned over and rested my cheek on Anthony's shoulder. I worried he thought I was insane, but instead of fleeing, he softly leaned his head over and rested it against mine.

I have no idea how long we stayed like that, Siamese twins joined at the scalp. It might have been just a few minutes, or it could have been a lot longer, but he never pulled away. My mom always said, *Never be the first one to leave a hug,* and all I could guess was that Anthony's mom said that too.

Anthony finally lifted his head and broke the silence. "What were your parents like?"

I pulled my head up and smiled a half smile. I thought for a moment. "Mom was available."

Anthony raised his eyebrows. "Available?"

"I mean, she was always there for me. Like, when I got up in the mornings, she was already up, making breakfast. And when I came home from school, she wanted to know about my classes, and my friends, and tennis. She liked to cook. She listened to books on CD all day long while she did housework. Dad said those stupid earphones made her deaf, and she couldn't hear thunder."

Anthony laughed.

"She *was* a bit volume-challenged," I said. "My dad, he was an engineer, kind of quiet, very organized. He would buy duplicates of things he liked. When he found a pair of sunglasses he liked, he'd buy ten pair of them. Every night he'd come home and empty the change from his pockets. Then he'd stack the coins into neat piles on his dresser. It used to drive my mom crazy, those stacks of coins. He would always surprise me."

"Surprise you? Like how?" Anthony asked.

I thought for a minute. "Well, one day we were eating dinner and we got on the topic of things we love. I said I loved jeans with a little bit of stretch, and I loved when I hit a backhand stroke right down the line. Mom said she loved movies that made her laugh and cry at the same time. I'm expecting Dad to say he loved a perfectly grilled steak or season tickets to the Eagles, when he said, *I love streets where the trees bend over and canopy the road. And I love Emily's laugh.* My mom got teary-eyed and said, *Yes, I love that too.*"

"Your parents sound like they were really great people." Anthony got up and retrieved his calculator off the floor. He looked at me with a hint of a smile. "*You* surprise me."

"Oh, yeah?" I asked. "How?"

He smiled sort of a secret smile. "You're different than most of the girls this side of Houston Street. You're honest and, I don't know, just a little bit crazy."

With horror, I felt a lump in the back of my throat. I looked away. "So, tell me about your parents."

Anthony leaned on the table and rested his chin in his hand.

"Mom's a hard worker—never complains about anything except her weight. She wants that gastric bypass surgery, but she says she can't get it because it would hurt business. She thinks people wouldn't buy from a skinny baker. She calls me. Constantly. Now she's discovered how to text. It's a total nightmare. She texts me jokes all the time. Whose mom does that?" He chewed on his pencil for a minute. "My dad was a firefighter."

"Was?" I asked.

Anthony nodded. "He died when I was five. He pulled a woman out of a burning building in Woodside, then went back to get the dog. He never came back out."

He said this matter-of-factly. I'm sure there was pain, but he was able to control his emotions as if we were discussing the weather. *Maybe time does heal all wounds*, I thought.

"I'm sorry about your dad," I said reflexively, even though I hated it when people apologized for my parents' death.

"It was a long time ago," he said. "I was really young, but I remember how hard it was. How unexpected—our total lack of preparation. Everything was so fresh, every detail available for scrutiny. You think it'll be that way forever—but here's the thing—life just keeps on going. People are forgotten and details get fuzzy. You have to work really hard to both let go and hold on."

I nodded, realizing that perhaps this was why I instantly felt so comfortable around Anthony, because we had experienced such similar things.

"I look at Dad's picture," Anthony said. "And that helps me remember his smile. But I can't hear his voice anymore."

I wondered when the scrawled writing on a tray table would become a distant memory and no longer pierce my heart daily. "Well, maybe it's better," I said suddenly.

Anthony wrinkled his forehead.

"Maybe it's better that you lost your dad while he was still a hero in your mind." I blinked back tears. "You grow up thinking everything is all perfect, but really everyone's just one horrible news flash away from finding out their parents are harboring secrets and lies."

Anthony leaned in close to me and put his hand on my shoulder. His eyes glistened with honey speckles, and I knew that at that minute he was understanding me better than anyone else. I felt a little exposed, and I wanted to look away, but I couldn't. It was like he had a rope and was pulling me toward him. He leaned in a little closer, and I think I saw him tilt his head a little.

The moment seemed almost orchestrated, like if we were in a movie, we would kiss. It would be a soft, fragile kiss. Suddenly, as if a montage clip in a movie, snapshots of scenes flashed through my mind: Anthony and me kissing, leaning against lockers. Lying on a couch. Waving goodbye as he drops me off at college. Long-distance letters. Late-night phone calls. An unexpected visit to my dorm room. A small square box. A large square diamond. Picking out china. Picking out an apartment. A wedding at the beach. A strapless gown. A honeymoon in Paris. A new home. A little pink line. A crying baby. Anthony placing her in my arms.

My stomach felt all jittery inside. I smiled at him and tilted my head seductively. "I'm sorry I'm so bad at chemistry."

"I wouldn't want any other partner," he said flirtatiously. He reached over and grabbed my lab book. "Let me show you." He lingered close, his arm rubbing against mine. As his fingers punched the numbers on the calculator, his elbow bumped the small white pastry box and the lid cracked open just a sliver. Just enough to release a puff of lemon-scented air.

Lemon pound cake. Like my mother. The mother who wouldn't be there to help me in my strapless gown. The father who wouldn't walk me down the aisle. The baby who would never know her grandparents.

I pushed him away from me. "I can't do this."

"Sure, you can, Em. Here, let me show you."

Outside the window another plane was flying over the river. "No, I really can't do this!" I dropped the calculator and it clattered noisily on the table.

"Look," he said calmly. "Really, if you break it down, it's just simple multiplication . . ."

I had to get away from him and the lemon cake that was overwhelming and distressing me. "YOU DO NOT UNDERSTAND!" I wailed, no longer recognizing my own voice. It was loud, and high-pitched, and frightening. I backed up quickly, my chair falling over behind me.

Anthony bolted upright with a look of panic. Not a panic like, *Oh, no, what's wrong? Can I help you?* More like, *Where the hell is the emergency exit?* That thought made me think of a plane, which made me think of my parents, and I started to wail all over again.

"JUST GO!" I shrieked, flailing my arms like a crazy person, trying to shove him out of his chair.

"But . . . ?" He looked so confused.

He wouldn't leave and I *needed* him to leave. So in a frenzy I picked up the beaker and smashed it down onto the kitchen table. The glass shattered everywhere, and the white crystallized powder spilled onto the table.

"Holy crap! Our compound!" Anthony panicked and frantically began scooping the compound into his hands. He cut his pinky finger on a glass shard and traces of red blood stained the white powder.

"LEAVE!" I screamed because the lemon fragrance was everywhere. "GO!" But he was concentrating too hard on saving our compound.

What happened next will compete with any of Georgia's SOAPnet storylines for craziest, most thoughtless, most insane moves ever. But I was desperate for Anthony to leave and for the memories to stop. So without thinking, I leaned over and with all my might, I blew the pile of crystallized compound like I was blowing out candles on a birthday cake. The room was completely silent as the powder exploded into a mushroom cloud of dust.

I will never forget the look of horror in Anthony's eyes. Or the sad way he turned and left, leaving his books and bag at my table. And I was left alone with tiny specks of crystals flying all around me like I was trapped inside a New York City snow globe.

chapter seven

"SERIOUSLY, GEORGIA, I was in full-on ugly cry mode. It was mortifying. Anthony probably thinks I'm nuts. Like certifiable." The phone was slippery in my hand. I was nervous about calling Georgia after our last phone call ended awkwardly, but Georgia acted as if everything was normal.

"So you really smashed the beaker?" Georgia asked.

"Uh-huh." I sighed.

"And blew the compound. You actually *blew*?"

"I know. It's humiliating."

"But you really think he was about to kiss you?" Georgia asked.

"What does it matter now? Unless I have a split personality for explanation, he's never going to speak to me again."

"Did he do the tilt-and-lean? Were his lips together or apart?"

"I'm not sure, but it was just a feeling. He had this penetrating look and I felt like I saw right through his honey brown eyes all the way into his soul—"

"Honey brown?" Georgia interrupted. "I thought he had

green eyes. Remember," she mimicked, *"Honestly, they're like emerald green."*

"That's Owen," I said.

"And this was . . . ?" Georgia asked.

"Anthony."

"I thought you liked Owen. Who the heck is Anthony? Jeez, when you lived here, you couldn't even *talk* to Steve McCaffity and now you're juggling two guys?"

"I am not juggling! I do like Owen. Owen is amazing and beautiful and sends shivers up my spine. Anthony is just a friend. He's my lab partner, remember?"

"Your chem labs are a little more *hands-on* than ours," Georgia said.

"Shut up. He probably had no intention of kissing me. I don't know what I was thinking. We were talking about our parents, and that stupid lemon pound cake kept prompting memories. I'm such a mess." I tried not to cry. "And now I've screwed up one of the only friendships here that I really felt comfortable with."

"Look," Georgia said, "just explain to him that all the talk about your parents made you a little crazy. Anyone with an ounce of compassion would understand."

"Yeah," I said, thinking back to our conversation. "Anthony thinks I never tried to understand Mom's apology. He said I was afraid."

It was silent on the other end.

"G?" I asked.

"Well, do you think maybe he has a point?"

I started to resist but stopped myself. I recalled the three months of numbness and inactivity. Was I subconsciously try-ing to avoid something that could possibly upset me?

"I don't know," I said. "Maybe. But isn't it too late? I can't go back and ransack the house now. I don't know how to *begin* to look for an answer."

"Have you thought about asking Jolie?" Georgia asked. "They were sisters. And friends."

"Right," I said. "I guess that would be a start." But my stomach turned just thinking about it. I sighed. "So what do I do about Anthony? How do we explain to the teacher why we no longer have our compound? Oh my God, he'll probably lose his scholarship for destruction of school property. This is a nightmare."

"I know," Georgia said. "Good luck." We hung up.

I sat on the bed and stared at the phone for a while. Both Georgia and Anthony thought I was avoiding Mom's apology. I went to the living room and waited for Jolie to come home.

"Hey," Jolie said, coming through the door and placing a pizza box on the table. "Did you get your lab done?"

"Not exactly." I walked over and sat at the table with her, glancing around to be sure I'd cleaned up the spill well enough. "Can I ask you something?"

"Sure." Jolie took a bite of pizza and handed me a napkin.

"Do you have any idea what Mom's apology meant?"

Jolie froze, a strand of cheese dangling from her lips. I guess she wondered why it took me almost four months to ask. She wiped her mouth, put her pizza down, and sat up a little straighter. "No," she said. "I wish I did."

"Oh," I said, sounding defeated. For a moment I thought

how nice it would be if the answer was here all along. "Did you keep our old address book so I could maybe call some of Mom's friends? Or do you remember the name of her college roommate?"

Jolie looked at me unblinking. "What's this all about?"

I drew circles with my finger in the remaining dusty compound debris on the kitchen table. "I'm just thinking about trying to find some answers. I mean I never really tried . . ."

Jolie's voice sounded stiff. "Em, we've worked so hard to move on and you're making great progress. I think digging for answers is a step in the wrong direction."

"Don't you want to know what she meant?"

"Of course I do." Jolie's voice softened. "I just don't know how we would ever be able to solve this mystery. I thought I knew everything about your mother, but some secrets are sacred, I guess."

I nodded slowly. We finished our meal in silence.

THE NEXT MORNING, I lugged Anthony's backpack to homeroom, but Anthony wasn't there.

The bell rang, so I lugged both bags on to history. Just when I decided he had dropped out of school to avoid me, I saw him slip in the door and quickly take his seat in front of me.

"Hey," I whispered over his shoulder. "I have your bag. I'm really—"

"Thanks," Anthony interrupted, and turned to grab it. Without making eye contact he swung back around and started scribbling furiously in his history notebook.

I've really screwed this up, I thought as my stomach dropped. Anthony sneezed.

I said, "Bless you," but he didn't thank me, just nodded once.

It was obvious that he was still upset at my behavior. *Who wouldn't be?* I thought. I acted like a lunatic and I jeopardized his grade. Oh, yeah, and practically shoved him out of the apartment while screaming.

The bell rang and Anthony jumped up and raced down the hall.

My next four classes dragged. I couldn't concentrate on any lectures; instead my mind swarmed with possible options of how to explain to Anthony why I smashed the beaker. I could tell him the truth, but I didn't want anyone to think of me as the old tragic Emily with poor coping strategies. I wanted only to be the new Emily.

Sixth-period chemistry class finally arrived, and I decided I would simply apologize. No extraneous details, just, *I'm really sorry*. But Mrs. Klein split us into groups, and I had no interaction with Anthony. By the day's end I realized that there were a zillion ways to apologize to someone, but none of them mattered if you never opened your mouth.

chapter eight

AFTER MY EXHAUSTING and unsuccessful day, I was outfitted in an old pair of velour sweatpants and planted on the couch with my laptop open and two frosted blueberry Pop-Tarts. If I couldn't rectify the Anthony situation, maybe I could unearth some answers about the apology. I started with a simple Google search. I typed in my mother's name, and four links popped up. A Columbia University alumni page, school board, and school PTA pages, and her name listed with a time for the 5K Turkey Trot. A lump formed in my throat. I stared at the screen. 24:08. That's how many minutes it took my mom to run the 5K. For some reason, seeing my mom in four little numbers made my heart hurt.

I started to feel dizzy so I threw myself onto the couch and turned on *Oprah*.

Jolie came through the door a few minutes later. "Pop-Tarts?" She thrust a white bag toward me. "Don't eat Pop-Tarts; I've got Joe Jr. burgers." She put the bag on the coffee table, then pushed a gray object over and sat on the table too. "What are you looking up?" she asked, peering over toward the laptop screen.

I shut the computer before she could see my Google search.

I changed the topic. "What is that?" I asked, pointing to the gray thing I had never noticed before.

She picked it up and spun it in her hands. "It's an ashtray."

"An ashtray? You don't smoke."

"I know, but isn't it just fabulous? Every coffee table deserves a great ashtray." She admired it. "Plus, when your mom was working at that art gallery so many years ago, she kept bugging me to come to a show, but I'm not really into art." She extended her hand toward the blank walls.

"How very minimalist of you," I teased.

She laughed. "So one day your mom said they were having some kind of domestic-exotic sculpture exhibition, and I thought, that just might be my thing. And that's where I found this." She handed it to me.

I held the heavy ashtray, running my fingers over the smooth surface, thinking that one day my mother held it too. I thought about her life at the art gallery and realized that I always imagined my mother as the happy homemaker on Arbor Way. I never really knew about the person she was before I arrived. That part of her was as unfamiliar to me as this cold, angular object in my hands. "I Googled her," I said.

"Who?" Jolie asked.

"Mom. I Googled Mom. I just . . . didn't know what else to do. What should I do?"

Jolie got up from the coffee table. "I think you should move on, that's what I think you should do."

"What if I can't move on, Jolie? What if this big wave is hovering over my head, ready to crash and I physically cannot move from this place until I understand her apology?"

I looked out at the Hudson. The waters were calm, but all I could see was the image of that plane diving for the water. I waited for Jolie to say something, but she didn't.

"You don't want to help me understand Mom's apology? FINE!" I screamed. "I've asked for *nothing* from you and the *one time* I ask you for help . . . Well, forget it. Go back to your nails and your makeup and live your life like I never interrupted it!" I grabbed my purse off the kitchen table and headed for the door. I heard Jolie calling my name as I slammed the door.

I burst through the lobby door to the street and started aimlessly walking, my mind racing with thoughts. Was Jolie right—was a search for answers useless? I looked down and realized I was still holding the gray ashtray. All at once, I knew where I wanted to go. I put the ashtray down next to the small landscaped pansy garden and tried to figure out how to hail a cab. I walked toward an intersection and awkwardly stuck my arm out. A yellow cab pulled up and I climbed in. The cabdriver looked over his shoulder at me for instruction, but I couldn't remember the name of the art gallery where Mom worked. I knew it was in an area called Museum Mile, and I thought I would recognize the building from when she had pointed it out to me several years ago.

"Museum Mile, please," I said.

"*Where* on Museum Mile?" he asked.

"Um, I'm not sure." My heart fluttered with embarrassment. Why did everything have to be so complicated here?

He gave me an impatient look.

"Just . . . anywhere on Museum Mile," I said.

We battled Midtown traffic, then soared up Park Avenue—it

was the first time I'd seen the famous street. The polished-looking white buildings and quaint corner cafés looked quiet and serene. The driver turned a corner toward Central Park and pulled up in front of the Metropolitan Museum of Art.

"Oh, yes. This will do fine." I paid, then walked several blocks north until I saw the familiar stucco facade and the arching window details and knew I had found the correct gallery.

Inside the gallery there was a beautiful winding staircase with an ornate wrought iron banister. I could envision my mother floating down the stairs, Scarlett O'Hara style. I wandered around not knowing what I was expecting to find, but trying to channel any details of my mother that I had never explored.

I was on the second floor, staring at the diamond-patterned floor and wondering why my mother gave up a career she loved, when a groomed man with a cleft chin rounded the corner and stopped. I looked up and met his eyes.

"I'm sorry," he said softly, running his hands through his thick, wavy brown hair. "I . . . I thought I recognized you."

"Oh," I said. *The relentless news coverage. The magazine exposés.* I turned and ran down the stairs, out the door, and didn't stop until I collapsed on the cold, concrete steps in front of the Metropolitan Museum of Art. The massive pillared building was a playground for hordes of tourists and school groups. As the visitors stepped past me, no one registered recognition. Like static or white noise, they bustled around me in a blur. No one knew me as the girl whose parents died or the girl whose mother left an unexplained apology. To them, I was just another visitor eager to soak in the beauty of art. I embraced the anonymity for hours. The numbness helped me stay calm until the sun started to sink and my fleece sweatshirt no longer kept me warm.

WHEN I GOT HOME, the apartment was dark. I walked down the hall. The radiant light from the TV in Jolie's room sparkled like a kaleidoscope on the dark hallway wall. The volume was set to mute. Through the open door, the flickering TV lights turned Jolie's face blue, then silver in a dizzying, fragmented pattern. Trent was sitting by her side on the bed, his arm draped over her shoulders. He was saying something with an unfamiliar serious demeanor. The TV brightened and I saw tears on Jolie's cheeks.

I walked closer to them, their backs to me.

"I thought it was the right thing," Jolie whispered. "She doesn't need any more grief, right?"

Trent rubbed the back of her hair.

"This is so hard!" Jolie whimpered. "Am I trying to protect her too much? Should I encourage her to look for answers? I don't know what to do. I'm not cut out for this mother stuff."

Trent pulled her hair back playfully so she was looking into his eyes. "It's true," he said. "You know squat about how to cook and you know nothing about how to raise a teen. You're clueless about how to mend that little girl's broken heart, let alone your own. But Jo, sweetie, the threads of your sister remain in Emily. So by God, you better figure it out."

Jolie's head dropped.

"It doesn't have to be Martha Stewart perfect," Trent continued. "Just be the grown-up."

I stood there, frozen, unsure what to feel. I was touched by

Jolie's desire to take care of me but also felt like a burden for requiring it.

I watched Jolie's petite shoulders quake. Then I turned and ran down the dark hallway and crawled into the still-unfamiliar bed. I pulled the blankets over my head to block out this new world—a world where a girl could live her whole life and never really know the truth about her own mother.

chapter nine

I DROPPED MY BAG down on the shiny marble floor and plopped into a seat at our usual lunch table.

"Why the grumpy face?" Andi asked. "Aren't you excited about tonight?"

"Tonight?" I asked, racking my brain. It was October 10th. Nothing registered.

"Tonight," Andi said. "The Team and Squad party at Owen's? Aren't you excited?"

"Oh, right, sorry," I said. "I think I bombed a quiz in history," I explained. That was not exactly what I was thinking about, but I couldn't begin to explain the whole mess my life had become. The fight with Jolie. The fact that Anthony was still barely talking to me now and was clearly uncomfortable in my presence. Oh, and the little problem of not understanding my mother's mysterious and public last words.

Lindsey came over and took a seat, adjusting her cute heavy cable-knit sweater. You were allowed to wear any kind of sweater or blazer over the green uniform shirts, thank goodness. "Hey, I heard Meyers nailed you with a pop quiz this morning," she said.

"Yeah," I said, shaking my head. That wasn't the half of it.

Andi turned to me. "I wish you could have come with us shopping. We had the best time. We went to Abracadabra's and found great stuff! I found this powder blue cheerleading outfit that looks straight out of the eighties!"

"So, what are you going to wear?" Lindsey asked me.

I tried to act casual, as if I had planned this all along. "Well, I thought I would wear my uniform from my old high school—last year's varsity basketball cheerleading uniform."

Andi inhaled. "Authentic! That's awesome."

"And sentimental," Lindsey added with a smile.

Oh, good, now if I could find it.

"Why don't we all get ready together?" Andi suggested. "We could go to my place after school—oh, shoot, no, we can't. My mom has the decorators scheduled."

Hmm. I had an idea. This might be exactly what I needed: a distraction. "We could go over to my place," I said, feeling a little bold. "Jolie, my aunt, she does makeup; maybe we could use some of her stuff."

Andi looked inquisitive. "What do you mean she *does makeup*?"

"She's a makeup artist," I said.

"Like at a counter?" Lindsey asked. "Which line? Ooh, could she get us some free samples?" It bewildered me that people who lived like Lindsay and Andi still got excited over free stuff.

"Well, actually, she kind of has her own line. You probably haven't heard of it; it's mostly for TV and movies . . ."

"TV and movies?" Andi asked, eager for details. "She does makeup for TV and movies? Oh my God. You're not talking about *Jolie Jane?* As in, *Jolie Jane, makeup artist to the stars?* As in, *only the best sheer, non-sticky gloss available in the universe, Jolie Jane?*" Andi's voice was rising.

I'm not normally paranoid, but I swore I could feel breath on my shoulder, so I turned around and my arm crashed into the new girl, Carly. She dropped her lunch tray. A turkey sandwich tumbled to the floor and a seltzer bottle rolled under the table.

"Oh," I said, "I'm so sorry." How long had she been standing behind me?

A crimson rash crawled up Carly's neck. She dropped down to her knees and tried desperately to reassemble the sandwich.

"Here," Lindsey said, bending down and retrieving the bottle.

Carly took the seltzer and pushed her giant glasses up on her nose. "Thank you," she said, and raced away.

Andi snickered. "Is that the girl Ethan is partnered with in chem?"

"Uh-huh," I said.

"My God, did you see those glasses?" Andi shook her head. "Has she never heard of Lasik?"

"She's new," I said. "Started here a few weeks ago. She's from Connecticut, I think. She seems nice."

A funny look spread across Andi's face. "Ethan told Aidan that she was flipping through a Victoria's Secret catalog in chem class and she dog-eared a page with thongs on it. Thongs—for her?! Then she had the gall to ask Ethan if he thought thongs were sexy or slutty." Andi smirked. "Where does *she* get off being so confident?"

I looked across the cafeteria at Carly eating alone.

Lindsey turned back to our previous conversation. "So, is Jolie Jane really your aunt?"

Lindsey and Andi waited in anticipation.

I nodded, and their mouths dropped.

"You've been holding out on us!" Andi exclaimed.

"No wonder your skin always looks so good," Lindsey raved.

"I love Jolie Jane cosmetics," Andi gushed. She rummaged through her purse, then waved a familiar-looking black and gold tube as confirmation. "Honestly, her glosses are killer."

It was so strange to see them hold Jolie in such high regard. I guess I never realized the full extent of her success. I knew she had money—but I didn't think she had notoriety. Jolie Jane cosmetics weren't sold at the mall back home in Pennsylvania, so to me, it seemed like unless you whipped out a magnifying glass and read the photo-shoot credits in the fashion magazines, Jolie had more of a behind-the-scenes kind of fame.

"My mother swears by her foundation sticks," Lindsey added.

"She's coming out with a new skin care line soon," I said casually.

"Awesome," Andi and Lindsey both said.

I laughed. "So why don't you guys come over around five thirty and maybe we can convince Jolie to do our makeup?"

They agreed.

I text messaged Jolie and asked her if we could *make up* at our house. I sensed that Jolie got my double meaning because she texted me back right away and said it was a date. Then, in a move reminiscent of my mother, Jolie added *XOXO*.

With the anticipation of the pre-party at my house in addition to the actual party at Owen's house, I managed to forget about the Anthony debacle until I walked into chemistry. I took my seat next to him at the lab bench. I saw he had a Band-Aid on his pinky finger where the broken beaker had cut him. The guilt hit me. I nervously tried to remember my rehearsed apology.

"Hey," Anthony said flatly. "I talked to Mrs. Klein yesterday. We have a new compound." He pointed at a beaker on the table. "She told me we can just combine last week's lab work with our next assignment so we have adequate time to catch up."

"Anthony . . ." I started.

"Don't worry about it," Anthony said brusquely.

I tried to write *I'm sorry*, but my pen was running out of ink. Anthony dug into his backpack and handed me a pen. I tried to smile at him, but he turned away.

Carly raced into class late and headed for her seat next to Ethan. I noticed that she was not wearing her glasses. I tried to recall if maybe she broke them today at lunch when we collided, but I didn't remember them falling off her face.

For the rest of the class, I kept trying to show Anthony my written apology, but he remained nose down in his book, twirling his chewed-up pencils in his hand.

• • •

WHEN I GOT HOME from school, I headed straight for my room to try and find my old cheerleading outfit. I opened the closet door and looked at the few remaining unpacked boxes. I wished I had labeled them somehow. Fortunately, the first box I picked contained the old uniform rolled up in a ball toward the bottom.

Jolie popped her head in my room. "Want to order pizza?" The question was casual, but I could still hear some post-fight hesitation.

"Pizza sounds good," I said. I waited for some sort of rehearsed monologue. An, *I'm sorry we fought last night. I was just taken off guard. Of course, I'll help you decipher your mother's apology.* But the speech never came. Jolie simply smiled and asked if I wanted pepperoni.

At five thirty sharp we buzzed Andi and Lindsey up.

Jolie greeted them casually, by name, ushering them in. Andi and Lindsey fawned unapologetically, raving about products and celebrity pictures Jolie had worked on. I guess there had been some insanely big *Vogue* interview last year—one that I'd been totally oblivious to back in my old life. Jolie laughed and hugged them both, waving off their compliments. On the one hand, it was great that Andi and Lindsey thought Jolie was so cool because that made me, by extension, acceptable. But I couldn't help feeling a little resentment, too—Jolie was so eager to help my friends, even if it was as superficial as doing their makeup, and yet she was unwilling to help me dig for answers to my mother's apology.

Andi, Lindsey, and I went into my room to change into the

cheerleading uniforms. My old uniform was laid out on my
bed. I touched it with a strange mix of affection and nostalgia.

Lindsey came over and sat on the bed, resting her hand on
the navy blue skirt. "Does it make you sad?" she asked.

"A little," I said, feeling the swirl of memories start to
overtake me.

"No time for sadness," Andi called from across the room,
slicing her hand through the air, and I noticed her fingernails
were painted blue to match her outfit.

Lindsey smiled at me and dug her uniform out of a white
plastic bag.

I pulled on the white and navy top and stepped into the
skirt. It fit a little more snugly than last winter, grazing the top
of my thighs and hugging my waist. I stared at myself in the
full-length mirror, wearing my old high school uniform.

"Okay," Andi said, pulling out a powder blue uniform from
her bag. "So I had this major underwear dilemma—I can't wear
a thong because the skirt is too short, right? Go with the full
coverage, cringe at the VPL, but realize that it's the only option
that's not totally slutty. Right?"

"Definitely," Lindsey shot back without thinking. "It's a
no-brainer."

What the heck is VPL?

"Absolutely," I answered with faked confidence, and
prayed that they didn't decide to raid my underwear drawer. I
could imagine the gasps when they saw my wide array of granny
panties. But I never understood the appeal of thongs; don't
they just give you a permanent wedgie?

"Plus," Lindsey continued, "with the flare of the skirt I don't think you'll have any *visible panty lines*. Don't worry."

"Exactly," I said, nodding. I wondered if Lindsey knew I needed her deciphering. I caught her eye in the mirror and smiled.

Andi wandered over to my closet and stared at my shoes with a perplexed look. "You have like thirty pairs of the same loafer," she said, clearly disturbed. "Where are the flip-flops? Where are the sandals? The sexy peep-toe pumps?"

Lindsey walked over, intrigued.

I think they were expecting some exotic explanation like I had a secret trapdoor that led to another closet. "Um, I have really ugly toes?" I said tentatively. "So I only wear closed-toe shoes."

"Let me see," Andi said.

"No!" I panicked, but Andi was walking toward me.

"Oh, come on! Ashton Kutcher has webbed feet and he's still gorgeous."

"Ashton Kutcher has webbed feet?" I asked, wobbling backward until I had landed on the side of my bed. While I was momentarily distracted, Andi plucked off my left shoe and wrestled off my sock.

Andi and Lindsey started laughing and teasing me.

"Stop!" I said, laughing.

"My God," Lindsey said. "It's like a free pass to lie—your toes are always crossed."

And as I doubled over and laughed, it felt good for us to have our first private joke, even if it *was* at the expense of my hideously freakish feet.

Jolie stuck her head in my room. "Ready for some makeup?"

We walked down the hall to Jolie's room. Andi and Lindsey stood motionless in the doorway, scanning the tables of brushes, palettes of color, and tubes of gloss. Lindsey hopped in the chair first.

Jolie clipped her hair back and studied her face. "You've got great, pillowy lips," she said. "So sexy."

Lindsey reflexively touched her lips.

In the mirror I saw Andi trace her own thin lips with her index finger.

Jolie turned toward her table and selected three pots with varying shades of tan powder. "I'm going to use a neutral palette on your eyes but make your lips really pop," she said.

Jolie used a long, thin brush to outline Lindsey's dark eyes in a mocha-colored liner, then used a larger brush to sweep a sable color across her lids. She filled Lindsey's lips with a matte ruby stain that made them look plump and dramatic. Lindsey swiveled around in the chair and said, "Look!"

"You look great!" Andi and I said in unison.

Andi walked over and playfully bumped Lindsey out of the chair.

Jolie stacked her pots of color back and grabbed some fresh brushes, placing them on the table in front of her. She smiled at Andi in the mirror.

Andi turned her lips in over her teeth and looked almost nervous.

"You have really great eyes," Jolie said.

"Really?" Andi asked. "You don't think they're too big?"

"Too big?" Jolie repeated. "You can never have eyes that are too big." She turned to her color collection and selected various jars and pots.

"When I was growing up, my brother used to call me bug eyes," Andi said.

Jolie turned back toward the mirror. "I bet all your brother's friends think differently."

Andi smiled.

"Okay," Jolie said. "Most people are afraid of color. You say blue or green and people get all sketchy on you. But I'm looking at you with your gorgeous hair and translucent skin and I'm thinking you need some sparkle, some drama. I'm going to put navy around your eyes and watch what it does." Jolie worked a thin brush into the top and bottom lash lines of Andi's eyes. Then she dusted a hint of dark plum powder into the creases of her lids.

Lindsey and I leaned in and saw Andi's cobalt blue eyes come alive. All the little speckles of green and gray buried in the blue irises jumped out at us.

Jolie picked up an eyelash curler. Like magic, the lashes curled toward the sky and her large eyes doubled in size.

Andi softly whispered, "Wow."

I could tell that Jolie was accustomed to working with fragile egos of celebrities because in a matter of minutes, she ignited a feeling of confidence and beauty in Andi. I had never thought of Andi needing reassurance because she was by far the most popular girl in school. But Lindsey had explained to me that

Andi's dreams of being a runway model were halted when she stopped growing at five feet. While she makes good money doing catalog modeling, to Andi, it's second best.

"Oh my God! The Laker Girls have flown east." Trent bounded through the door.

"We're going to a costume party," I said to Trent, then turned to the girls and said, "This is Trent," offering no other explanation because, really, how do you explain Trent?

"Obviously," he said picking up a pom-pom.

"Hi," Lindsey said, holding out her hand, but Andi's eyes were transfixed on a shelf mounted high above Jolie's worktable.

Andi pointed in the direction of the shelf. "Is that . . . an EMMY?"

Jolie smiled and nodded.

"What?" I asked.

Trent turned toward Jolie. "Have you never told your niece of all your accolades? Modesty—hmm—really, that surprises me a bit." Trent looked toward me. "Your auntie won an Emmy last year for her makeup work on *Good Morning with Rick and Riley*."

Wow, I can't believe I didn't know that.

"AN EMMY???!!" Andi screamed, then turned to Lindsey and repeated, "AN EMMY!"

"Well, you can't get all gussied up and not let me fix your hair," Trent said. He stuck a finger out at Lindsey. "You, Sporty Spice, come here and sit."

Lindsey sat down, and Trent dramatically combed his fingers through her long, dark hair.

"Oh, honey. You are too one dimensional. You must come

to my salon and let me fix your color." He paused, staring at her. "You look a lot like Leighton Meester. Has anyone ever told you that?"

"The Gossip Girl?" Lindsey smiled. "I don't think so."

"Now the question is, do you want to continue being the poster child for headbands and Chanel scarves or do you want to look your own age?"

"What do you mean? I don't know . . ." Lindsey said doubtfully.

"Oh, honey, it's hair. It'll grow back," Trent said. "A little chop here and there will give you *so* much more oomph."

"Okay," Lindsey said hesitantly, and before she could rethink her answer, he took a razor and sliced across a handful of hair.

Andi and I gasped.

"Amateurs," Trent said, and grabbed a flatiron. He smoothed the iron over the newly chopped hair, and in thirty seconds Lindsey was completely transformed from cool and conservative into edgy-pretty.

"What'd I tell you," Trent said. "Come on, blondie, you're next."

Andi sat in the chair, looking at us with a *this is unbelievable* look in her eyes.

"Oh," Trent said, examining Andi's hair. "Good color—perfection. Your cut's divine, too. You just need some height." He started teasing and spraying. "Trust me, bed head is sexy."

And again, he was right.

"And you," Trent said, turning to me. "I'm a little disappointed in you. Your friends had no idea who I was. Do they think you got your style at Great Clips? I think not. Nobody does long beach hair layers like I do." He pulled me into the chair and did a quick blowout, scrunching my hair in his hands.

"Hey, Trent," Andi said. "I *totally* would have nominated *you* for an Emmy too."

"I know, sweetie," he said. "I know."

chapter ten

WE CHIPPED IN AND TOOK A CAB to Owen's apartment. The cabdriver kept staring at us, dressed in three different cheerleading ensembles, but we offered no explanation.

Owen lived in a fancy, high-rise building with a rotating glass entryway in the west Twenties. Where Jolie's building was sleek and modern, Owen's was ornate and opulent. Andi pressed the PH button in the elevator and we rode all the way to the top floor. The doors opened and deposited us in a plush hallway lined with busy wallpaper. Our feet clomped loudly on the beige marble floors.

Lindsey leaned in toward the dark wooden door. "I don't hear anyone inside."

"That's weird," Andi said. "We're not early." She looked down at her watch. She tried the doorknob, and the door swung open to an extravagant but vacant apartment. There was a round table in the center of the foyer with a towering floral arrangement. Taped to the vase was a note: GO BACK OUT TO THE HALLWAY, TAKE SECOND DOOR ON LEFT.

I had no clue what was going on, but at least it seemed like neither did Andi or Lindsey. We walked back into the hallway and found the second door on the left. It opened to a narrow staircase. Andi turned to us and raised her eyebrows.

Lindsey and I shrugged back. In single file we climbed the creaky staircase. As we rose higher, the air became cooler, and we could hear the thumping of loud music. The door at the top of the staircase opened to a huge rooftop garden, surrounded by the most magnificent views of the city I had ever seen.

The three of us gasped all at once. From one side of the roof you could see the Empire State Building blinking in the dark, amid the severe skyline of Midtown Manhattan. Lit-up domes and skyscrapers made the whole sky look jagged and bright. In the opposite direction you could see all the way to the West Side Highway, where cars raced by.

Hordes of people filled the terrace, lounging on wrought iron benches and chairs, meandering under the low trees in one corner—I'd never seen a tree *on a roof* before! Some people were dancing, and I thought I saw a group clustered around what looked like a shiny keg. Many of them were dressed in a sea of different-colored cheerleader uniforms, but there were crowds of people dressed in jeans and sweaters, too.

"Oh my God." Andi scrunched her nose as a shaggy boy with scruffy facial hair jostled her shoulder passing by. "Half of these people don't even go to Darlington!"

"I bet half these people aren't even in *school* anymore," Lindsey said.

Andi spotted Aidan over in the far corner. She strutted across the rooftop, the pleats of her miniskirt slapping against her swaying hips. Heads, both male and female, swiveled and followed her strides. She fluffed her teased hair, enjoying the attention, and smiled at the onlookers.

I scanned around looking for Owen but didn't see him anywhere. What I *did* see was unlike anything I had ever witnessed outside of a movie theater. I thought wild high school parties with chaos and mayhem were all products of the imaginations of screenwriters. But here, perched amid the amazing city skyline, mayhem was everywhere. There were swarms of people singing, dancing, and making out. Straight ahead someone had somehow propped a mattress up, leaning against two benches turned on their sides. A hose was jimmied up at the top, creating a real-life water slide. Two burly guys were hoisting up a girl I recognized from my history class and throwing her down the mattress slide. She yelled as the water splashed and drenched her. There was a long line of eager participants, so I guess the bitter late October air didn't bother them.

I thought about the "parties" I had gone to back in Pennsylvania and felt so lame. Justin Henderson's so-called rager last year had maybe thirty people max. And while some of my friends could be considered more rebellious than I was, I clearly remember a provocative coed game of Twister at Selena Thompson's Christmas party creating a buzz around school. The party at my house, the night of the accident, was considered extreme, and that was because we danced on the kitchen counter. These partyers were probably dancing on counters by the age of ten. Quickly I forced my mind to stop recalling the past for fear that Andi and Lindsey would somehow telepathically pick up on how sheltered I was.

"Come on, let's dance!" Lindsey said, taking my arm

and walking toward the right side of the roof, where several benches and terra-cotta pots had been pushed aside to form a dance floor.

I absolutely hated dancing in public because I was pretty sure I looked like I was being electrocuted, but I followed Lindsey and tried very hard not to do anything moronic like snap my fingers. The music was retro eighties, and more groups of girls gradually drifted toward the music. Crowds of guys hovered around the perimeter of the dance area, gawking.

We danced for a long time, then the music shuffled to a hard techno beat and some guys entered the scene, pressing up behind girls and gyrating. Lindsey rolled her eyes at me. I laughed, and we walked over toward the edge of the roof. Numerous carved pumpkins were lined up along the brick ledge. Candles glowed inside the jack-o'-lanterns, sending beams of orange light across the roof onto people's shirts and faces. There were long aluminum heaters wrapping around the floor edge. It made me think of the time that my parents and I went to my cousin's wedding in New Jersey. The reception was held in a big, white tent and they had those same electric heaters. I started to get that tingly numb feeling I got whenever a memory emerged to haunt me. *Couldn't they just have the party indoors like normal people?* my dad had said. As an engineer, he was always super-concerned about wasteful energy-sucking devices. But my mom had touched him on the nose and declared that an outdoor party had the perfect ambience. I didn't understand what she meant at the time, but now, as I scanned the roof again for Owen, I realized that an outdoor gathering definitely sparked romance and excitement even in New York, where you couldn't see the stars.

Lindsey rubbed her hands together over the red electric glow. "Ooh, that feels good," she sighed. "I'm going to have to leave soon. My mom makes me come home by midnight if I have a practice on Saturday."

"Practice, like for a sport?" I asked, realizing that Jolie had not mentioned a curfew.

"Horseback riding, yeah. I have lessons in Scarsdale. Hey, do you want to come? It's beautiful out there. You could meet Ginny, my horse. And my really hot instructor." She grinned. "Or would that be totally boring for you?" she asked, running her fingers through her hair.

"No, I would love to come," I answered quickly. "Your new haircut really looks great, by the way."

Lindsey smiled. "I'll call you in the morning so we can come pick you up on our way," she said.

"Okay, great," I said, feeling a surge of happiness and *belonging*—one I hadn't felt in a long time. We both turned around toward the dance floor and finally, I saw Owen in the far corner, his attention turned to a pretty girl dressed in a tight maroon sweater with a yellow 22 printed on it and a tiny maroon pleated skirt with yellow trim. She kept touching him on the chest. Her mouth spoke with exaggeration: *Owen, you are soooo funny*.

My stomach did a flip.

Lindsey followed my gaze. "That's Carrie Lisbet; what's she doing here? She's a freshman!" Lindsey looked over at my face. "You really like him, don't you?" she asked.

I looked at his short blond hair and angular jaw. "I don't know, maybe."

Lindsey laughed. "Yeah, right."

"Well, I think he's really hot. I mean, who doesn't, right?" I asked.

Lindsey nodded in agreement.

"But there are a lot of hot guys at this school," I said. "It's just that Owen is the only one who makes me all jittery inside."

"I know the feeling," Lindsey said wistfully.

"Really? Who?"

She tapped her foot for a minute and said, "Okay, don't tell Andi because she'll freak, but I have this thing for my instructor."

"Why would Andi freak?"

"Because he's twenty-three, and Andi says that's too old, plus she says he's just a riding instructor and I should only focus on top-tier guys."

"That's kind of crappy," I said, though I did think it was kind of wild of her to be interested in a guy that old.

She looked across the room at Andi, who was surrounded by a group of fawning admirers. Lindsey had an unreadable look on her face. I knew all of Georgia's crazy expressions—like how she crinkled her nose when she was confused or how she tugged her left ear when she was embarrassed. But my friendship with Lindsey was still so new, that faraway look on her face was unrecognizable to me. I wondered if she was thinking the same thing I was: why was Lindsey here with me, the new girl, while her best friend was off flirting with hordes of guys?

Lindsey turned back toward me. "It *is* a little crappy. But that's Andi. She has her *ideas*," she air quoted, "about what's acceptable. But I just can't help it. Jason—that's my instructor—is so adorable and his biceps, my God, don't get me started. Sometimes, I fake being wobbly on the saddle just so he'll spot me."

"Well, he may be hot," I said. "But *hello*, twenty-three! When we were peeing in a diaper, he was practically doing multiplication tables!"

· Lindsey laughed. "God, I know. I can't help myself, though. He's that cute."

"I will definitely come with you tomorrow," I said. "I've gotta meet this guy for myself."

I felt a light touch on my shoulder. I turned around and saw Owen smiling. *Spark. Spark. Spark.* His eyes were so light and clear I swore I could see the moon's reflection.

The music suddenly blared, the bass thumping under our feet.

"Hi," Owen screamed over the music, inching closer toward me.

I tried to say hi, but it came out like a cough.

"Are you cold?" he yelled, putting his arm around me.

I nodded and pretended I was.

"I need to make a phone call," Lindsey said, and walked away, giving me a quick smile.

Someone adjusted the music volume. Owen smiled and said, "That's better."

We leaned over and rested our elbows on the ledge, staring out at the twinkling lights of the city. The view from Jolie's apartment was all cobblestone streets, trees, and river, but Owen's building looked like it was dropped right in the middle of the city, with buildings shooting up all around us. Windows glowed everywhere, and twenty stories below cars scurried across streets.

Owen looked at my empty hands. "Do you want me to get you a drink?" he asked.

"Oh, no thanks, I'm fine."

He nodded and tilted his head with a touch of sympathy. "AA?"

AA??!! "Um, no, I just don't drink."

Owen looked confused for a second like he had never heard such a crazy thing. Then he changed the subject. "So, how is Darlington's new darling? Have you fallen madly in love with our school yet?"

"I'm getting used to it," I answered. I wanted to say, *You are making it so much easier to forget all my problems,* but his flirtatious tone made me nervous so instead I stammered, "Your, um, I mean, this roof thingy, it's really amazing."

"You'll have to see it in the spring when all the flowers are blooming," Owen said.

Was that an invitation?

I could imagine the roof garden in full bloom: an oasis in the middle of the sky. I didn't say that because he would think that was cheesy, so I said, "Someday, when I get older, I'm going to have a rooftop just like this." Which, let's face it, is even more cheesy. Argh! If only I'd asked Georgia to help me script something cute to say.

"Oh, yeah?" he said, his eyes crinkling. "There are lots of things I like to do up here."

Oh, man, he was definitely flirting. "Like what?" I said,

trying to sound comfortable, like I had conversations like these with guys all the time.

"Talk to pretty girls like you, for one thing."

He thought I was pretty. That's what he was implying. Right? Oh. My. God. My face must have turned a horrifying scarlet, but he didn't seem to notice. "Nice outfit, by the way."

"Th-thanks," I stammered. "It's from my old school. I was on the team. Briefly. I kept, like, tripping and messing up the sequences, though. So you know, I quit."

Owen chuckled lightly and leaned toward me. "You're funny. You're the kind of person I'd like to get to know better. You aren't like the other girls." He was staring into my eyes now, leaning closer so I could smell his breath: sweet and citrus.

Oh my God, he was going to kiss me, right there in front of everyone. He saw something was different about me, and just then, I didn't care if it was because I was an orphan or if he'd somehow heard about my crooked toes. All *I* knew was that he was looking at me with those piercing green eyes and I suddenly really, *really* wanted him to kiss me . . .

But did it have to be so *exposed*? What if I turned my head the wrong way and we bumped noses? Not only would Owen realize how clueless I am, but practically the entire student body of Darlington would witness my incompetence.

He was inching closer, still grinning that slightly mischievous grin. *Get a grip,* I thought, *this is Owen, mega-popular, beautiful Owen, and this might be my only chance.*

I saw his lips part, just a fraction, and I could see a hint of his top teeth. He was doing the tilt-and-lean. *Note to self—Tell Georgia his lips were parted. Shut up!* I thought as I saw his eyelids close. *Quick, close your eyes!* But I couldn't because I was oddly fascinated by the scene next to me, where a group of guys had started piling the glowing jack-o'-lanterns on top of each other to form a pyramid. A guy with a Darlington football uniform on began stacking beer cans in between the pumpkins, and I have to say all the candlelight bouncing off the aluminum cans made a spectacular light show.

But then, as if in slow motion, I noticed a guy dressed only in jeans and shoulder pads walking toward the pumpkin pyramid with a bottle outstretched. I squinted and saw it was a whiskey bottle, 100 proof. My mind was racing. Alcohol and heat, that wasn't a good combination, was it? I knew I wasn't very good at chemistry, but I did have experience watching the Food Network and the word that kept coming to mind was *flambé*. Shoulder pad guy added the whiskey bottle to the jack-o'-lantern display and in an instant, flames erupted bursting ten feet above our heads with a loud *poof*.

There were screams. There was running. And then, there was the smell. The smell of burning hair.

Lindsey barreled toward me. "OH MY GOD, EMILY!" And then I fainted.

When I came to, Lindsay was on top of me, using the pleats of her skirt to extinguish my burning hair.

It took a while, and someone came running and dumped water on us, too. I was coughing, sputtering. Between the smoke in my eyes and the water in my clothes, I was confused, shivery. It was hard to see, and with all the commotion, I could barely tell which way was up. Already I could hear a siren in the air.

I didn't see it, but I heard later that the hose from the water slide was the only thing that prevented the whole building from bursting into flames.

When Lindsey finally rolled off me, I lifted my head off the ground and looked at my body, covered in orange pulp and slippery seeds. I reached around and felt the singed tips of my hair. "Trent is going to kill me," was all I could think to say.

Lindsey gave a sympathetic smile. We both lay there for a while, stunned.

Smoke seemed to be rising off the floor like steam. Shards of glass and slices of aluminum cans littered the floor. A huge line of people jostled each other trying to exit single file down the narrow staircase.

I looked over my shoulder. Owen was being interrogated by police officers and firefighters. *They got here fast.* I guess when rich people are in danger, the cops come running quick.

Lindsey followed my glance over to where Owen was standing with his hands in his pockets, looking surprisingly calm. "Just shy of contact, huh?"

I contemplated asking her if my pre-kiss head tilt had looked right, before the flames had gone up, that is.

Instead, I peered through the haze of smoke toward the sky. Given the proximity of the rooftop to the great beyond, I wondered if my parents had a clearer, bird's-eye view of all the rowdiness. I looked over at Owen again. I could visualize my parents sitting in lawn chairs, popcorn in hand, shaking their heads. *First she forces the kind, smart boy out of the apartment like a crazy person,* I imagined my parents' thoughts. *Then she carouses with drunken fire starters. What's happened to our little girl?*

I inhaled deeply and linked my arm through Lindsey's. "Let's get out of here," I said. "I have a ten-minute cab ride to invent an excuse for why my hair is burned and I'm covered in pumpkin."

In the cab, Lindsey and I tried to concoct a feasible explanation for my singed hair while brushing leftover pumpkin goo off of ourselves.

"Oh my God, you're like Cinderella!" Georgia exclaimed over the phone when I called her for some advice. "And why didn't you *stop, drop, and roll*?!! Everybody knows: you catch on fire, you *stop, drop, and roll!* Did you sleep through elementary school?" Georgia's voice was shrill.

In the end, Lindsey and I decided on a modified version of the truth. We invented a story involving a slippery floor and a single jack-o'-lantern whose top had been removed.

The cab pulled up to my apartment and Lindsey wished me luck. I rehearsed my story on the elevator ride up. Funny thing is, I never even needed the details because Jolie was more obsessed with *what* happened rather than *how.*

"Your hair! Your hair!" she kept repeating after seeing me trudge into the apartment. She raced over to me. "Thank God, not your face." She put her hands on either side of my face and tried to assess the damage. Then she wrapped me in an amazingly soft blanket and called an emergency session with Trent. He showed up twenty minutes later.

"I'm not happy about being called over at one in the OH

MY GOD, your hair!" He practically *ran* over to where I was perched at the kitchen bar and started molesting my head. He walked around me four times, then took a breath and said, "Well, at first I thought we could go funky, asymmetrical, but I keep getting eighties flashbacks, so that's a no go." He sucked in a breath. "I think we're just going to have to whack it off. I think you could pull off a wedged bob."

Jolie saw my face and tried to reassure me. "Lindsey went shorter with her hair and she looks great."

"Yeah, but not *that short.* Plus, I don't have her bone struc-ture," I whined. "My face is all cheeks. And I love my long hair. Just the other day, a lady at the bus stop told me my hair looked like Gisele's—the model."

Trent's eyes widened. "Gisele? Oh, honey, let's not get car-ried away."

So, with no other options, I let Trent whack my hair into a bob.

The whole time I watched my wavy locks fall to the shiny kitchen floor, I thought of Owen—and what would have hap-pened if the fire hadn't interrupted us.

chapter eleven

I WOKE THE NEXT MORNING with the smell of smoke still lingering in my clothes and thoughts of Owen lingering on my mind. What *would* have happened if the fire hadn't erupted? Was it possible that gorgeous, popular Owen really wanted to kiss me? I thought of all those sleepless nights back in Pennsylvania when I was afraid I'd never have a boyfriend. Now in this new life, could it be that romantic possibilities were within reach?

I climbed out of bed and joined Jolie at the kitchen table.

She smiled. "I like the shorter hair. It makes you look smarter. Hey, I just got in a sample of the cucumber-mint exfoliating mask from my new skin care line." She held up a black jar. "They need my final approval for the go-ahead. Want to try it out with me first?"

We went into the bathroom and finger painted our foreheads, noses, and chins with a green, tingly paste. We were supposed to let it sit for an hour, so we plopped on the couch, Jolie with a mug of coffee, me with a bowl of Froot Loops, turned on the TV, and let the mask work its magic.

Suddenly, we heard a knock on the door and both instinctively looked at the ornate clock on the living room wall. It was only ten. I shrugged and decided to open the door.

In retrospect, I should have checked the peephole. But I didn't. So when I opened the door with green paste covering my face and wearing my pink flannel duck pajamas, I was completely unprepared to see Owen's flirtatious smile. I threw my hands over my face and screamed. Owen burst out laughing.

Jolie set her mug down with a quizzical look.

"Sorry to show up so early and unannounced," Owen said with a wry grin. "I told the doorman I wanted to surprise you. Guess I have a trustworthy face."

Jolie got up and crossed the room, her hand outstretched. I stayed frozen in the doorway.

Owen extended his hand. "Owen Nichols. And you're Emily's aunt, I presume?" He sounded so mature and articulate. "Emily and I had some unfinished business."

Jolie raised her eyebrows at me.

Oh my God. Unfinished business. The tilt-and-lean, the parting lips. We were just shy of contact, Lindsey had said. I blushed.

"Remember, Em?" Owen said. "Last night, I told you I would show you around the city?" He leaned toward me and touched the end of a bobbed lock of my hair in his fingertips. His eyes twinkled with mischief.

Jolie looked back and forth from Owen to me, and I wondered if she was thinking about our *players* conversation.

"Oh, right," I said with exaggeration. "Did we say ten? I thought it was eleven! Let me shower and rinse this mask off."

As I ran into my bedroom, my cell phone rang. I saw the caller ID listed Lindsey. I picked it up. "Hey, I can't go to your riding lesson with you this morning. Now ask me why."

"Okay," Lindsey said. "Why?"

"Because *Owen* is in my kitchen eating an English muffin with Jolie! He showed up this morning, totally unexpected, and said *we had unfinished business!*"

"Oh my God," Lindsey panted.

"Do you think he really likes me?!" I whispered frantically.

"OF COURSE he likes you! Don't be such an idiot!!"

"You've got to help me." I hyperventilated. "I don't want to screw this up. Tell me what to do."

"Okay, wear that pretty lip gloss Jolie used last night. Make sure you have gum. Oh, and if all else fails, just laugh like everything he says is hilarious. Good luck!"

"Thanks!" I said, and we hung up.

Forty-five minutes later I emerged from the bathroom. Any signs of Jolie's hesitation were erased; she was transfixed by Owen's charm and had clearly forgotten to even bother removing her own cucumber-mint mask. They were in the kitchen, Owen's sleeves of his blue oxford were rolled to his elbows, and he was cracking eggs into a glass dish. He reached past her and grabbed a wire whisk from a container of utensils.

"Seriously, kid," Owen said, his back still to me. "How can you not know how to scramble an egg?"

Did Owen just call my aunt kid?

Jolie threw her head back and laughed.

Owen looked over his shoulder at me and smiled. "Ready?"

He handed the whisk to Jolie, then covered her hand with his and swirled it in the eggs. Then he patted her on the back two times. "Remember, nobody likes runny eggs."

Jolie laughed again.

We closed the door behind us and Owen turned to me. He took my hand in his.

"Hey," he said, smiling. "I was worried about you last night." He reached over and stroked my short hair again. "After the cops and firemen left, I looked everywhere for you—but you were gone. I'm glad to see you weren't hurt. And that you even had time to get your hair done." He grinned again.

I shook my head. "Yeah, I'm okay. It was just, a minor hair catastrophe . . ." He laughed, and I waited for him to say something else, like about whether he'd gotten in trouble for having the party, but the elevator doors opened with a *ping* and we walked in.

"So what are we doing?" I asked tentatively.

He flashed that flirtatious smile. "Stuff."

My stomach felt all knotty with anticipation. What did he have planned? I felt this enormous pressure not to crush his expectations. What if he thought I was boring? Oh my God, he was going to think I was an inexperienced, immature simpleton. I wished I had time to call Georgia. I needed to know what Silvia Rodero did to make all the men of Rio adore her! Didn't she do some flippy thing with her hair and call everyone *cara mia*?

Owen looked at me funny. I took my finger down from my imaginary glasses and pretended to rub between my eyebrows.

"Did I get all that green stuff off?" I asked.

He nodded, amused.

The elevator doors opened and we walked through the lobby into the crisp air. The sky was a magnificent cobalt blue and the sun peeped in and out behind cotton bundle clouds. There was practically no breeze, but somehow the leaves were falling from the trees and circling around us in patterns of gold and red. We walked over toward Hudson River Park.

He put his arm around me as we walked along the bike path flanked with towering elm trees. It was a breathtakingly romantic walk, and if the maniac bike riders left us alone for two seconds, I'm sure we would have concluded our previously attempted kiss. But on they rode.

Looking out to the dark water of the Hudson made me think back to the peaceful, calm Delaware River. My relationship with the Hudson had been much more tumultuous. *Please,* I prayed. *Just for today, let these waters sweep me away to a fairy-tale land with no plane crashes, no mysteries, and a popular boy who adores me.*

Owen sat down on a bench. "This place is awesome," he said.

"Yes, it is," I said breathlessly.

"I know what you're thinking," Owen said.

That this is the beginning of something new, something perfect, something unexpected . . .

Owen smiled. "They do like tons of photo shoots here all the time." He nodded toward a stretch of lawn. "Some days this place is just loaded with hot chicks everywhere. Even in the winter when it's cold as balls, they've got these models with skimpy little bikinis on and man, you can really tell when they're cold." He snickered.

Okay, not exactly what I was thinking.

A few minutes of awkward silence passed. I tried to think of something to say.

"So, the party was fun last night." *What am I talking about??!! Does he really think I would say I had fun after I caught on fire??!!* My stomach felt tight and anxious.

"Yeah. It was fun. Crazy fun."

Silence again. Two bike riders whizzed by us. Owen pulled his cell phone from his back pocket and made a call. "Yeah, Clyde? We'll be there in ten."

Clyde? Who was Clyde?

When we walked back to the road, there was a black Town Car waiting for us. A man jumped out of the car and held the door open for us.

I gave Owen a suspicious look.

"My dad lets me use the car for special occasions," he said, sticking his arm out to let me get in first. *Special occasions!* I was so worried that Owen wasn't having a good time, that he noticed the awkward silences and stilted conversations. But he called this day a *special occasion.*

"Take us to the ferry," Owen told Clyde, the driver. He held my hand as we drove farther downtown, apparently to a place called Battery Park.

"We're taking a ferry?" I asked.

"To see the statue," Owen explained, smiling. "What's more New York than good old Lady Liberty?" he asked, looking out the window.

The Statue of Liberty. *The most famous symbol of freedom.* That's what Owen was trying to tell me—I deserved freedom from my grief, freedom from the burden of my mother's apology. Freedom to begin a romantic journey . . .

While waiting in line to board the ferry, the salty air blew my hair and pricked my cheeks. In the distance, the green statue seemed to smile toward me. The line of tourists wrapped around us, but I hardly noticed. Maybe I was getting used to this busy city after all. Owen told stories and jokes and cheered for the street performers near the station. He never asked about the accident or the apology, and I truly felt like the new Emily.

I was so caught up in the pure romance that I forgot an important detail: I get seasick. Like deathly ill, fall-on-the-floor seasick. I looked across the turbulent water toward the statue. It couldn't be that long of a trip, I thought.

Fifteen minutes aboard the ship and I was in full-blown agony, hand to my mouth, praying. *Hey, Big Guy, please, please don't make me throw up. Not in front of Owen. Just this once, let me not puke.*

"Poor baby," Owen said, rubbing my back.

The boat finally docked at Liberty Island. Once my feet hit the solid ground, my stomach settled a little. We walked inside the statue and began to climb the never-ending stairs. The first wrapping staircase led to a double corkscrew staircase with small triangular steps, and I wished I had known where we were going so I could have worn sneakers. Or at least something with a flat, rubber sole. Not the black boots with skinny kitten heels that kept catching in the open steel stairs. I wanted to have meaningful, romantic conversations with Owen, but I was so frustrated with the stairs I found myself wishing I was at home, on the couch, watching *E! True Hollywood Story*. Luckily Owen didn't seem to notice I was lagging. He kept talking about all the cool things there were to do in the city.

"At the back of the café, there's this hidden door that leads to a swanky little bar where they don't even card," he was in the middle of saying. "It's pretty sweet."

"How cool!" I answered, a little out of breath. I wasn't sure what café he had been telling me about, but as I looked over at Owen's dimple in his left cheek, I felt really guilty. He was trying. Trying to show me all the opportunities that lay ahead of me. Of *us*. If we were to go on another date sometime, that is.

I thought about the fact that even a month ago, I wouldn't have been out and about at a busy tourist destination with a hot guy—I was barely able to leave the house at all. It seemed like a miracle that a guy like him would even put up with a girl who had as much baggage as me.

He swatted me with a cheesy foam Statue of Liberty crown as we stepped off the ferry and walked toward Clyde. I giggled, trying to ignore the nausea that was still with me from the trip back. "This has been such a great day, Owen. I mean it. And I was definitely a little less sick on the ride back," I added. "So, thanks."

"What? Are you ready to go home already?" he asked, teasing me. "I'm kind of hungry."

The thought of food was not appealing, but I didn't want to

disappoint Owen. So I followed him to the car and Clyde drove us back toward Greenwich Village. We pulled up to an old carriage house that had a line of people waiting to get in.

"Wait, I need to freshen up. After the ferry, I feel kind of gross."

Owen came close. "You," he said, "look perfect." My spine tingled and I followed him in.

Inside the restaurant, we were seated at a small table in the corner under a huge wall of exposed brick. I sat in the plush, red velvet chair and stared up at the enormous stained glass windows that formed the shape of a flower.

Owen had a satisfied look on his face. "I know," he said, nodding. "I know what you're thinking. One if by land, two if by sea . . ." He looked at me with anticipation.

No, I had no idea what he was talking about. "Paul Revere? Right? I think I remember that being a *Who Wants to Be a Millionaire?* question . . ." Owen was looking at me like I was crazy. Then I glanced down and saw that was the name of the restaurant. One If by Land, Two If by Sea. "Oh, right, the restaurant." I hoped he thought I was being funny again.

Owen smiled wide. "My dad knows the owner."

I forced an impressed nod. I opened the menu and noticed that the food descriptions were extravagant with words I didn't understand like *infusion* and *aubergines*. It kind of reminded me of the spa menu at Cornelia Day where Jolie had taken me weeks ago—totally over my head. After the horrendous ferry ride, I really just wanted a burger and fries, but this did not appear to be an option.

A statuesque blond approached our table. "My name is

Claire and I'll be your server tonight." She spoke in a raspy voice and looked only at Owen.

"Well, hi, Claire," Owen said in his usual flirtatious way.

"Hey. You look so familiar," she said. "Do I know you?" She leaned over resting one elbow on the table so there was a view straight down the line of her enormous chest.

Owen's eyes followed the trail of cleavage. He leaned closer toward her. "My name is Owen Nichols." He smiled flirtatiously. "I come here sometimes . . ."

"I bet you do," she said. She was so seductive, so blatant. I felt a lump in my throat like I wanted to cry. Owen probably didn't even remember that I was there with him; he was too busy eyeing the hills and valleys of our waitress.

"Wait," she said, putting a finger into the air. "Are you in my theater class? I swear, I've seen you outside this restaurant. I'm a film student at NYU."

"An aspiring actress," Owen said, nodding. "Nice."

She laughed, her skirted white apron bouncing on her hips.

I stared down at the menu. Owen had said I looked perfect. Not five minutes ago, he said the word *perfect*. My eyes filled with tears, making the words on the menu swim around. I couldn't pronounce anything on the menu; I *was* a simpleton. Why did I think I could go to a restaurant that served *goat cheese tortellini dusted in wild fennel pollen*? Pollen? Wasn't pollen the stuff that turned cars yellow and made my dad's eyes itchy? Just thinking about my dad and how out of place he'd feel in a restaurant like this made my throat constrict. I started to feel that dizzy, numb feeling again. I looked at the menu once more. *Purple asparagus; turnips stuffed with pig's feet.* Purple asparagus? Pig's feet? What was I doing here?

"Well, Owen," the temptress was saying. "Would you like to hear our specials?"

"I would love to," Owen said.

Without glancing at any notes, she began reciting with theatrical emphasis. "Tonight we have a *spicy* sumac squab breast *romanced* by a hot-chili-flecked pasta that will make you *lose your self-control.*" She stopped to exhale a long breath and Owen leaned back in his chair as if waiting for her to bend down and kiss him.

Do not cry. Do not cry.

I stiffened up. "Guess those acting lessons are really paying off," I said.

Two pairs of eyes shot toward me in surprise. It was like they both forgot that I was there.

Claire glared at me. "Humph," she grunted, turning back toward Owen. "What would you like to eat, Owen?"

I tried to focus on the menu. *Pick something, anything,* I commanded, but all I could concentrate on was trying to swallow the lump in my throat. I looked up. Owen had just ordered something *medium rare.*

Claire turned to me with an agitated expression. "And what do you want?"

"Um." Focus. Order something. Not the pollen thing. "Ahh, I'll just have the special. You know—so I can *lose my self-control* and all."

The waitress gave me a snarky look, shoved her pencil in her apron pocket, and turned on her heel. Owen watched her cross the room and disappear behind double doors. Then he turned to me, a smile plastered on his face, shaking his head

"I really think I know that chick." He couldn't stop grinning. He shook his head again and laughed. "We just can't figure out where we met!"

"Right," I said. "I was here—for that conversation."

"Right." He nodded. "You're funny, Emily."

"Um, excuse me. I need to go to the bathroom." I bolted across the room and flung open the bathroom door. There was a woman in a uniform sitting on a chair, but I didn't care. I plopped down on an upholstered couch and whipped out my cell phone.

First I texted Lindsay, not sure if she'd be back from her lesson. Then I hit 3 on my speed dial.

"Jolie! It's a complete disaster!" I wailed. "He's totally flirting with our waitress who's this blond bombshell film student with enormous boobs and a habit of licking her lips. Maybe he is just a player like Trent said and he doesn't even care *who* he's with."

"Whoa, Em, calm down. He's there with YOU, not some slutty waitress. Don't freak. If she's flirting with him, maybe you just need to flirt more."

"How 'bout a REAL solution! I am utterly *inadequate* to start a seduction scene with the hottest guy in our whole class—possibly the whole universe. This is a disaster. I shouldn't have come." Tears threatened worse than before. Who was I kidding? I wasn't ready to live like a normal person and go on normal dates. Let alone go out with Darlington royalty.

"Remember last night you and your friends were posing

and making camera faces and we all said that you could be a model?"

I sniffled. *"A pre-pubescent, tween model for Gymboree* is what Trent said." I saw the uniformed bathroom attendant smile.

"Oh, come on! You know he was just joking," Jolie said. "Listen, sweetie. The point is, when you relax and have fun, you sparkle!"

"Sparkle? I don't think so."

"Yes. You sparkle. Now go—channel that. Relax and have fun. Owen picked you."

"Okay. I'll relax. Thanks. I feel better," I said, even though I wasn't sure if I did. I felt so alone as soon as we hung up.

The uniformed lady handed me a tissue. "The boys," she said in a thick accent. "They always cause the heartaches."

I nodded. "Thanks." I dabbed at my nose. Then I took a deep, sniffly breath in. I checked my bobbed haircut in the mirror, then strode back out toward our table with my head held high. *Owen picked me.*

Our meal arrived just after I sat down. What had I ordered? I stared down at the plate. It looked sort of like chicken. I cut into the meat and tentatively tasted it. At first, I thought, *Okay, not too bad,* and then I remembered *spicy something or other that might just make you lose your self-control.*

And lose it, I did.

First my nose started running. Then I began coughing. Big sweat bullets dripped down my forehead. It felt like I had dumped a whole jar of jalapeño peppers down my throat. I grabbed for my water and guzzled. I wiped my eyes. I looked down at my food, then up at Owen. And then we both started to laugh. My big crazy laugh came flying out of me like it hadn't in a long while, and because I was leaning on the table, the vase rattled and I made a move to grab it before it fell over, making Owen laugh more.

I pointed down at my plate. "What IS this?" I asked, dabbing at my eyes, now wet from the spiciness and the laughing fest.

"That was the special," Owen said. "The spicy squab."

I shook my head. "I don't even know what that means."

He gave me a look like, *How could you have lived this long and not know what squab is?*

"Seriously," I said. "I don't know." And there it was—the clear delineation between Owen's world and mine. He lived in a world of fancy restaurants with strange meals and I, clearly, did not. I guzzled more water.

"It's pigeon. A baby pigeon, actually." Owen smiled.

OH MY GOD. "I just ate a *pigeon*?" I tried not to barf right there onto the fancy linen tablecloth. "How could you let me order pigeon?"

Owen burst out laughing all over again. "I know. I thought it was a little suspect."

I watched him cracking up, then I started to laugh too.

Owen cut his steak and forked half of it onto my bread plate. And just like that, I relaxed.

Claire reappeared later after we'd turned down dessert, this time wearing freshly applied lipstick and flushed cheeks. She laid the check down in front of Owen.

"I hope the service was satisfactory," she crooned, lowering her eyelids into a seductive half closure. God, she was so *obvious.* Why didn't she just write down her name and number and give it to him?

"Hey," Owen said, handing a credit card to Claire. "Why don't you write down your name and number."

WHAT?!

"I'm going to write a letter to your manager and tell him what a great job you did," Owen said.

Claire glanced my way and raised her eyebrows as if to say, *What do you think about that?*

I shot her a *I think you're pathetic* scowl.

Claire pulled out her pen and scrawled her information on a scrap of paper. "I put my cell and e-mail there too." She looked over at me, then back to Owen. "Just in case."

"Cool," said Owen, oblivious to the nonverbal fight Claire and I were having.

We grabbed our coats and left. Owen waved in Claire's direction.

Owen asked if anything was wrong on the walk home, after letting Clyde know where to meet him to take him back. I told Owen I was fine. I wanted to be happy. And it had been a good date, sort of. I mean, it was way better than when Justin Chapman took me bowling and we split a pitcher of Pepsi and a pizza. It was even nicer than when Scotty Dayton took me to the Newtown Diner and told me I could order anything I wanted, including an appetizer. But with those guys it was so easy. I could just be myself and not worry that everything I said would sound stupid. And I never felt like I had lost some competition to a sultry waitress. Why couldn't it be both ways? Have easy comfort *and* sparks of electricity?

We arrived back at the apartment to find Jolie and Trent in the middle of a Scrabble game.

"*Wishy-washy* IS a word," Trent was saying. "Like, stop being so *wishy-washy* about the rules of this game."

They both turned and looked at us.

"Hi," Owen said. "Thanks for letting me borrow Emily for the day. I hope we can do it again soon." He smiled his thousand-watt smile, rubbed my arm, then waved goodbye as he shut the door.

"OH MY GOD," Trent said, dropping his Scrabble tile on the floor. "That is one fine-looking boy. He's so polished and groomed for his age—dashing in a soap-opera-handsome kind of way." He started fanning himself. "Whew, good for you, tiger. Am I sweating? I think I'm sweating. Was that Owen?"

I nodded.

"I knew it was him, I just knew it," Trent said.

"So," Jolie said, "what did you guys do all day, before the, ah, trip to One If by Land, Two If by Sea?"

I recounted our day's events and was glad Jolie hadn't made a big deal of my freak-out call from the restaurant bathroom.

Jolie *was* looking at me intently, though, rolling the letter *S* tile between her fingers. I noticed her freckles were showing and she looked young sitting there on her living room floor with Trent. "Would your mom let you go out with this guy—spend all day with him?" Her eyes darted back and forth between me and Trent.

"It wasn't a big deal—just a fun day together," I explained.

"Seriously," Trent added. "It's not like she's jumping into bed with him; didn't you see, he didn't even give her a kiss goodbye." He turned toward me. "Why was that, hon, do you need a mint?"

Maybe it's because I had pigeon breath, I thought.

Jolie dropped her *S* tile on the ground. "Can we please not say things like *jump into bed*?"

Trent rolled his eyes. "Jump into the new millennium, Jo. She's sixteen! Turn on the TV—tits and ass everywhere."

"Can we *please* not say *tits and ass*!" Jolie clenched her teeth.

Trent shooed his hand at Jolie. "Get some medication and chill." He looked back down at the Scrabble board. "Look! That was a triple word score! I'm beating you so bad."

I walked down the hall toward my room with Trent's words buzzing in my ears. *He didn't even kiss her goodbye.*

chapter twelve

KISS, KISS, KISS. I wrote the words in the condensation on the bathroom mirror with my finger the next morning. *Why didn't Owen kiss me?* I was so confused. Did I even want him to kiss me? After his flirtatious behavior with the waitress, maybe he *was* just a player. I thought back to the car ride when he looked at me with those green eyes and told me I was perfect. I didn't care if he was a player or not, I wanted him to kiss me!

I wiped my hand in a circle and stared into the mirror. Even with my wet hair slicked back, I didn't look too awful. Not hideous, anyway. I had decent eyes and a small, unobtrusive nose. My face was not the problem, I decided. Clearly, Owen had been repulsed by my body. LACK of body, actually. I bet from the moment he wrapped his arm around my bony ribs he thought, *If I wanted a scrawny companion, I could have picked up a stray dog at the rescue mission.* I looked over my shoulder and wondered how much butt implants would cost.

My cell phone rang in my bedroom. I grabbed a robe and raced to get it.

"So," Lindsey said. "What happened? Did you tell the

skanky waitress to leave your guy alone?" So she'd gotten my text the night before.

"Before or after Owen asked for her number?"

"WHAT?"

I replayed the night's end. When I got to the part about Owen waving goodbye without a kiss, Lindsey groaned.

"I know," I said. "That can't be good, right?"

I heard a clicking noise, like Lindsey was tapping a pen on her desk. "Well, maybe he's taking a new approach."

"Huh?"

"When Owen dated Cecilia Rallins, I think they pretty much jumped right to it, if you know what I mean. But come on, Cecilia is easier access than an East Village dive bar. Plus, they only went out for like a month. I think he really likes you— the Statue of Liberty, the restaurant—it's all so romantic."

"Cecilia Rallins? Owen dated Cecilia Rallins?" I panicked. An image of her hunter green polo stretching over her DD-size chest flashed in my mind. "Oh my God. First the busty waitress, now this. Obviously, I'm not his type. I mean, Cecilia Rallins? Come on! I heard for a fact that she has her bras custom made."

"She's dumb as dirt," Lindsey said. "I'm pretty sure she has a tutor for home ec"

"Darlington teaches home ec?"

"Whatever, you get my point. Don't worry about her. Plus, I'm sure if Owen knew all about your football star ex-boyfriend in Pennsylvania, he'd feel insecure too."

I sighed. "Maybe."

"So what are you doing today?" Lindsey asked. "Do you want to go shopping and take your mind off this?"

"I was supposed to meet with Anthony to finish our chem report that's due tomorrow, but I'm not sure if that's going to happen," I said vaguely.

"Why?" Lindsey asked.

"Well." I took a breath. "Last week we sort of had a little . . . disagreement."

"About what?"

"Oh," I said, "I messed up our chem project. I kind of spazzed out. I mean, it was totally my fault. I probably should just call him, apologize and get it over with."

"Or you could forget about chemistry and shop with me."

As much as I would have loved to avoid the discussion with Anthony, I told Lindsey I really needed to straighten things out with him. At least that was one issue I might have the ability to solve. Unlike my mother's apology, which seemed so unattainable.

"Well, good luck," Lindsey said, and we hung up.

I stared at the phone, afraid to speak to Anthony after the way he avoided me in class. I chickened out and texted.

I tried for a solid hour to work on the chemistry lab but couldn't concentrate. I looked at the clock on the wall and started to panic. Still no word from Anthony. In my entire academic history, I had never failed to complete an assignment before. I decided I needed a change of location. So I gathered up my books and headed outside. I still hadn't quite figured out the subway system, so I took a cab to the New York Public Library.

As I entered under the towering stone archways, I instantly felt smarter, convinced I could complete the chemistry assignment on my own. I found a seat in the Rose Reading Room and laid out my books. I looked around. Boy, it was pretty fancy for a library. The ceiling was painted with clouds, and crystal chandeliers glowed like something you would see in a ballroom. *Ballroom—how romantic.* I tapped my foot and wondered why Owen hadn't kissed me. Or complimented me on my haircut. Or called me.

My cell phone rang and snapped me out of my daydream. It took me a few minutes to find the phone in my bag and the ring echoed through the immense room. An old lady at the table across from me glared in my direction. I gave her an apologetic shrug.

"Hello?" I answered.

"Hey, it's Anthony."

My heart started to race. "Um, Anthony, I want to say—"

Anthony cut me off. "I know what you're going to say. I said some things that upset you. I should never have accused you of not wanting to understand the apology. But then I thought you were okay, but my mom always says, *Girls may act like they're okay, but if you hurt their feelings, they're NOT okay.* So you obviously were NOT OKAY. But I didn't know that you were not okay, and I'm sorry. I know you overreacted, and I know you're probably embarrassed. When I said you were a little crazy, boy, I didn't know the half of it. But you felt comfortable enough to talk to me about your parents, and of course I'm happy about that. So we don't need to make a big deal out of the whole *smashing of the beaker thing.* I'll admit, I was a little upset, but after rethinking it, I'll just let it go. And if you gain some respect for me for being so awesome, well, I'm good with that."

I smiled. "Actually, I was just going to tell you that you left some of your chewed-up pencils at my house."

"Oh."

"I'm just kidding!" I laughed, and with the vast twenty-foot ceiling, my honking laughter echoed for what seemed like miles. Hundreds of eyes scolded me.

"I'm *really* sorry," I said to Anthony, lowering my voice and leaning over the heavy wooden table. "You must think I'm a nutcase."

"Well, I've known that all along," he said, laughing.

I relaxed. "I guess just talking about . . . you know, all of it . . . the memories . . ." I took a deep breath.

"You don't have to explain anything to me," Anthony said.

"I just keep wondering if maybe you're right. I actually did try and search for some clues." I doodled on a blank page of my notebook.

"What did you do?" Anthony asked.

"Just searched the Internet, but I didn't come up with much. I don't know if I can handle trying again."

He thought for a moment. "You'll do what you need to, when you're ready."

I sighed. "So what do we do about the lab report?"

"It's already done. I've printed a copy for you."

"What? I WOULD have done it!!" I insisted.

The grumpy lady held her finger up to her lips. *Ssshhhhh!*

"Yeah, right," Anthony said, laughing.

I bent my head closer to the table and whispered, "I spent

all weekend reviewing my notes and I'm all caught up. I know EXACTLY what's going on with the molecular weight calculation thingy. I'm totally up to speed."

"I have no doubt," he said sarcastically.

"Well, I'll do the next report. You can take the week off, I swear."

"Look," Anthony said. "Just promise me: no more hissy fits, no more destruction of property, and I'll be there next Sunday."

"Deal," I said, and we hung up.

As I clicked the phone off, it rang again immediately. This time the whole table next to me snickered. I hit the talk button and heard Georgia on the other end.

"So," she said. "I totally figured out why Owen didn't kiss you."

"Okay, why?" I whispered.

"I was watching my TiVo'd episode of *Rhapsody in Rio* when suddenly, it hit me. This is exactly like the story line from last summer when Luis was falling for June—"

I cut her off. "Georgia, we are both white. This is not a *he's afraid to cross racial boundaries* thing."

The woman at the table next to me sighed loudly and collected her things to leave.

"Well, if you'd LET ME FINISH," Georgia shouted. "Once Luis and June decided to date, Luis was afraid to let June get close enough to see the scar above his lip from cleft palate surgery."

"Oh, jeez," I said. There was a clear lack of comprehension here. "First of all, Owen has NOT had cleft palate surgery. In fact, he probably doesn't have a single scar anywhere on his body. He's *flawless*. The only reason he didn't kiss me is either A—he suddenly recognized that I am completely unworthy of his godliness and affection . . ."

I heard giggles from behind me.

"Not true," Georgia said.

"Or B—he thinks I'm totally inexperienced and is afraid I'll be a bad, messy kisser." More laughter around me. "Or C—he thinks I'm a complete prude. Neither of which is a very good option."

"Although not that far off . . ." Georgia said.

"That's REALLY nice," I said. A girl walked up to me and handed me a slip of paper that said, *D—he's just not that into you*. I scowled at her and balled the paper up.

"I'm just kidding. Chill out." Georgia laughed. "He's obviously attracted to you or he wouldn't have taken you out."

"Yeah, but he didn't even compliment me on my hair! I had like eight inches taken off and he barely noticed."

"On *Rhapsody in Rio*, Selena got a nose job, a lip job, a boob job, and a tummy tuck and Ricardo asked her if she took a nap because she looked so well rested. Guys are oblivious."

"I guess. So, I talked to Anthony and mended things."

"Good for you. I knew there was an ounce of maturity in you."

"Get this," I said. "He did the lab report for me. Even after I freaked out and everything."

"What do you mean, HE DID THE LAB REPORT? You're NOT SERIOUSLY considering handing in someone else's work as your own, are you? Haven't you heard of plagiarism? Oh my

God. You could get kicked out of every college before you even get accepted."

"I'm not plagiarizing!" I shouted. Twenty heads turned in my direction.

A grungy student from across the table growled, "Library, dude, library."

I lowered my voice and cupped the phone. "We're lab partners. We did most of the work together . . . He just, you know, tweaked it a bit." I tossed my books into my backpack, holding the phone against my ear with my shoulder.

"Uh huh. Because we all know how good you are with those chemistry calculations."

"We're *partners*! Whatever. I just thought it was cool of him." I got up to leave and people clapped, actually *clapped.*

"I suppose, if you disregard the whole dishonesty thing, it was a nice gesture, considering you flipped out and destroyed your compound," Georgia said.

"Well, now that the whole Anthony fiasco is over, I can really focus on Owen. I mean, why would he show up at my apartment if he wasn't attracted to me?"

"Ugh! Give it up! Paralysis by analysis!" Georgia shouted.

"I am so demoting you from best friend status," I declared, stepping out onto the broad sunny stone steps in front of the library, cabs and other cars whizzing by below.

"Ooooh. Threaten away," Georgia teased. "You can't live without me and you know it."

chapter thirteen

MONDAY MORNING, IN HOMEROOM, Anthony turned around and secretly slid the lab report into my back-pack. He held a finger to his lips and mouthed, *Ssshhh.*

For a moment, I had an ounce of guilt and wondered if Georgia was right. But it was too late; the report was due by sixth period. So I smiled and whispered, "Thank you." Then I silently prayed. *Hey, Big Guy. I swear, I'm only accepting this because of the dire circumstances.* I thought about adding that it would be super-great if I got an A on this report but decided not to press my luck.

WHEN I SAT DOWN at the lunch table later, Andi was fran-tically text messaging on her iPhone as Lindsey read over her shoulder.

Andi looked up at me. "Okay," she said, very business-like, tapping the screen of her phone. "When Aidan stopped by to visit me at the Roxy shoot yesterday, he said that Owen had not mentioned anything about the date or lack of a kiss. So we're seeing if he mentions it today."

"That's good, right?" Lindsey asked.

I looked across the room and saw Aidan staring down at his phone. Owen sat next to him, dipping his fry in ketchup.

"You're texting Aidan NOW?" I shrieked. "STOP! Owen is right there! He'll think I'm a stalker!"

Andi slid her phone into her purse. "Aidan said he's going to casually bring up the party, then say, *So, did you spend all day Saturday cleaning up?* That'll give Owen an opportunity to tell them he spent Saturday with you. If he doesn't mention anything—"

I interjected. "Then we'll assume he's embarrassed to be seen with me and thinks I'm a total loser."

"Not true!" Lindsey said.

Andi fingered her blond hair. "But if he DOES bring up the date, Aidan will be able to tell if he likes you or not by how Owen talks about you."

I felt my stomach do a flip.

Andi's cell phone remained silent for the remainder of lunch.

"They're probably just talking football," Lindsey said reassuringly.

We glanced over at their lunch table and saw the guys talking animatedly. Aidan and Ethan high-fived, then Ethan stood up, reached into the back pocket of his khakis, and pulled out a fifty-dollar bill. He smacked it down on the table in front of Aidan.

"See," Andi said, flipping her shiny blond hair as she turned back to face us. "Football bets. We'll just have to wait."

AT THE START OF CHEMISTRY CLASS, Mrs. Klein requested the lab reports. As I turned around to collect the reports behind me, I noticed Carly again was not wearing her glasses. But obviously, she couldn't see. Her eyes were all squinty, and she pushed her pages back and forth to try and focus. Ethan tapped Carly's shoulder, and immediately she stopped squinting, turned, and looked at him, flushing. Ethan flung his lab report toward her and the stapled pages missed her desk, floating toward the ground.

Carly jumped out of her seat. "I'm so sorry," she said. "I'm such a klutz."

Anthony nudged my arm, waiting for me to pass the reports ahead. He followed my gaze toward the back of the room. "Yeah," Anthony said. "She's got it bad for him."

"You think?" I asked.

"No doubt," he said, passing the stack of papers forward. "She started wearing makeup, she changed her hair. And the glasses thing—it's a dead giveaway."

"Hmm," I said, surprised by Anthony's acute observations.

"Poor girl," Anthony whispered. "He'll break her heart."

"Why would you say that?" I asked.

Anthony gave me an incredulous look. "Come on, Emily. Guys like Ethan don't date girls like Carly."

"Why?" I said quickly. "Because he's a big-time basketball star and she's unpopular and a little, ya know, pudgy?"

"Pretty much."

I sighed. "That is so wrong, though. What if she's really nice? Maybe he could actually like her for who she is," I said, my voice rising despite myself. I wasn't sure why I was coming to her defense—I'd barely met her.

"You and I both know nice is not enough," Anthony said, matter-of-fact.

"Would YOU date her?" I asked with a touch of hostility I hadn't meant to show.

"Why, because I'm not as popular as Ethan, it would be acceptable?"

"No, I'm asking if you would date someone who was maybe average looking but had a good personality?" I asked, trying to control my sudden anger at the situation.

"Why are you getting so mad? You don't even know her."

Why was I getting mad? It was true, I didn't know her. My mind was spinning. Back in Pennsylvania, while I wasn't unpopular and I had never been overweight, I always felt like I just blended in. I remembered what it felt like to sit on the sidelines and wait to be noticed. Now in New York, with Jolie's makeup and Trent's hairstyle, I was embraced by the popular crowd and pursued by a very popular boy. But I couldn't help but wonder if we were back in Pennsylvania, would Owen even give me a second glance?

I leaned over and whispered in Anthony's ear. "What if Carly weighed less, and had a mini-makeover? Look at her— she really could be pretty with a little help. Or is she still not dateable because she's not popular?"

"Wow, are you like bipolar, or do I just bring out the crazy in you?" Anthony started laughing.

"Mr. Rucelli?" Mrs. Klein said. "Would you like to share with the class what's so funny?"

Anthony turned his head back toward the front of the room. "What's so funny," he said, deadpan, "is how a girl can go from pleasant to pissed off faster than a Porsche can go zero to sixty."

All eyes fell on me.

Mrs. Klein smiled. "Well, Mr. Rucelli, as my husband says, that is what sets us women apart from men: violent mood swings and neediness."

The class laughed.

I jabbed Anthony in the back with the cap of my pen and knew he was smiling.

After Mrs. Klein dismissed us, Anthony and I walked down the hallway together. All the talk of popularity reminded me of the thoughts I'd been having for weeks now.

"Hey," I said tentatively. "How come I never see you at lunch?"

"I eat in the library," he answered with no shame.

"Why?" I tried not to sound judgmental.

He shrugged as we turned the corner. "I do my homework at lunch so when I get home from school, I have time to chill. I go to bed early since I get up so early."

We stopped at my maroon-colored locker and I turned toward him.

"Don't you worry that people could make fun of you?"

"Do you honestly think people are tracking my lunchtime rituals?" He chuckled. "And if they are, who cares?"

I care, I thought as I opened my locker to throw some books in. But Anthony just shrugged again, unaffected by other people's opinions. My stomach dropped knowing that even though I might enjoy Anthony's company more, I'd rather sit and listen to never-ending recounts of modeling jobs and horseback lessons than worry that my classmates were mocking me.

"Hey," Owen said, walking up to me from the other side. "Just the person I wanted to see."

"Really?" I asked, smiling. My heart skipped a beat.

Owen leaned against the metal locker next to mine. God, he looked all sparkly and perfect.

"I had a really good time Saturday," Owen said.

"You did?" My heart continued to thump. I tried to lick my lips. "Um, I had a great time too. Thanks for showing up."
Thanks for showing up?!

If he thought I was an idiot, he didn't let on. Owen reached over and gently touched my arm. It was a simple gesture, but it sent my heart drumming to a techno beat.

He smiled. "I was wondering if you wanted to come to my swim meet next week? Andi comes a lot to watch Aidan, so you guys could come together."

You in a swimsuit—I'm there.

Owen started laughing.

Oops, did I say that out loud? *Make an exit before you humiliate yourself any more!*

"I'd love to go," I said. "Thanks." I turned to walk to my next class.

I looked for Anthony to finish our conversation, but he had walked on without me.

"**HONEY, I'M HOME,**" I called as I practically skipped through the front door of the apartment that afternoon. "How was your day? Mine was blissfully wonderfully awesome!" I'd been grinning pretty much nonstop since the encounter with Owen at my locker. I had immediately told Lindsay about it, who said she'd come to the swim meet next week too and we could head over to her place afterward.

"It was fine. I styled Cameron today," Jolie answered from the other room as I threw my book bag on the floor.

I walked into the living room. *"Diaz?"* I opened the takeout box on the coffee table and grimaced. Falafel. I hated falafel.

"Yes, Cameron Diaz, for a *Vogue* shoot. She's hilarious; she ripped the butt of her pants and had to borrow mine when she left. Not even kidding," Jolie said, coming out of her studio.

"Cameron Diaz wore *your pants*?" I laughed as I poked at a falafel ball with my finger.

"Yeah, only they fit her like capris." Jolie grabbed the remote and flipped through a few channels, still standing behind the couch. "So I, uh, got a call today. The house sold."

I dropped the carton, caught off guard.

Suddenly the entire noisy city seemed to go silent, from the cabs honking and sirens usually racing down the block to the little yappy dog in the building next door. It was just dead quiet.

Jolie cleared her throat. *"Your* house. It actually sold a few weeks ago, but the deal finally went through . . ." She didn't make eye contact with me. "Since your parents had no surviving relatives, you're the solitary heir." Jolie still didn't look at me. "I put the money in a trust fund for you."

I stared at Jolie and then at the TV, feeling empty, numb. My high from the day totally vanished—as far away as my childhood home seemed now. As far away as my childhood itself. I didn't know how to feel.

After a couple hours of staring at the television and nibbling halfheartedly at the takeout, I dialed Georgia. She was silent at first, and somehow I just knew she knew why I was calling.

"The new family moved in a couple days ago." She sighed. "I wasn't sure if I should tell you. They put an American flag on your front porch and garden gnomes in the shrubs."

"Garden gnomes?" For some reason, it hadn't seemed real until she'd said *garden gnomes*. They made it seem so . . . final. The whole world I'd grown up with all my life—everything I'd known up to the tragedy—replaced with the new.

Replaced with garden gnomes.

chapter fourteen

"LOOK," ANDI SAID, pointing to where a group of guys in green swimsuits and caps emerged from a locker room. "There they are." Andi, Lindsey, and I had climbed into the stands at one end of the Olympic-size swimming pool in the Darlington Athletic Center. It was one block away from the school in an enormous facility that housed an indoor track, a basketball court, a gymnastics area, and then the huge pool. The humid air smelled strongly of chlorine, and the cream-tiled walls were damp with perspiration. The dark skinny jeans I'd changed into after school stuck to the backs of my legs. Suddenly, the black cashmere hoodie sweater Jolie had bought me to survive the late October chill didn't seem as smart an outfit choice as I'd thought either.

I watched as Aidan scanned the crowd, his eyes shifting up and finding us. He waved. Aidan nudged Owen, who looked up at us, nodded, and grinned.

I caught my breath, noticing Owen's body was a perfect, athletic V: strong, bulky shoulders tapering to a trim and sculpted waist.

The team members swimming in the free-style race climbed onto their platforms and crouched into ready position. The muscles of Owen's back contracted in anticipation. God, he was toned.

The shrill whistle blew, and the swimmers sprang into the water and began their laps. As they swam, I thought back to Pleasant Meadows Summer Camp, where Georgia had dragged me over the summer between sixth and seventh grade. I'd thrown a fit because swimming lessons were required, and they forced me to remove my sneakers. Several of the kids had made fun of my toes, and when I returned home crying, Mom had simply laughed and told me to be thankful for the things that make us each unique. She told me that keeping my weird-o toes a secret would just make things harder.

"He won! He won!" Lindsey clapped, jolting me from my memories.

"What?" I turned my head.

Andi waved, jingling her two sterling silver bangles. I'd never seen her look so eager. "Did you see that?" she said, tugging at the sleeve of my hoodie. "He was totally checking to make sure you saw him win." Andi sat back down with a perplexed look on her otherwise perfect face. "I just don't get it. He seems really into you—but no kiss, and it's been, what— almost a week since your date?" She made air quotes when she said *date*. "And he hasn't called or texted you once?"

"No," I said, suddenly feeling on the defensive.

"Maybe," Lindsey said, pushing back her now-layered dark locks from her face, "he just doesn't want to move too fast."

Andi rolled her big blue eyes and gave us a look like, *What guy do you know that doesn't want to move fast?* But then the crowd was dispersing and exiting the bleachers. We walked down. As we reached the bottom bleacher, Aidan and Owen walked over, freshly showered and dressed in loose-fit jeans.

"Congratulations!" I said to Owen. His blond hair looked dark and dripped onto his shoulders.

"Thanks," Owen said. "I'm so glad you came. Hey, do you want to come over later to, like, celebrate?"

I felt the heat rise in my cheeks. I was stumped. This was one of those times where I had to make a decision. Do the right thing and stick with the plans previously made to have dinner with Lindsey or follow my lust into the strong arms of the swim champ that actually seemed interested in me.

"I'd love to," I said. "But . . . I'm going over to Lindsey's tonight for dinner." *Damn my moral upbringing!*

Andi's eyes widened in shock and she mouthed, *What are you doing??!!*

Lindsey turned around and looked as if she was going to protest, but Owen interrupted her. He put his hand on my shoulder. "Okay, we'll do it another time," he said.

"Okay," I said, a little breathy, immediately regretting my decision. But then I saw Lindsey's face, sweet and genuine, and knew I had done the right thing.

We all walked down the corridor of the athletic building. Lindsey's diamond earring fell out and I bent down to help her find it. Owen walked ahead and joined Aidan and Andi.

"You should go over to Owen's tonight," Lindsey whispered.

"But you're all by yourself tonight," I said.

"I'm *always* by myself. Really, you should go."

"No," I said. "We made plans. Anyway, I want to hear about Mister Stud Jockey Jason."

Lindsey beamed. "I can't believe I actually asked him out. I mean, if a note counts as asking."

I laughed. In the distance, there was a repetitive *boom, boom, swish* reverberating from the basketball court ahead. As we rounded the corner, there she was, nose pressed to the door of the basketball court, her breath fogging up the glass window: the new girl, Carly.

In front of me, Aidan elbowed Owen.

We all knew the unmistakable *dribble, dribble, swish* coming from behind the door could only be Ethan. He was the only one who never missed.

Carly heard our footsteps and looked up. Her face froze; she knew she'd been caught staring. She turned and without a word scrambled away.

"That girl can move pretty fast," Aidan said.

Given her size was left implied.

I felt bad for her. She had done nothing to deserve their ridicule. But at the same time, I knew in some dark recess of my mind, I was relieved not to be the one they were mocking.

WHEN I GOT HOME from Lindsey's, my cheerleading uniform was wrapped in plastic and lying on the kitchen table.

There was a note next to it. *The dry cleaner said pumpkin stains are a pain in the butt!! I went out. Love, J.*

I picked up the outfit and wandered back toward my room. When I shoved the uniform in the back of the closet, I accidentally kicked the small unmarked box I had pulled out a few days before. The box turned to its side and a paintbrush rolled out. I picked it up. It was crusted with dried phthalo green paint. I remembered now. This was a box I had packed with some of my parents' things that I couldn't part with. I pulled the box over and reached inside. There was a Ziploc bag I had filled with my dad's last stack of coins and his ID work badge from Hadford Engineering. I picked up the heavy Gustave Courbet art book that Mom had propped under her stool to give her more height. The book was fat and dusty. I thumbed through the pages, and two cards fluttered to the ground. The first card was old with curling edges and a picture of a single red rose on the front. I opened it up. Inside, in perfect script, it read: *Dear Jill, Thanks for playing hooky with me. —D.* Hooky? And who was "D"?

I quickly reached for the second card. This card's cover was a New York City skyline. When I opened it, there was a photo tucked inside. As I looked at it, my heart quickened. My mother was standing arm in arm with a tall, handsome man. Behind them was a long rope, a line of acrobats, and, in the distance, the Statue of Liberty.

I looked inside the card. *Jill, What a perfect day. You are perfect. D.*

I dusted off the photo and examined it closely. There was something oddly familiar about the man, like I had seen him on TV or in the movies, but I couldn't place it. In the lower left corner the date was electronically printed on the photo. I did the math and confirmed my horrible suspicion. At that time, my parents were married.

Who was this man? And why had my mom kept these cards for all these years? I got in bed and crawled under the covers, clutching the photo in my hands as I waited for Jolie to come home and give me some answers.

But in the wee hours of the night, I finally drifted off to sleep thinking, *Just a week ago, I stood in that same line outside the Statue of Liberty with a handsome guy of my own. Would I have enjoyed that day as much if I'd known whatever happened at that exact location so many years ago?*

chapter fifteen

"GOD, WHAT'S WRONG? You look awful," Andi said
to me as I placed my salad on our usual cafeteria table halfway through lunch on Thursday. I plopped down in the chair
between her and Lindsey and stared as Andi adjusted the little
camel skirt she wore over textured white leggings and boots.
Her white cable-knit sweater fell loosely off one shoulder as
she scanned the crowd, taking in the scene. I'd been trying
really hard to dress well, varying up the khaki skirts and polo
shirts. But seeing Andi during lunch always made me realize
how far behind I still was.

Today, though, I didn't really care. "Ugh. I couldn't sleep
last night," I said, recalling the hours I spent analyzing my
mother's cards and photo. I patted at the puffy bags under my
eyes. I'd been so preoccupied, I hadn't gotten any chemistry
homework done, which meant I'd been trying to work on it in
between classes.

"Why?" Lindsey asked, her brown eyes soft with genuine
concern.

But before I could answer, Andi said, "This will cheer you up, my dear," and nodded in the direction behind me.

I whipped around, relieved for a distraction, and saw Aidan, Owen, and Ethan carrying their books and drinks toward us. I grabbed my cheeks and tried to pinch some color into them.

"Hey," the guys all mumbled as they pulled a few extra ornate wooden chairs over and squished around our table.

Owen smiled at me. "Missed you last night after the meet. Me and a few buddies chilled at my place."

I blushed. "Um, yeah, sorry I missed it." Lindsey, Andi, and the rest of the crew faded from my peripheral vision, and it was all Owen and his huge, delicious grin. But this time, I felt a pang of something. Not quite distrust, but something else. I guess it was that he reminded me of that mysterious man who'd written notes to my mom. The mysterious "D."

The bell rang, and even though I'd barely eaten, we collected our things and started to walk to our next classes. Owen and I walked in silence for a few minutes.

"I had such a good time on our, you know, date," I stuttered, trying to make natural-sounding conversation. I took a breath. "I've been wondering, like, why or how, I guess, did you decide we were going to the Statue of Liberty that day. I mean, did you plan to take me there, or was it spontaneous?" I tried to sound casual, not wanting to reveal that after seeing Mom's photo of a similar date, I couldn't help but think, Statue of Liberty—how cliché is that? "D" had planned the same date years ago.

We reached my locker and all at once, Owen was leaning me against the cold, dark red metal, staring at me and saying, "Hey, who doesn't like the Statue of Liberty, kid? Even a beautiful, mysterious girl like you. You know, I don't even have your number."

Suddenly, the fact that he planned a cliché date vanished. I was melting into his deep green eyes. "Uh. Uh." The only number I could recall was my old home number from Pennsylvania. "Uh." THINK!

"Here." Owen reached over, grazing my arms slightly, and grabbed my cell phone out of my purse. He flipped it open. Then he took his BlackBerry and programmed my number while I leaned against my locker, immobile. He handed me my phone. "Thanks, kid." Then he leaned over and with the softest, fullest lips gently kissed me. My heart stopped. Like, *flatline.* Then he pulled away slightly, looking into my eyes, and my heart bounced back so fast I just knew I was having a heart attack. My head felt all woozy, and for a brief moment I contemplated calling 911.

The bell rang. Owen raced down the hallway.

I leaned against the locker for a full five minutes before I regained the use of my legs.

ONE KISS WAS ALL IT TOOK to catapult me from new girl in the popular crowd status to couple royalty. Walking down the hall the rest of the week, I saw underclassmen point and whisper.

In the girls' bathroom on Thursday a nervous freshman with jet black hair in a braid asked me where I got my awesome lipstick. I told her I bought it at CVS. I didn't want to say it was from Jolie's latest line and then seem like I was bragging. I politely turned on the sink.

"Do you work out like five hours a day?" she asked, ogling me in the mirror and biting her lip. I shrugged, smiled, dried my hands, and walked out. Since when did random strangers talk to me in the bathroom? Oh, yeah, since I was a Darlington monarch.

Owen still had not booked an official second date, but apparently to the Darlington world, we were a couple.

WHEN JOLIE WALKED IN THE DOOR late Friday night, I flung myself toward her. All the attention I'd been getting at school must have given me confidence. I held up the picture of Mom with the handsome gentleman and the cards signed by "D." The items I'd been obsessing over since I'd found them two nights before.

"What's this?!" I demanded while she was still unwinding her long black scarf.

Jolie took the photo and looked at it for a long time. Her light hair was static from the cold. "Where did you get this?"

"It was tucked into one of Mom's old art books." I tried to read her expression. "Did you know this guy?"

Jolie shook her head. "Maybe it was just some old boyfriend." She kicked off her gold-flecked flats as she edged past me into the living room and sat down on the leather recliner, tucking her feet up under her.

"But look," I said, pointing at the photo in my hand. "Look at the date."

I stood there in the entryway while Jolie tapped on her laptop and started checking her e-mails. Was she blatantly ignoring me?

"Who is D?" I asked.

Jolie shrugged and didn't look at me.

"Well, did you know any of Mom's friends who may have lived in the city around that time?"

"I don't know," Jolie said shaking her head.

"It's suspicious," I said, my voice wavering. "Isn't it? Or am I being crazy? Do you not think this is weird?"

"I don't know, Emily."

"Jolie," I said, my voice practically a whisper now. "Did Mom cheat on Dad?" Just saying it seemed ridiculous, but what else was I to think?

Jolie didn't answer. She just turned and looked out the window at the Hudson.

A new kind of dread took over. For the first time in a long time, I felt truly awake, like all my nerve endings were on fire. It wasn't a good feeling.

I took the photo and stormed down the hall. I buried it back inside the cardboard box and shoved it deep into my closet. Then I slammed the closet door and sat down on the bed, staring hard at the back of the closet door, breathing slowly, and letting the fire inside me burn.

chapter sixteen

SUNDAY MORNING, Anthony showed up for our scheduled lab report meeting. His arms were full of white cardboard boxes tied with string and marked with a green logo that read: *CornerShop Bakery*.

Anthony plopped the boxes onto the kitchen table. "Mom watched *When Harry Met Sally* on TNT last night," he said, tearing the string and opening the boxes, revealing mountains of pastries, but I noticed no lemon pound cake. "Every time she watches that stupid movie," Anthony continued, "she gets all teary-eyed and starts baking. She starts yelling at the TV, telling Harry not to be such a fool. And while she bawls, she keeps throwing more pans in the oven. I swear, what is it with you women and chick flicks?"

"I love *When Harry Met Sally*," Jolie said, peering over the assortment of pastries and grabbing an apple fritter. "Milk?" she asked both of us, going to the fridge.

Anthony and I both nodded.

"Oh, jackpot," I said, finding a whole box of donuts. "I've never seen *When Harry Met Sally*. What's the big deal?"

"You've never seen *When Harry Met Sally?*" Jolie asked, shocked. "It's a classic New York love story! I can't believe that. Well, I know I have it on DVD somewhere, we can watch it tonight, if you want." Her voice was hesitant. We hadn't talked much since I hounded her about my mom's suspicious cards and photo.

"Okay," I said, picking up my glass of milk and handing the other glass to Anthony.

We headed to my room.

"So, this is Emily's room," Anthony said, looking around. "Man, you could fit a basketball court in here." As he glanced around at my things, a smile crept across his face.

"What?" I asked, feeling analyzed.

Anthony pointed. "You have seven unused canvases. Ten unused paintbrushes." His lips moved silently as he counted. "Twelve Bic gel pens. *Twelve?* Stacks of books and two of the same iPods. Do you like buy in bulk or something?"

I picked up the iPods. "One is for music, one is for audio-books." I looked around. "If I like something, I want to have a duplicate. You know, in case something happens to the first one."

Anthony got a look on his face—his dark eyes kind of crinkled for a second and his eyebrows scrunched together. Then it passed. "What about the canvases—they're all blank. Are you ever going to paint something?"

"I guess I'm just waiting to see if someday I'll discover I have my mom's artistic ability."

He walked over toward my bookshelves and leaned in to examine my photos. He pointed to the picture of my parents that I took the summer before the accident. In the photo, Mom is on her knees in her tomato garden. She has on a big straw hat and lime green gardening gloves. She's so engrossed in her tomatoes that she doesn't see my dad sneaking behind her, about to spray her with a water hose.

"Your parents?"

I nodded and smiled.

"Wow, your mom is really pretty."

I didn't correct the tense.

I leaned over his shoulder, taking in Mom's shoulder-length blond hair and the way her smile lit up her whole face.

Anthony used his thumb to wipe off the thin layer of dust and examined it closely. "You look like her."

A big lump stuck in my throat and my eyes started to well up. Anthony glanced up at me.

"You know, if your eyebrows weren't so bushy and your cheeks weren't all pouchy like you had nuts hidden back there." He put the frame down and playfully filled his cheeks up with air and messed up his eyebrows. "You're sort of a squirrel-like version of your mom."

I slapped him on the shoulder. "God, you're so annoying."

"Hey," he said. "I knew it was about time for you to start freaking out."

I thought back to that day a few weeks ago and laughed. Imagine: Anthony kissing me. It seemed so ridiculous now. He was like a big brother, warm and comfortable. Then thinking about kissing brought an image of Owen's soft lips to mind. I blushed.

"Okay," I said, refocusing and taking out my lab book. "I'm totally ready to conquer this report."

Unfortunately, I was wrong. After three straight hours of Anthony walking me through the calculations, my head throbbed and I still didn't know the difference between pressure and volume. And now Anthony was throwing around the word *solubility*. I massaged my temples.

"Let's take a break," Anthony suggested. "If you don't mind walking a few blocks, I know a place I think you'd like."

It was overcast and breezy. Anthony shoved his ungloved hands into his coat pockets. We walked briskly down 11th Street to the intersection with Bleecker Street. Most of the trees had lost their leaves, and scattered Halloween decorations popped up in window displays. Anthony stopped in front of a small bookstore. A black awning draped over the green-painted building. In white print it read: *Biography Bookshop*. Hundreds of books were stacked on a table out front. Anthony opened the door, and I stepped inside. The warm air enveloped my body.

"This place is really cool," I said, looking at the thousands of books crammed into the wooden shelves.

"I know. It's awesome," Anthony said. He held up a book: *Chemistry for Dummies*.

"*Ha Ha,*" I snickered.

After browsing around for about thirty minutes, we met up at the cash register. I found two novels. Anthony was holding *101 New Italian Meals*.

"It's my mom's birthday next week," he said.

We paid for our books and headed outside. I followed Anthony across the street.

"Okay, I'm probably asking for trouble getting you all hopped up on sugar, but this place is unbelievable." He opened the white door.

"Magnolia Bakery?" I asked. "Why does that sound familiar?"

"Because," he said. "It's where all the celebrities go to break their diets."

"I can't believe you shop the competition," I teased.

"It's the cupcakes," he said, smiling. "They're the best."

We each ordered a vanilla cupcake and then crossed the street to the small park. We sat on a bench. Across from us a white-haired man in a suit had his tassled loafers propped up on a stone table.

Looking at Anthony, with a small blob of frosting below his nose, I felt a certain kind of ease. And even though I had spent more physical time with Andi and Lindsey and more mental time obsessing about Owen, with Anthony, I felt a level of comfort that is typically reserved for early childhood friends—someone who knows your history and requires no explanation.

"Can I ask you something?" I looked up from my cupcake.

Anthony smirked. "Only if my answer will not turn you into a raging lunatic, like it has before."

"Seriously," I said.

"Okay, what?"

"Say you were dating someone . . ." I started.

"Now, why do you make that sound so far-fetched?" he interrupted.

"Hush! Let me finish! Okay, say you were in a *committed relationship* . . ."

Anthony shook his head, laughing.

I continued. "Would there ever be an innocent reason for you to do something with a *different* girl? Like, could it be just a *friends* thing?"

"What is it with you girls and your drama?" Anthony leaned back on the wooden bench and took a bite of his cupcake.

There was shouting and we saw a tall man dressed like Tina Turner arguing with another man dressed like Cher. They entered the park.

"Is today Halloween?" I asked, confused. I'd thought it was only October 26th, but considering how disconnected I tended to be lately, it was hard to say. I took one look at Anthony, though, and realized I was wrong.

Anthony laughed at my reaction. "Every day here is an education for you." He chuckled again. "Jolie said you guys were going to watch *When Harry Met Sally* tonight, right?"

"What does that have to do with it?" I asked.

"The whole basis of that movie is that guys and girls can't just be friends."

"Really?" That sounded intriguing. "Do you believe that?" A breeze blew and a few crinkly leaves landed in my lap.

"I'm here with you, aren't I? Unless you don't consider me a friend," he joked. "Just your chemistry warrior."

I smirked at him. "I tolerate you the best I can. Now, back

to my question: Does, say, touring the Statue of Liberty qualify as a friendship activity, or is it too romantic?"

"Is this about Owen? Because I don't think he tours the city with Aidan. Especially not at One If by Land, Two If by Sea."

My mouth dropped open.

"Yes, I know that you guys went out. It's a small school, Em."

I swallowed and ran my fingers through my hair.

The two drag queens passed by our bench. "Mmm. Lovers and their cupcakes. Too cute!" the shorter one said, grinning at the other as they left the park.

I blushed and looked back at Anthony. He raised his eyebrows and I giggled. "Actually," I said. "This is not about Owen."

He crinkled his forehead with curiosity.

I explained about finding Mom's cards and photo. "The date on the photo," I started.

"Were your parents married at the time?" Anthony asked tentatively.

My stomach tightened. I nodded. "But it could have just been a friends kind of thing, right? It doesn't mean that she . . ." I trailed off, not wanting to finish my own thoughts.

He rubbed his mouth with his hand. "That's a little dicey. I don't know . . ." He paused.

I felt the back of my throat start to burn like I was getting ready to cry. The cold air nipped at the back of my neck.

"I don't know, Em," he said again. "Maybe you should give up on the search for answers to your mom's apology. You're not really getting anywhere, and you might stumble into some stuff that maybe you don't want to know."

I knew that he was trying to protect me, but suddenly I was angry. I swallowed hard and blotted at my eyes. "You were the one that told me you would ransack the house. You told me to Google her name. YOU told me I should stop being afraid!"

The two college-age girls sitting on the bench next to us glanced over.

Anthony smiled a sad smile. "Sorry, Em. Sometimes my advice is all wrong."

I couldn't look at him for a minute. I just stared down at the little heart that was carved into the wood of the bench, pressing into it with my chapped finger. I was so angry. Look for answers, don't be afraid. Don't look for answers, they might hurt you. I felt like I was trying to rock a vending machine to free a jammed bag of candy. Back and forth. The harder I pushed, the more the candy got wrapped around the wire coil.

Anthony's phone rang. He glanced at the screen, sighed, and put his phone away.

I tossed a napkin across the bench at him. "Wipe your mouth," I said. I got up from the bench. Birds cawed through the cool gray October sky. "And go call your mom back," I added. "I'm sure she's wondering where you are."

I walked away, toward the park gate, and rested my hand on the cold railing, staring at the people bustling by in their fall jackets and scarves. I wondered how many of them were hurrying home to their mothers.

chapter
seventeen

ANTHONY WAS UNUSUALLY QUIET as we walked back to the apartment.

"Sorry," I said finally. "Sorry I snapped."

The corners of Anthony's mouth quivered, then he burst out laughing. "Man, you are hanging on by a thread! But how come I'm always the one around when it snaps?"

I smacked him. "Shut up."

Back at the apartment, Anthony handed me a sheet of study notes to help me prepare for our quiz on Tuesday.

After he left, I called Georgia and told her about finding the cards and picture. I was waiting for her to cheer me up, tell me a long story about the latest drama going on at school, but Georgia was unusually quiet.

"G, you knew my parents better than anyone," I went on. "You know how Mom stuck Post-it notes in Dad's briefcase every day. And how she sat through all those Eagles games even

though she hated sports. And remember on his fortieth birthday when she made that two-tier cake from scratch? I mean,
she really loved him. Right? She wouldn't have cheated on him,
would she? Do you think this is linked to the apology?"

Georgia let out a long breath. "I don't know. Maybe the Statue
of Liberty thing was just an innocent friends thing." She said
what I wanted to hear, but her voice was flat and unconvincing.

"That's what I was thinking." I stared at my oversized
shadow on the long bedroom wall. I could hear Georgia breathing. Again, I imagined rocking the jammed vending machine.
When would the candy bar finally break free and rid me of this
permanent state of dangle? I changed the topic. "Speaking of
friends, have you ever seen *When Harry Met Sally*?"

"No. Why?"

"Jolie and Anthony said the whole movie is about whether
guys and girls can be friends. It's supposed to be really good. I
want you to rent it and tonight at seven call me so we can watch
it together."

"Sounds like a plan. Oh, and Em?" She lowered her voice
slightly. "Maybe you should lay off trying to understand your
mom's apology."

I swallowed. "Well, what am I supposed to do now? Give up
on finding my answers?" Now that I had finally found the courage to start searching, I knew there was no way I could stop—
not with the feeling of possible revelation growing deep inside
my gut—a feeling of both fascination and fear.

It was silent on the other end for a few seconds. Georgia let
out another exhale. "Do what you have to do, Em. Okay, talk to
you at seven."

I invited Lindsey over, because to Jolie's shock, she hadn't seen the movie either.

Lindsey and I camped out on the floor, dressed in sweats, propped up against the coffee table. Jolie came home with two large boxes of pizza and paper plates.

At seven sharp, Georgia called. I handed the phone to Lindsey and my two friends finally met.

Lindsey handed the phone back to me. I plugged in my earpiece and we popped the DVD in.

Trent bounded through the door, a bag of popcorn in one hand and a six-pack of Diet Coke in the other. "I can't believe you started the movie without me," he whined.

"It's just the opening credits," Jolie said.

Trent pointed a finger at my phone and earpiece. "I need the 411 on this."

"Georgia's going to watch the movie with us," I explained.

"Thank God for free nights and weekends," Trent said, sitting on the couch next to Jolie. "The evolution of Sally's hair through the years is the best part of this movie."

"Shut up and let us watch," Jolie said.

From the moment Harry and Sally took off toward a new life in New York, I knew I was going to like the movie. Trent grabbed my earpiece and debated with Georgia about which haircut best suited Sally.

Jolie, Lindsey, and I argued whether men and women could just be friends. After all, in the movie, Harry and Sally did get married.

"I just hope one day I can find my own Harry," Lindsey said, turning around and propping her elbows on the coffee table.

"Me too," I agreed.

"What do you mean?! You HAVE found your Harry! O-wen!" Lindsey sang.

"But he hasn't called all weekend. And I gave him my number," I said.

Trent flipped my phone shut. "Who hasn't called? The hot player?"

Lindsey laughed.

"That's because he's off PLAYING!" Trent said. "I warned you about him . . ."

I felt my heart sink.

Jolie pointed to the door. "Out. See you tomorrow."

Trent kissed Lindsey's and my cheeks and made a playful scowl at Jolie.

"Well," I said, standing up and stretching. "Maybe after your date with your horse guy, you'll have your own Harry."

"It's not until Thursday. I still can't get over that he said he would meet me in the city. Anyway, keep your freakish toes crossed for me," Lindsey said, laughing. I tried not to seem scandalized by the tryst she was planning with a twenty-three-year-old riding instructor as Lindsey thanked us for the movie and left.

Jolie and I cleaned up the pizza boxes, then I went into my room. I lay on my bed, my mind racing. How does a girl prioritize her scrambling mind? (1) Wallow in the mystery of my dead mother's apology? (2) Agonize over what seemed to be the impeding revelation that said mother was an adulterer? Or (3) Obsess over the mixed messages of Owen, hot God and apparent, but not positive, boyfriend?

Just then, my phone rang. The caller ID displayed Owen's name. Obviously, my priorities shifted to number three.

"Hi," I answered, trying to sound casual.

"Hey," Owen said, sounding equally casual. "How was your weekend?"

"Boring," I sighed, "and non-eventful."

"Well, I was upstate visiting relatives, but I couldn't stop thinking about you...."

"Oh, yeah?"

He couldn't stop thinking about me!!! Take a breath.

We chatted for a few minutes about his trip and an upcoming test at school, then we hung up. I glided into the bathroom replaying every word of our conversation. As I washed my face for bed, all my other worries floated to the far corners of my mind and I found myself humming the song from *When Harry Met Sally*, "It Had to Be You."

"HEY, GUESS WHAT," I said, breaking open a bag of chips the following Monday at lunch.

Lindsey and Andi both turned to me, probably shocked that these weren't the reduced-fat kind.

"Owen called me last night. He said he thought about me all weekend!"

"Ooh, that's awesome!" Lindsey exclaimed while opening a bottle of seltzer.

"Did he book another date?" Andi asked.

"Not exactly ..." I said, and stuck a chip in my mouth.

"Hmm," Andi grumbled. "He's obviously interested ...

You need to make him jealous, Emily. Let him realize that you're not just sitting around and waiting for him."

Unfortunately, sitting around and waiting is EXACTLY what I'm doing, I thought.

"But how?" I asked.

Andi twirled her long blond hair around her finger. "When the guys come over, just follow my lead."

Lindsey and I exchanged doubtful glances.

As if on cue, the guys got up from their table and worked their way across the lunchroom.

"Quick," Andi said. "Start laughing." She opened her mouth and let out a loud, "Ha ha ha!"

Lindsey and I looked at each other and cracked up.

"What's so funny?" Aidan asked, leaning over to peck Andi on her cheek.

"That's a powerful laugh, kid," Owen said.

I blushed.

Andi turned toward the guys. "We were just talking about Emily's ex-boyfriend, Steve."

Owen's eyes narrowed to slits.

"Why is that so funny?" Ethan asked, shooting a crumpled brown bag across the room into the trash can.

"Because," Andi explained, twirling her blond hair. "He wants Emily back sooooooo bad. He keeps calling and sending her stuff. Right, Em?"

All eyes turned to me. "Um, right," I mumbled.

Andi continued. "This weekend, he sent her a teddy bear with a note that said, *Remember last New Year's and my parents' hot tub.*" She paused for a minute, the words *hot tub* lingering in the air. "A teddy bear! I mean, COME ON! The only time a teddy bear works is if there is a very sparkly piece of jewelry attached." Andi threw her head back and laughed again.

She was pretty convincing. I made a mental note to encourage her to check out the drama department.

"Hot tub! That sounds interesting," Ethan said, giving me a smarmy look.

My face started to burn. If they only knew that last New Year's, Georgia and I spent the night watching *New Year's Rockin' Eve.*

Owen caught my eye. "And I thought you said your weekend was uneventful. While all along, you were receiving romantic packages . . ."

The bell rang and I quickly gathered up my things.

"Here, I'll take that," Owen said, grabbing my lunch tray.

"Thanks," I said, picking up my backpack.

He walked slowly, waiting for me to catch up. He opened the door and we walked into the hallway.

"So how come I never knew about this Steve guy?" Owen asked.

I put on my best game face. "We broke up before I even moved here."

"But apparently, that was not his decision . . ." Owen said, following me to my locker.

He leaned against the metal locker next to mine and locked eyes with me.

Thirteen . . . twenty-seven . . . six. The door wouldn't budge. *Damn. Think!*

Thirteen . . . twenty-seven . . . five. Nothing. *Shoot.* I swear I heard Owen laughing.

"My parents have dinner plans Friday night," he said. "And I get scared when I'm alone on Halloween. You want to come over? Help me give out candy to all the adorable brats who live in my building?"

"What?" I asked, sounding way too breathy.

"You—me—my house—Friday night?"

I cannot believe Andi's plan worked! I smiled and shrugged. I hadn't made any other Halloween plans anyway.

"Okay," Owen said. "It's a date." Then he turned around and walked off to his class.

I whipped out my phone and text messaged Andi that she was brilliant.

Hey, Big Guy, I'm very sorry I lied about the whole Steve thing, but technically, it wasn't my fault. I promise to try and avoid situations in the future that involve such blatant fabrication. By the way, do you think you could jog my memory about this combination? I really need my notebook.

The bell rang and I was late.

As my literature teacher droned on, I thought about the emotional power of jealousy. My mind wandered to the photo of Mom and the handsome man named "D." Perhaps Mom also had a friend who had concocted an elaborate ruse to inspire jealousy and help re-ignite some extinguished sparks in her married life?

THAT AFTERNOON, I instant messaged Georgia and replayed my conversation with Owen.

Tennisfan500: Then he invited me over Fri. night to give out candy to the trick-or-treaters in his building. Cute, right?

CutiepieG: That's GREAT! What are you going to wear?

Tennisfan500: NO IDEA. Maybe I'll go shopping with Andi and Lindsey for something. Am I supposed to dress up? Like in a costume?

CutiepieG: I dunno. Sounds like you'll be on the other side of the fence and should just look normal. 'Member in the movie when Harry tells Sally she should wear skirts more often? Maybe you should wear a skirt. By the way, did you tell Anthony we loved the movie? Does Anthony hang with Owen? You never mention them together.

Tennisfan500: It's weird. Anthony is so nice, but he doesn't seem to have any close friends. I mean, he gets along with everyone—it's not like he's a geek or something, but he's never at any of the parties or anything.

CutiepieG: Maybe he's a loner.

Tennisfan500: He doesn't seem like loner material. Maybe I should wear a skirt . . .

CutiepieG: Scratch that. I changed my mind. No skirt, because remember my *don't shave your legs* policy. That way you know things won't go too far . . .

Tennisfan500: Give me a break.

CutiepieG: Just in case you get caught up in the moment, remember: hairy legs means the jeans stay on.

"THIS SAYS TO COOK THE STUFFING *inside* the turkey. Seriously, that can't be right," Jolie said, her nose pressed between the pages of *The Joy of Cooking*, a notebook in one hand.

"You've gotten at least fifty invitations to Thanksgiving dinners," I said, gesturing toward a pile of fancy stationery stacked on top of the microwave. "And Thanksgiving isn't for three more weeks."

"None of those matter. We've always spent Thanksgiving as a family and that's how it's going to be," Jolie insisted. "I just need to prepare. Now what's that casserole thing your mom always made?"

"Sweet potato casserole." I closed my chemistry book, crumpled up my paper, and threw it in the trash.

Jolie flipped to the index in the back of the book.

"Owen asked me to come over to his house Friday night," I said.

Jolie looked up. "The player?" She air quoted *player*. "Asked you for another date?"

I shrugged casually. "Just a low-key Halloween thing."

"We need to tell Trent his theory, as always, was wrong." She flipped back toward the front of the cookbook. "Are Owen's parents going to be there?"

In life you are thrown so many opportunities to travel down the wrong path. I knew that if I simply said, *Yes, they'll be there,* she would never check. I bit my lip, remembering my silent promise to the Big Guy, less than twenty-four hours ago, to stop telling so many little lies.

"Actually, I don't think his parents will be there." *There, Big Guy. Are you happy? Now I probably just blew my opportunity for a date with Owen.*

"Is he having a party?" Jolie asked, sticking a bookmark between the pages and laying the book down.

"No." I got up from the table and sat on the couch. I turned on the TV and tried to act casual.

Jolie pursed her lips and was silent for what felt like an hour. "So it'll be just the two of you?"

"You know, I'm not positive. I think he invited some other people . . ." *He might have,* I thought defensively, looking upward toward the ceiling, not sure whether I was defending myself to the Big Guy or my parents. Maybe both.

Jolie dug into her pocket and pulled out lip gloss. She rolled the tube over her lips, back and forth about twenty times. She capped the tube and returned it to her pocket.

"Fine," she said authoritatively, smacking her lips. She locked eyes with me, looking nervous. "But if you are ever in a situation where you feel . . . uncomfortable . . . I want you to call me. Immediately. And I'll come, no questions asked. Understood?"

This felt so—rehearsed—I wondered if Jolie had been secretly watching *Gilmore Girls.* My heart swelled.

I got up and gave her a hug. "Thank you."

chapter
eighteen

BY THE NEXT DAY, the entire student body knew of my approaching date with Owen. Apparently Halloween was not a "cool" holiday to celebrate in the city, because everyone had seen the big parade a million times before and just wanted to avoid traffic. Andi and Lindsey were going to rent some horror movies and chill. It was kind of sad for me, since Halloween back home had been a really big deal, and everyone at school wore costumes to the dance and played around with fake blood and drank dry ice punch. All that cheesy stuff.

That was why I was even more grateful to Owen for his invitation to spend Halloween together. It was so adorable that he wanted to give out candy to kids. All week, I marveled how, in the face of post-traumatic events, cryptic apologies, and mysterious findings, I, Emily Carson, was about to embark on a second date with the most eligible guy at school.

So, it was no surprise to me when my first few days of

restored glory came crashing down like a curtain dropped at the end of a play.

I awoke Wednesday morning in a world of physical pain.

It was a foreign sensation that felt like I had slept all night with an apple lodged between my teeth. My jaw felt rigid and creaky, and when I attempted to massage the area in front of my ears, I heard two loud POP, POPs.

"Jolie!" I called from my bed.

She flew into my room. "What's wrong?" She pressed her hand to my forehead.

"My mouth hurts."

She scrunched up her face. "Mouth? Like a toothache?"

"Not exactly," I mumbled painfully. "I feel like I got punched on both sides of my face."

Jolie's forehead creased. She touched my cheeks and felt around my chin. "It doesn't feel swollen." She pursed her lips in thought, then grabbed my phone off the charger. "I'm going to make you an appointment with the dentist. I'll see if they can squeeze you in this morning."

I grimaced. "I have a quiz in English I really can't miss."

"Okay, I'll make it for after school." She walked out.

I dragged myself out of bed and into the bathroom. I was sitting on the edge of the tub, holding my cheeks, when Jolie reappeared with a Post-it note that listed the dentist's name, address, number, and my four-thirty appointment time.

"I'll do my best to meet you there," Jolie said. "I may be a few minutes late." She leaned down and kissed my cheek. "Gotta run."

I searched in the medicine cabinet for some Advil but only

found skin care products, dental floss, and a tube of tooth-paste. I wandered down the hall to Jolie's bathroom. It was a smaller version of the master bath with the same beige tile and decorative black diamond accents, only there was no over-sized Jacuzzi tub, just a glass shower. I opened her medicine cabinet and found a similar array of beauty supplies. I tried the cabinet under the sink. There was a plastic Tupperware tub filled with an assortment of cold remedies and pain reliev-ers. When I pulled the tub out of the dark cabinet, an oversized manila envelope dropped down from behind a pile of towels. It seemed like an odd place for an envelope to be. I reached back and grabbed it with curiosity, sending the towels tumbling to the floor. The envelope was fat and sealed with a strip of heavy packing tape. My heart began to race. Whatever was in this envelope seemed to be deliberately hidden. Hidden by Jolie. Since I was the only one Jolie had ever lived with, the envelope was hidden from *me.* My stomach turned. I tried to tear the top of the envelope, but the tape was too strong. I rifled through Jolie's cabinets looking for scissors, finally settling on a pair of tweezers. I shoved the tweezers under the tape and ripped it open. The contents flew out and spilled on the floor. Letters. Maybe ten of them—each addressed to Jill Carson in the same perfect script I saw on the cards. D's handwriting. *Oh my God.* My jaw throbbed. I grabbed the letters and a bottle of Advil and ran to my bedroom. I gave up on going to school, dove onto my bed with the letters, and started reading.

BY THE TIME I made it to my dentist appointment, I had read and reread all the letters. The first two seemed innocent enough, talking mostly about recent exhibits at the art gallery where Mom worked. But by the third letter there was some intangible tone that made me feel uneasy. In his writing there definitely was a palpable romantic tension. Then came letter number eight. Horrible letter number eight. My gut felt twisted in a million directions. On top of that, my whole face throbbed with pain despite the Advil.

The dentist's serene blue and green waiting room did nothing to soothe my nerves. The receptionist opened a clear glass window. "Can I help you?" she asked.

"I have a four-thirty appointment. Emily Carson."

I filled out a clipboard of information and planted myself in a chair, replaying the letters in my head. One in particular, the eighth letter, that was dated January 15, 1993. I couldn't get one line out of my brain. *Even in the cold drizzle, your soft kiss was enough to melt my heart.*

Clearly, I wasn't adhering to Georgia and Anthony's advice about abandoning the search for answers, but what could I say? Now that I had inadvertently stumbled on something that seemed scandalous, I felt like I might be headed toward some kind of revelation. My need to understand my mother's apology outweighed my fear of the train wreck that might loom ahead.

"Emily Carson?" a tall brunette dressed in scrubs called from the doorway.

My stomach clenched. I followed the hygienist to an exam room.

She motioned for me to sit in the large chair. Poised with her pen to the paper, she asked, "So what's bothering you today?"

My mother kissed another man.

She waited patiently for a minute or so, then finally said, "Is it one tooth in particular?"

I cleared my throat and forced my brain to work. "It hurts here," I said, motioning to the sides of my jaw. "I feel like I have toothpicks propping open my mouth."

She chuckled and took an x-ray of each side of my mouth. "Okay. Dr. Reeves will be with you in a few minutes."

I reached for my backpack, where I'd stashed the letters. Maybe I misread something. As my hand reached the zipper, a lanky man dressed in aqua scrubs flew through the door and sat on a wheeled stool. He slid over to my chair and extended his hand.

I dropped my backpack to the floor.

"I'm Dr. Reeves," he said, flashing two deep dimples. His salt and pepper hair was cut short and he looked like a slightly less handsome version of George Clooney. "Woke up with an achy jaw, huh?"

I nodded.

"Can I feel around a bit?" he asked, motioning to my mouth.

"Okay."

He poked his gloved fingers inside my mouth and prodded around. He removed his hands and looked at me with a sympathetic face. "Have you been under any stress lately?"

Um, kind of. I nodded.

He nodded back. "It seems like you've developed what's called TMJ. That's temperomandibular joint dysfunction. TMJ usually results from grinding your teeth at night from built-up anxiety." He paused, as if waiting for me to comment, but I was not about to launch into the numerous anxiety-causing problems of my life.

Dr. Reeves continued. "We're going to have to fit you with a night guard to help reduce the grinding."

Better make it a good one, because I just found out my mom kissed another man. Stress levels are at a record high.

Dr. Reeves held an x-ray up to the light. "Sorry, Emily, looks like you have a cavity, too."

See what you're doing to me, Mom! Cavities and weird jaw problems. How could you do this to me? How could you kiss another man? I thought you loved Dad. Suddenly, the next thought I had stopped me cold: maybe I didn't know my mother at all.

"Let me take a quick peek," Dr. Reeves said, inserting a metal probe into my mouth.

Maybe she was apologizing because she never really loved my dad or me.

My eyes welled up and tears spilled out.

"Oh," Dr. Reeves said. "I'm sorry, did that hurt?"

I lied and nodded.

He pulled the probe out of my mouth and patted my shoulder. "I'm sorry, Emily."

I wanted to grab his arms and ask him to hug me and tell me everything would be okay. Instead, we both stood and walked out to the waiting room.

Jolie stood and smiled at me. I looked away. She reached to shake Dr. Reeves's hand.

"Mrs. Carson?" Dr. Reeves asked.

"Actually, I'm Emily's aunt. Just call me Jolie."

He smiled his dimpled smile. Dr. Reeves went on to explain

the TMJ, the teeth grinding, and the cavity. Jolie smiled and twirled her hair and I wanted to scream, *How can you stand there and flirt with this man when you know you've been hiding things from me!*

I planned my attack. I'd wait until she was sitting on the couch, then I'd dump the letters in her lap and make her explain.

On the cab ride home Jolie said, "That dentist was very nice."

"You mean he was hot," I said, hoping to make her feel superficial.

"Hot? You think?"

"Wow," I said nastily. "You work with way too many beautiful people. Your perspective is all messed up." I shook my head like I was scolding her. "You can't even recognize a normal, attractive person."

"God," she said, running her hands through her hair. "All that silicone and Botox. You may be right." She sounded apologetic, which made me feel just a little bad because she didn't even know why I was attacking her.

I turned away from Jolie and looked out the window for the remainder of the ride home. When we got home, Jolie planted herself on the couch. I went into my room and dug the letters out of my backpack. I unfolded the crumpled page.

Your soft kiss was enough to melt my heart.

My heart broke. I knew from the photo that "D" had a Hollywood glamour appeal, but I wondered why it was enough to lure Mom away from Dad. I laid my head down on the pillow and softly cried myself to sleep.

chapter
nineteen

"OKAY, CALM DOWN," Lindsey said.

"CALM DOWN?" I screamed through locked jaws. "How can I calm down? I can't open my mouth!" I paced my room.

"You must chill!" Lindsey demanded, hands on my shoulders, forcing me to sit. "Take a breath. In—out. Good."

I felt myself relax slightly.

"I thought you got something at the dentist's to help with this jaw thing?" Lindsey asked.

"My appointment to get fitted for the night guard is next week. Seriously, Lin, if I open my mouth any wider than this," I parted my lips approximately an inch, "I get this shooting pain."

"So don't open your mouth."

"I am going to Owen's in two hours!! I can't go over there like this. WHAT IF HE TRIES TO KISS ME?!" *Oh my God, what if he tries to kiss me?* I started to hyperventilate.

"He's going to try and kiss me and either A—I'm physically not going to be able to open my mouth and he'll think I'm a TOTAL PRUDE, or B—we'll be mid—make out, the pain will escalate, and my jaw will give out and come crashing down. I'LL PROBABLY SEVER HIS TONGUE!"

"YOU MUST CHILL!" Lindsey commanded, grabbing my phone off my desk.

"Who are you calling?"

She ignored me, pushing buttons.

"Hey, Georgia?" Lindsey said. "We have a situation here." Lindsey explained my predicament.

Since when did Lindsey and Georgia talk?

Silence followed on our end, Lindsey nodding in agreement with whatever crazy suggestion Georgia was making.

"You're right. Okay, hold on." Lindsey went over to my bed and picked up a pillow. "We have to improvise to see how dire the situation is."

"Oh, if you think I'm kissing that pillow . . ." I started.

I heard Georgia's loud protests through the phone.

Lindsey thrust my cell toward my ear.

"Do you really think we want to witness you kissing a pillow?" Georgia ranted, ignoring the fact that she was, indeed, two states away. "It's *painful.* I mean it physically hurts just thinking of you pressing your lips to a flannel-covered bundle of cotton, but I'm trying to help you avoid a catastrophic situation. So I suggest you quit your belly aching and pucker up!"

I laid the phone on my bed and veered toward Lindsey, who was holding the pillow in front of her face like a mask.

"Close your eyes! Make it authentic!" Georgia bellowed across the phone lines.

I closed my eyes, tilted my head, and made contact. The pillowcase was dry and scratchy. Lint stuck to my glossed lips. I tried to imagine Owen's hands at the nape of my neck, stroking my hair. I parted my lips and imagined his mouth, hot and moist . . .

"OOOWWWWW!"

Lindsey jumped back, dropping the pillow. "Are you okay?" she asked.

I massaged my jawbone.

Georgia was babbling over the phone.

I reached over and put her on speaker.

"That decides it," Georgia said. "You need to postpone the date."

"Postpone? I can't postpone," I whined.

Lindsey vigorously shook her head, agreeing with me. "No, you HAVE to go."

The three of us argued about what to do. Tell him the truth? Postpone? Smile through the agony?

"Postpone," Georgia said. "That's my final answer." She sighed and hung up.

Lindsey, who had gone to the bathroom, returned holding an orange medicine bottle in her hand. "What's this?" she asked, pointing to the prescription label.

"It's a muscle relaxer Dr. Reeves gave me to help me sleep until I get my night guard," I explained.

"HELLO!!!" Lindsey shouted. "You've been kissing pillows

when you had a whole bottle of muscle relaxers sitting in the next room?!"

"I take those at night. They make me a little loopy."

"That's a bonus, Emily. You're going to be nervous—not only will this relax your mouth, it will relax *your mind.*"

I contemplated. "Nah, I can't. I'll be all giddy. Owen will think I'm a nut."

Lindsey waved the pills in one hand and the phone in the other. "Muscle relaxers or postpone. You pick."

"Fine," I said, grabbing the medicine bottle. I popped the tablet in my mouth and chugged some water. "This night is going to be a disaster. I can just feel it."

"Stop being so dramatic. You'll be fine. Just let these little babies work their magic," Lindsey said, tapping the medicine bottle. She flung my jeans toward me. "Come on, get dressed."

The ensemble that Andi and Lindsey had selected, including the Blue Cult jeans, Dolce & Gabbana top, and Anthropologie cowboy boots, cost more than I had spent on clothes in an entire year. At the time I had felt guilty for charging Jolie's credit card for so much. But now, knowing she hid those letters from me, I felt no remorse. Oh, and there was the extra sixty-five dollars for the water bra Andi insisted I purchase. I slid into the clothes, eyeing myself in the mirror.

Lindsey pulled a necklace out of her bag and wrapped it around my neck. "There," she said. "That looks great."

I unclasped my mom's pearls and gently placed them in my jewelry box.

We both turned toward the mirror. She was right, I looked pretty darn good. I smiled and noticed my mouth tension was easing.

Jolie popped her head in my bedroom. "Hey, want some makeup?"

Maybe it was the muscle relaxers kicking in, but suddenly my pent-up anger toward Jolie for hiding the letters seemed to lessen. *In fact,* I thought, *when I confront her this weekend, maybe I'll give her a chance to explain.* "Sure!" I said. "Makeup is *awesome.*"

Lindsey walked over and reread the medicine label with a look of concern.

I grabbed her arm and we followed Jolie into her studio.

Jolie fluttered around shaking her brushes on my cheeks and around my eyes, but I noticed that she wasn't applying much color.

When my eyes still looked virginally clean, I grabbed the brush from Jolie. "Hey! There's no eyeliner on this!"

Jolie looked at the brush, faking innocence. "Oops," she said, and lightly dabbed the brush into a pot of mocha-colored powder.

"Are you purposefully trying to make me look young and innocent?"

Lindsey chuckled.

Jolie looked like she had just swallowed an ice cube. "Fine!" she said, dipping the brush back into the pot. "But don't even think about asking for red lips."

Lindsey and I laughed.

Jolie darkened my eyes but left my lips a glossy nude. It was flattering and age appropriate, she said. By the time Jolie had finished with my makeup, my mouth was positively pain free.

Lindsey and I walked back into my room to grab my purse before I left.

"Look," I said. "Watch." I opened my mouth, then shut it. Open, shut, open, shut. I started to laugh.

Lindsey patted my shoulder. "Muscle relaxers kicked in, huh? Maybe you should have something to eat before you go."

"Nah," I said. "Owen said there was lots of candy and his maid put leftovers in the fridge or something." I did a small dance around my room.

Lindsey gave me a suspicious look. "Are you sure you don't want a few crackers?"

I shook my head. With my expensive outfit, my hair and makeup done, and my restored jaw function, I felt a rush of excitement. I was ready. *Look out, Owen, here I come.*

Owen answered the door in baggy jeans and a crew neck black shirt that stretched across his broad shoulders. He was barefoot and his hair was still wet, like he had just gotten out of the shower. The hint of water shimmered in his short blond hair, setting off the yellow flecks in his bright, green eyes.

I followed him into the living room and sat on the couch.

"Want something to drink?" he asked.

"Sure."

He headed for the kitchen.

"So when will the kids be coming by?" I asked, looking around the room. It was very airy and modern—even more so than Jolie's place. But then there was a huge portrait of a soldier over the mantel against the far wall that looked like it had to have been in the family for centuries. It didn't seem to fit with the sleek furniture with metal detailing and enormous flat-screen TV on the other end of the room.

"Huh?" Owen called from the kitchen, where I heard the sound of a refrigerator closing.

"The um, trick-or-treaters?"

"Oh, they're around," he said, coming back into the room. "You missed the mad rush at around five o'clock." He smiled, and I felt light-headed just looking at him. "I'm sure we'll still get some stragglers, though." He set the drinks down on coasters on the shiny black coffee table and touched my chin.

"Oh." I picked up the remote and started flipping through the channels anxiously. If he was nervous at all, he hid it well, talking animatedly, occasionally touching my arms or nudging my leg playfully with his.

We fell into a rhythm of conversation that was much easier than on our Statue of Liberty date. We each ate a few mini Snickers bars and started talking about food: Owen had never, in his entire life, cooked a meal. His family's cook prepared pretty much all the food they ate in their home. His favorites were Belgian waffles and strawberries for breakfast. He recently discovered Japonais in Union Square. I told him Jolie never cooked either. My favorite meal was my mom's lasagna. I was tired of takeout and craved anything homemade or not from a carton.

We talked about travel: Owen had skied in Switzerland, backpacked through Europe, and cruised the Greek islands. I told him I went to Disney World when I was seven, but aside from the occasional Florida trip, my family spent most of our vacations on the Jersey shore. When I segued into a monologue about which place served the best saltwater taffy on the board-walk, I noticed that the living room was getting a little wobbly. No, actually it was spinning.

In retrospect, I should have realized something was up. I mean, who puts ice cubes in a regular glass of orange juice? And it had tasted slightly medicinal, leaving a lasting burn at the back of my throat. After my third refill, my jaw was not only feeling relaxed, it was downright numb. In fact, I couldn't exactly feel my tongue.

"Would you 'scuse me for one sec?" I slurred, attempting to stand.

"Whoa," Owen said, steadying me back on my feet. "Want some help?"

I flashed him a big, loopy grin. "I'm great. Thanksh."

I staggered down the hall into the powder room. As I sat on the toilet, the room started to spin again. I reached out for the wall and accidentally knocked a photo frame off the coun-ter. The glass shattered on the ground. *Crap!* I gently picked up the glass shards, throwing them in the trash, then shoved the picture and frame into my purse. I grabbed my cell phone and speed dialed Georgia.

"Hey, what's up?" she asked.

"Little problem."

She waited. I explained about the mystery orange juice drinks and the spinning room.

"Oh my God. He's trying to intoxicate you! He wants to take advantage of you! I knew this would happen. Okay, the room is spinning, but how do you feel? Are you light-headed?"

"Yessh."

"Oh, jeez. This is bad. I bet he slipped you a ruffie."

"He did not shlip me a ruffie! You watch too much TV! It's just the mushcle relaxer I took. You're not shupposed to mix it with alcohol . . ."

"THE WHAT?!!!"

"Dr. Reeves gave me a mushcle relaxer for my jaw. Lindshey made me take it."

"OH MY GOD. Oprah did an entire episode on housewives addicted to pain pills. You can't just go popping pills, then downing a whole liquor cabinet; it's a recipe for disaster. We need to call the hospital. We need to get you into detox."

"Shhhut up!" I garbled. "It wash one pill. ONE. I'm not a closhet addict. And I wahsn't planning on drinking any alcohol."

"Owen pressured you, didn't he? You gave in to the peer pressure," Georgia insisted.

"I DIDN'T KNOW THERE WASH ANY ALCOHOL IN THE DRINK!!"

"Relax. You need to eat. Something to soak up the alcohol. Like bread."

"Okay," I said.

"Maybe you should call Jolie . . ."

"NO! We're having a good time. I'll be fine. You're right, I jusht need to eat." I hung up. When I stumbled out of the bath-room, Owen was setting a couple of plates at the table in the opposite corner of the living room, nearest to the kitchen.

"Hungry?" he asked.

"Starved," I said slowly, trying not to slur. I planted myself in a chair.

Owen pulled out a dish from the oven. He removed the foil. "Tanya made Turkish lamb chops. And I think this is a cauliflower puree."

I didn't know who Tanya was, but I didn't care. I dove in, praying the sustenance would return my equilibrium. And it did. At least momentarily.

The dishes were still on the table and I'd only had a couple bites of the minty, tender meat when Owen got up and walked over to me. He pulled me up out of the chair, leaned me against the kitchen doorway, and kissed me. Hard and eager. His mouth was firm and aggressive, and my mouth cooperated with such ease, I felt relaxed and confident. *I might be the best kisser he's ever kissed,* I thought with bravado.

Minus that small amount of . . . did I just drool? Guess he didn't notice.

He steered me backward, out of the kitchen, into the living room. Then he leaned me down on the couch. The decline sent my stomach into orbit, but I decided it was butterflies, nothing to worry about. I kept kissing him. His hands roamed around my waist, inching up to my chest. There was an undeniable swishing sound. *Crap. Why? Why did I let Andi convince me to purchase a water bra? The manufacturers of this contraption, while quite clever at creating cleavage, obviously failed to recall the groping that can occur with teenage romp sessions.* Owen's hands roamed. Swish. *Please, Big Guy, please don't let my water bra pop. Please, I'll feed the hungry, clothe the naked . . .*

There was another swishing sound, but this time it wasn't my bra. A tidal wave stirred deep in my stomach, and the walls started to spin again.

I cannot believe this is happening.

I thrust Owen off of me. He went crashing to the floor, just missing the coffee table.

Hoisting myself up off the couch, I clapped my hand to my mouth and barely, *barely* made it to the bathroom. And that's the last thing I remembered.

By the time I was coherent again, I was tucked into my bed, a water glass and a bottle of Advil on my nightstand.

I heard Owen's voice out in the living room. He was thanking Trent for picking me up.

"Shoot," Trent said. "No big deal. I was thirty before I could handle my liquor. So I was on Em's speed dial? Man, it's good to be important."

Small chuckle from Owen. Owen said goodbye and the front door slammed.

Trent's face peered into my room. "You okay, sweetie?"

I groaned. I didn't know which hurt worse: my jaw, my head, or my ego. "Maybe we don't need to tell Jolie?" I suggested.

"Sorry, sugar." Trent grimaced. "She knows. She was a little freaked out. She's on her way home now." He made a big frown. "She left the big boss's party already. So, honestly, the best thing you can do now is pray."

I pulled the pillow over my eyes.

"But more importantly," Trent continued. "Tell me, did Owen hold your hair while you puked?"

chapter twenty

"WHAT EXACTLY WERE YOU DOING, EMILY?"
Jolie's voice was shrill and my head was pounding. "When I
allowed you to go over to Owen's house, against my better judgment, I might add, it was because I *trusted* you."

Pound. Pound. I reached for the water bottle on the coffee
table and swished water around in my cotton-dry mouth.

"I certainly didn't expect that you would get liquored up
and half naked . . ."

"I wasn't half naked! My clothes were covered in puke, so
Owen gave me a sweatshirt." At least that's what I thought—
my memory was a tad hazy. My tongue stuck to the roof of my
mouth as I spoke. Why did my teeth feel like they were wearing
fuzzy slippers? Pound. Pound.

"Well, that's just lovely, Emily. And why exactly did you
puke, huh? Just how much alcohol did you consume? What was
it you were planning to do once you felt all loose and happy?
Forget it." She shook her head violently. "I don't even want to
know."

"Look." I clenched my forehead with one hand, my jaw with

the other. "I wasn't intending to get drunk. You KNOW I don't drink. This is going to sound ridiculous, but I didn't even know there was alcohol in the drink. Owen offered me a drink before dinner and that was it. I thought it was just orange juice."

"You're sixteen! Not thirty. You don't have cocktails before a meal!"

I held my head. I wasn't even about to explain the muscle relaxers.

Jolie took two long breaths. "Okay." Her voice was calmer. "Don't you think it was a little *irresponsible* to let yourself get into that position with that kind of guy?"

"What do you mean, *that kind of guy*? I thought you liked Owen."

"Yeah, I like Owen. Trust me, I've liked a lot of Owens." Her mouth was set into a straight, thin line.

"What's *that* supposed to mean? So you agree with Trent? You think Owen's a player? That he's USING me? That he couldn't actually LIKE me?"

Jolie exhaled deeply. "That's not what I'm saying." She ran her fingers through her hair. "A boy who looks like that and acts like that, he's used to getting what he wants. And at sixteen, there's pretty much just one thing that he wants. I know your mom didn't raise you to be the kind of girl who gets drunk and swaps clothes with the local hottie."

So, she was going to play the dead mother card. Lay on the guilt. Well, it worked. My eyes welled.

Jolie's face softened. She ran her fingers through her hair again. "Look, I know you're a responsible person and this was not in character, but my God, Emily, use your head. Think about what you're doing and who you're doing it with. Sometimes it's just better to stay away from the golden boys and find the nice, shy kid in the corner. He's the one that will treat you right."

"I don't see you dating any shy geeks. So maybe I learned from a good teacher," I said with bite.

Jolie looked away, defeat written on her face. "Emily, I don't want you to live like I live. Sure, it's got a lot of fun, but it has a lot of heartache, too. Live like your mother—true love and stability."

"Yeah, right!" I yelled.

Jolie looked back at me, confused.

I got up and raced for my bedroom with my brain knocking against my skull in rhythm with my footsteps. I ran back into the living room with the incriminating letter in my hand. "I know what you did—hiding this from me! I know what *she* did with that 'D' guy!"

Jolie looked frantic. "What? What do you have?" She reached for the letter and scanned it. "Where did you get this?"

"Oh, play dumb!" I yelled. "I found it where you hid it! In your bathroom cabinet!"

Jolie sat down on the couch, her face flushing red. "The envelope," she mumbled. She turned toward me and tried to take my hand, but I pulled it away fast, knocking the remote off the coffee table.

"Why didn't you show me this?! Who is this guy? Are you hiding anything else? What do you know?" I fired questions at her, but she just stared out at the Hudson.

"LOOK AT ME WHEN I'M TALKING TO YOU!" I yelled. It was my mother's words; we both knew it.

Jolie's face crumpled into her hands.

"Just tell me," I said, softer. "What do you know?"

Jolie picked up the letter and tore it in half. "That's what I know." The letter floated to the ground.

I eased myself back down on the couch and laid my head on the soft, green, chenille pillows. My mom had married the nice, shy kid who kept his coins neatly stacked on the dresser. Then on the sly she romped around with the charismatic golden boy. I wiped my eyes on the pillow, thinking of my golden boy. Bits and pieces of the previous night re-entered my mind. Laughing. Lamb chops. Kissing, groping. Oh God, the water bra. Did it pop? I don't think it popped. Sitting on the toilet. Projectile vomiting. Something crashing. Red puke on Trent's leather seats.

I rolled over and buried my face into the couch. I didn't know which was worse: the splitting headache, the throbbing jaw, listening to Jolie cry, or the tortuous fragmented memories of a ruined opportunity.

"SO, HOW'S MY GIRL?" Owen cooed through the phone that night. "The one with zero tolerance for vodka?"

Uhhh. So it was vodka. My stomach turned. But did Owen just call me *his girl*?! *Even after the disastrous date?*

"I've been through half a bottle of Advil," I moaned. "But at least I can stand now."

"You are so lucky that your puke didn't stain my mom's carpet or you'd be over here, steam cleaning." Owen laughed.

Oh God. "I am so embarrassed," I said. "I took a muscle relaxer . . ." I started to explain.

"Yeah, I know. I saw Lindsey at the gym this morning."

"Owen? Can I ask you a favor?"

"Shoot."

"Could we keep the muscle relaxer/alcohol disaster our little secret? Please? I'm so horrified."

"You got it, kid. I was thinking, maybe you should come over tomorrow, hit the re-do button."

"I really want to, but I have to work on my chem lab report," I said. "It's due really soon and we're totally behind. It's kind of my Sunday ritual from now until Thanksgiving."

"Oh, too bad."

Wow, maybe I really was a good kisser, even in my mildly uncoordinated state.

"Maybe sometime next week?" I suggested.

"That works. The only thing that'll get me through the next week is knowing that we'll be picking up where we left off."

I giggled. "I'll see you at school." I hung up both exhilarated and frightened. I thought about what Jolie said. *Think about what you're doing and who you're doing it with.* I wanted to make out with Owen and have fun. I wanted him to think I was sexy and confident. But I also needed to be smart, to recognize what his true intent was. I wanted to know how to set limits, how to be a girlfriend to someone popular and experienced but remain true to myself. I needed my mother to sit with me on our back porch and tell me what to do. I needed her to make me her best buttery noodles and say, "Just trust your gut and let the blank canvas guide you." All at once I was furious at her. I was furious that she wasn't alive and I was devastated that the memory of her was tarnished by a few letters. How could I be so mad at my mother but somehow still need her to be there, to be the way she was, the way I knew her before I laid my eyes on those words of deception?

I reached into my purse for a tissue and saw the metal picture frame I had broken in Owen's bathroom. I took it out and studied it. Owen was squinting into the sun, kneeling down next to a boy in a wheelchair. They both had Special Olympics T-shirts on, and a volunteer badge hung from a string around Owen's neck.

The phone rang in my purse, startling me. It was Anthony.

"Hey," he said. "Just wanted to make sure we're still on for tomorrow. And you still want to come to my house?"

"Um, sure. And where exactly do you live?"

"Brooklyn."

I recalled the black and white photo of the Brooklyn Bridge hanging on the wall in Trent's salon. I imagined myself sauntering across the bridge, the cityscape a theatrical backdrop and the breeze rustling my hair.

"So you get on the F train at Washington Square Park." He broke my reverie.

F train? "Now when you say *train* . . ."

"Oh, jeez. The subway, Em."

Crap. Who was I kidding? I couldn't navigate myself out of a cardboard box; I certainly couldn't travel to another *borough*. Anthony was spitting out directions. I was about to suggest we meet at a more central location when Anthony interrupted my thoughts.

"Hey, Em? Thanks so much for coming my way. That's really cool of you."

I dropped my head, defeated. "No problem."

I wrote down the directions, asking for spellings and clarifications.

"I promise you won't get lost."

As if I weren't lost enough already.

chapter twenty-one

I WALKED DOWN THE CONCRETE STEPS into the underground world of subway travelers. I looked around nervously. Anywhere that was dark at noon creeped me out. I pressed through the cold, silver turnstile. The metal gave me an electric shock and my hand shot back like a slingshot. The man behind me cackled. I looked over my shoulder.

"My dad used to say when you got shocked, it meant you were full of spark. Ha ha."

The man gave me a crazy look.

Why am I talking to random people in the subway terminal? Okay, shut up and act like you know what you're doing! I looked at all the signs and tried not to panic. There was no mass transit in Newtown, Pennsylvania, and aside from one disastrous ride with Georgia on Amtrak, I had never been on a train, much less a subway, so this was all uncharted territory. How would I know when to get off?

I boarded the train and found a seat. I clenched and unclenched the written directions in my hands. *I can do this*, I thought. *I'm not a complete idiot.* Sure, I had failed to recognize my OJ was spiked. And I had allowed my falsified cleavage to be discovered. And I had drooled on Owen while attempting to kiss him. But *surely* I could travel to Anthony's house without handholding or a GPS.

They announced my stop and I got off, again rereading the directions. *Head west toward Clinton Street.* I hated when people gave directions like that; why couldn't they just say go left or right? Did he assume there was a compass floating in my water bra?

I looked further on the written directions. *Just past the park on Clinton Street . . .*

I tapped a safe-looking man on the shoulder. "Excuse me, is there a park close by?"

He turned toward me, stuck out his pointer finger directing me, then walked on without a word.

I followed the line of his finger. "Right, obviously. Thanks!" I called, but he was already halfway down the block. I walked down the street, passing restaurants and local shops flanked by beautiful old brownstones. As I rounded the corner onto Anthony's road, I saw a group of guys playing basketball in the street, a portable net resting on the edge of the sidewalk. The sight of it made me ache for my days of kickball on Arbor Way.

As I walked closer, I could make out Anthony, dressed in old jeans and a gray sweatshirt. His face was flushed with activity and his ears were red from the cold. One of the other basketball players motioned to him. Anthony stopped dribbling, held the ball in his hands, and turned around.

I waved.

He walked toward me.

"Go on," I said. "Finish your game. I'll watch."

He smiled and turned back to his game, tossing the ball to his friend.

I took a seat on the stoop in front of an old, four-story brownstone. A copper mailbox with *Rucelli* engraved on the front hung next to the door.

The basketball game was competitive, with lots of yelling and high-fiving. They teased each other with such familiarity, it was clear they were old friends. Watching Anthony here, in his own environment, was such a contrast to how I perceived him at school—as a loner. I felt like an idiot for assuming that Anthony's actions within the confines of Darlington's walls paralleled how his life was elsewhere. And suddenly I understood. He didn't ostracize himself to the library because he had no friends. His friends just weren't available at lunch. He didn't care what people at Darlington thought about him because his security was here. I envied him, wishing I had the pride to not obsess about how others viewed me.

Across the street, two pretty girls walked by, slowing down as they approached the basketball net. One of Anthony's friends tapped a sweaty teammate on the shoulder, then nodded his chin toward the opposite sidewalk. The sweaty guy smiled, seeing the girls, then said, "Molly and Adrienne," to no one in particular.

Anthony's head swung around toward the girls.

The taller girl, with long, wavy black hair, waved and smiled, then whispered something to her friend. The shorter girl, the prettier of the two, had olive skin framed by shiny, stick straight auburn locks. Her eyes were wide and dark, and she had a sexy, pouty mouth. She smiled then called out, "Hi, Anthony."

I couldn't see Anthony's face when he responded, "Hey, Adrienne."

The short, pretty one, Adrienne, smiled toward Anthony, then nudged her friend with her elbow, gesturing across the street in my direction. The girls looked at each other and burst into a fit of laughter. They waved goodbye to the guys and sauntered down the road.

My face burned. *Were they laughing at me?*

The guys stood there, motionless, the basketball resting on the street, and watched Molly and Adrienne walk, their curvy backsides swaying as if to music, until they turned the corner and disappeared out of sight.

I felt a sudden surge of inadequacy. I always thought I had a decent butt, small and firm, but I was quite certain it lacked the raw sex appeal of those two curvy, confident girls. And I was abruptly aware of how the cold weather leaves me looking so pasty and lifeless. My hair darkens to the color of soggy Cheerios. How bland is that? *Note to self: Harass Trent for highlights that don't fade!* Compared to those girls, I was about as appealing as unbuttered toast. *Second note to self: Buy some self-tanner! Buy* Buns of Steel!

Anthony walked over toward me. "You survived the subway!" he teased.

I'm sure Adrienne rides the subway every day and doesn't require a map or written notes, I thought bitterly. I mustered up a smile and nodded. "Didn't wind up in Queens, did I?"

He laughed and opened the door. I followed him inside the long and narrow brownstone, dropping my backpack on the couch. The living room had beautiful architecture, archways and elaborate moldings, but the paint was chipping in spots and the ceiling looked old and musty. Only the kitchen showed signs of recent updates, with a huge gas range, double ovens and an enormous counter top, cluttered with cookbooks and baking accessories.

"This is really nice," I said. "Your home. The neighborhood."

Anthony smiled. "Yeah, we lived here way before it was cool to live here. They've cleaned it up pretty nice. All the yuppies started moving in from Manhattan a couple of years back. It's been really good for the bakery. Hey, do you mind if I take a quick shower before we get started?" he asked, pointing down the hall.

"I was hoping you would," I teased, feeling more relaxed to be inside and away from the two voluptuous local beauties.

I went back into the living room and sat on the couch. I knew I should review my chemistry notes, but I opted instead to read through a *People* magazine.

The phone rang.

I heard the water shut off, and the bathroom door swung open. Steam poured out, followed by Anthony, dripping wet, a towel wrapped around his waist. He raced into the kitchen and picked up the cordless phone.

He scribbled on a pad of Post-it notes, saying, "Uh, huh, okay, okay. Great. I'll let her know. Thanks."

I tried really hard not to stare in total shock and amazement, but his body, oh my God, his body. A broad chest with a sprinkle of dark hair across the top and huge, sculpted biceps. Did he do push-ups and arm curls while baking muffins every morning? It had never occurred to me that under his boring hunter green school polo hid such a masterpiece of perfection.

Anthony set the phone down and I averted my eyes.

"That was a really important call for my mom," he explained. "She threatened my life if I missed it."

I nodded, absentmindedly staring at the ceiling.

He walked back toward his room.

Stop thinking about his chest! Stop thinking about his broad, sculpted, wet chest. STOP!

I bet ADRIENNE has seen his amazing chest.

Anthony walked back into the room, jeans and a white T-shirt on. Why had I always just felt like Anthony was the big brother type and not some poster-worthy heartthrob? How had I never noticed his sleeves stretch taut over his biceps before? And why did I assume that just because he ate lunch in the library that he wasn't datable? I thought back to the day I pushed him out of Jolie's apartment. Had he really intended to kiss me, or was I just delusional from post-traumatic stress? I looked at him rifling through his chemistry notebook. I wanted to talk to Anthony about finding Mom's letters, but suddenly I felt myself closing up. I always assumed Anthony and I had a special relationship—that I held an important place in his life. But that was before I saw his life outside of Darlington, filled with neighborhood friends and voluptuous girls. Maybe I wasn't special to him at all.

He pulled out a crumpled piece of newspaper, smiled, and handed it to me. "I saw this and thought of you." It was a comic strip. A frazzled-looking girl was sitting at a desk, books open, pens and paper everywhere. The girl's head was sizzling and a stream of smoke floated to the sky. The caption said: *Academic overload.*

Anthony laughed. "It wouldn't be the first time your head caught fire."

"Very funny," I said, thinking, *No, I don't think he ever intended to kiss me. He definitely just thinks of me as a friend.* And suddenly, a teeny tiny part of me was queasy. Why didn't Anthony want to kiss me? Owen wanted to kiss me, so I couldn't be too pasty. I crumpled up the comic and tossed it at Anthony's head.

He laughed again, then opened his chemistry book and started chewing on a pencil. Somehow that annoying little habit didn't seem so annoying now. His full lips seemed kind of sexy as he gnawed on the pencil. With his arms resting on the table, his short sleeves hiked up slightly, showing the swell of his biceps. The biceps of the guy who never actually wanted to kiss me. I was never going to be able to concentrate. *Stop!* I told myself. *Why does it matter?* I had a date planned with the hottest guy in the whole junior class whose biceps were equally as impressive. At least I thought they were, as best as I could remember the night I saw them.

My stomach dropped a notch. Suddenly, I envisioned Owen

clipping out a comic strip of an inexperienced girl, slobbering in a fit of inebriation all over a gorgeous guy as she attempts to seduce him. Oh God. I was in over my head. *Third note to self: Schedule an emergency session with Lindsey and Andi. Put your pride aside, admit your inexperience, and beg for some kissing guidance.*

Anthony tapped his pencil on the table, bringing me back to reality.

"Ready?" he asked.

I am ready for nothing, I thought.

But I nodded and tried my best not to let my brain catch fire.

CHAPTER TWENTY-TWO

THE SCHOOL WAS BUZZING all week and into the next.

As I walked down the pristine halls, people stared, whispered, and sometimes blatantly pointed. I got to my locker and the school's most notorious gossipers—Sammy Greensboro and Vera Stewart—were stalking me like hawks. The two girls cornered me against my locker like prey. It had already been a week and I still couldn't open my own locker without harassment.

Vera leaned one arm against my locker, shook her red hair, and pursed her thin lips. "Is it true that you got wasted and totally hooked up with Owen last week?"

"I heard that you broke five thousand dollars' worth of crystal in a drunken rage." Sammy widened her hazel eyes and hopped up and down a little. She was the shorter of the two and clearly Vera's sidekick.

"I heard Owen had to call the cops to personally escort you out."

"ENOUGH!" Andi bellowed, inserting herself into the huddle. I was just as startled as the stalkers that such a booming sound could come out of Andi's teeny tiny body.

The girls and some other stragglers scattered.

"Thanks," I said gratefully.

"That's the price you pay when you date the school's most eligible bachelor," Andi said, fluffing her hair in my locker mirror.

"I'm surprised he still wants to date me after that night."

"Are you kidding? He said you were hilarious."

My heart plummeted. Hilarious. Not sexy. Not sultry. Hilarious. "What do you mean, hilarious? Not *the whole world is watching me puke on YouTube* hilarious, right?"

"Relax. We know it wasn't your fault. You know, the reaction."

"Reaction?" I asked tentatively.

"Owen said you had an allergic reaction to something . . . was it the nuts?"

I nodded furiously, and my heart swelled that he honored his promise.

"Anyway," Andi continued. "He just said you were wobbly and klutzy and all over the place."

All over the place. *Like with my kissing skills? Oh God. What if I truly am a terrible kisser and next time I don't have the alcohol to blame?* I looked around to make sure no one was eavesdropping. "Hey." I leaned in close, whispering. "Do you think you, Lindsey, and I could have a talk? Sometime soon?"

Andi's forehead furrowed with curiosity. "What about?"

"Girl stuff," I whispered, giving her a look that said, *No details amid the stalkers.*

She got my drift. "How about this weekend at my place."

"Great," I said. "I'll text Lindsey."

DR. REEVES'S HANDS were bulkier than I remembered as he jammed a slab of plastic into my mouth that Friday after school.

"See," he said. "That will keep your jaw stationary and reduce the grinding."

Whatever, I thought, *just make it better. I have to go out with Owen again soon and muscle relaxers are not an option.*

As he removed the night guard from my mouth, there was a knock on the exam room door. A hygienist ushered Jolie in. She was tucked into a glamorous knee-length light gray wool coat.

"Sorry I'm late," she said, taking a seat in a chair by the window.

"Actually, we're just finishing up," Dr. Reeves said, sliding his stool over to Jolie. He opened the plastic container, pulled out the night guard, and began his demonstration again.

I watched as Jolie's eyes scanned Dr. Reeves from the top of his salt and pepper hair down to the tippy toes of his shiny leather shoes. He wasn't wearing scrubs today; instead he wore tan pants, an expensive-looking tailored shirt, open at the collar, no tie.

"Any questions?" Dr. Reeves asked as his eyes locked on Jolie.

"No," I said.

He turned around quickly, almost startled, as if he forgot I was in the room. Then he stood up and offered to help me out of the exam chair. He escorted us down the hall to the receptionist and told us to make an appointment in one month for a recheck. He lingered for a moment, then extended his hand to Jolie.

"I hope you have a wonderful Thanksgiving," he said, apparently addressing both of us but looking only at Jolie.

"I hope you have a great holiday too." Jolie's voice sounded artificial and juvenile.

"Don't eat too much pie," Dr. Reeves joked, still holding her hand.

"But I like pie." Jolie laughed. I saw her flick her light hair, and her eyes seemed to twinkle more than usual. She dropped his hand and quickly pulled her hair into an easy ponytail, trying to look busy.

The patients in the waiting room fell to a hush, all eyes observing this exchange. All at once, Dr. Reeves released his gaze on her, patted me on the back, and walked down the corridor. Jolie watched him until he disappeared into the exam room, hearing him greet his next patient with his deep, cheerful hello.

Jolie made my appointment and we went home. During the cab ride down 7th Avenue, I gazed at her face through my peripheral vision. I was still mad at her. But it was strange to see her cheeks glowing in the light of the stores as we drove past. I realized what I was looking at was hope.

chapter
twenty-three

ALL DAY SATURDAY, I practiced non-humiliating ways to ask Andi and Lindsey for a little help in the hooking-up department. *It's been a long time since I made out with Steve and I'm just a little worried I've forgotten how. Ha ha. Yes, I know Owen and I made out last weekend, but let's face it, I wasn't exactly coherent.*

As Lindsey and I took a cab to Andi's condo, I became a little panicky. "Why did Andi tell us to bring a bathing suit? She's not going to, like, give me a bikini wax or something, is she?"

Lindsey laughed. "Relax. I think she just wants us to hang out at the pool."

"The pool? It's November." I shivered just thinking about it.

"It's an indoor pool. What's wrong? You seem jittery or nervous or something."

I pushed my sunglasses up my nose. "No, I'm fine." *You are going to totally think I'm an immature, inexperienced idiot, but I'm fine.*

We walked into the contemporary lobby decorated all in shades of white and cream. Andi was standing in front of a waterfall fountain, flirting with the concierge.

"Hey, guys!" Andi called.

We followed her into the elevator and rode to the floor marked *Fitness Level.* We walked past the gym to a door with a large engraved plaque that read *Lap Pool.* I couldn't imagine anyone exercising in such an opulent setting. There were two crystal chandeliers hanging above the long, rectangular pool. There was an ornate gold-framed wall-size mirror at one end of the pool and three round tufted cream ottomans at the other end. We changed into our bathing suits in the locker room— I was relieved to see Lindsay wore a tankini like me—then wrapped ourselves in plush terry-cloth robes and each took an ottoman to sit on.

I wanted to spout my rehearsed monologue about being out of practice, but I anxiously blurted out, "I'm totally inexperienced and I don't think I'm a very good kisser. I don't want Owen to laugh at me. And I can't keep delaying our next date!" I hugged my arms around my legs.

Andi sat up, adjusting her white bikini top. "Well, then let's start with what you *are* proficient at."

"Proficient? I haven't even taken a test drive!" I said, panicking.

Lindsey looked interested and Andi looked confused.

I bit my lip. "I know you guys probably think I'm totally lame, but I just haven't really fooled around much with guys."

Andi's brow furrowed. "So, are you asking for help with the *physical mechanics* of hooking up?" she asked, looking unsure.

I nodded furiously. "Yes. Exactly. Like the breathing. My tennis coach used to say in through the nose, out through the mouth. And kissing is, in a sense, exercise, right? But out through the mouth seems all wrong, and while I contemplated this on our date night, I got all panicked and tried to convince my lungs to go oxygen free for just a few minutes and I practically suffocated."

Lindsey burst out laughing, practically falling off the ottoman.

Andi smiled. "I really don't think Owen noticed." She walked over to a refrigerator, inserted a card, and opened it. She took out three Diet Cokes and handed them to us.

"Why? What did he say?" I leaned forward in anticipation. Owen and I were still at a stage where we didn't exactly talk much at school. In fact, it only happened if he initiated conversation.

"Well, he didn't say anything specifically," Andi said. "But Aidan said he talked about you a lot."

"So he didn't say anything about a bad head tilt or a distracting nose position?"

Lindsey giggled again.

"Hmm," Andi grunted. She leaned forward and grabbed the pillow behind her back. "Okay, say this is Owen . . ."

"Oh, we've been down that road." Lindsey laughed.

"Not nice, Lin," I bellowed. "Okay, so this is Owen." I walked up to the pillow.

Andi lifted my chin, cocked my head, and showed proper lip-parting techniques. She looked like she was about to launch into a further tutorial.

"Okay." I stopped her. "That's good. Thanks."

Andi gave me a strange look, her blue eyes squinting.

Ugh. How to explain the battleground in my mind between hormones and morals? "I want to make out with Owen, but I don't want him to think it's going to go any further. Because it won't." I bit my lip, afraid of their reaction.

"Oh," Andi said. "I get it. Like a promise ring? That's really big right now."

"I totally get it too," Lindsey said. "You know when it happens, it'll be *amazing*, but you just aren't ready for it to happen yet."

Andi started laughing. "Um, I know that when you watch movies, it looks *amazing*, like your body is *exploding with pleasure*, but just a heads-up: they're wrong. Well, at least for the first fifty times or so—then it gets good."

"Fifty times!" Lindsey shouted. "Are you like a nympho or something?"

Andi shook her head, still laughing. "Well, like I said, it does get good, it just takes some practice."

The three of us fell on the tiled floor laughing.

Andi pointed over at me. "And even if you're *not* ready for *amazing*, you still need a bikini wax."

I looked over at Lindsey and we burst out laughing again.

Lindsey propped up on her elbow, her short, dark hair grazing her shoulder. "Even if I *am* ready, I don't think it'll ever happen."

"What do you mean?" I asked, dipping my toes into the pool water.

"Jason never showed up last night," Lindsey said, joining me by the poolside.

"I completely forgot about your date. I'm so sorry," I said.

"Did he call and explain?" Andi leaned in with curiosity.

"Nothing," Lindsey said. "No call. No text. Can you imagine? I just sat there waiting in the lobby of Café Loup like a loser."

"I'm so sorry," I whispered.

"Yeah," said Lindsey. "Me too."

On my way home I felt a sense of relief. Neither of them teased me for my inexperience, and I was worried that Andi would think I was a prude. But she didn't seem to pass any judgment; in fact, she seemed to really enjoy helping me.

I decided to call Georgia and let her in on some of my new-found knowledge. If I was struggling in the make-out department, Georgia was totally clueless.

"Oh my God!" Georgia wailed. "You're going to become a statistic!"

"A what?" I asked.

"Pregnant at sixteen is not becoming, Emily. I thought we agreed we wouldn't be like those trashy girls that gave it up to the first guy that showed interest."

"I'm not giving anything up. Jeez, calm down. I'm not a trashy girl. Don't you know me at all? I just thought I could share a little insight about the art of a good make-out session."

"Oh, sure, call it a make-out session, but when Silvia on *Rhapsody in Rio* decided to quote-unquote *make out* with

Miguel, nine months later they wound up with triplet boys and an ugly custody hearing."

I shook my head. "Stop freaking."

But Georgia continued to freak, without a breath, until I swore on my first unborn child, which I assured her would not arrive for at least another decade, that I would *not,* in the heat of the moment, allow Owen to deflower me.

chapter
twenty-four

"HAPPY THANKSGIVING!" Trent bellowed as he walked in carrying an apple pie and a stack of DVDs. "Football's on all day." He frowned. "So I brought movies." He joined us in the living room, helping himself to a plate of chips and salsa.

I could hardly believe it was already Thanksgiving. It seemed like just yesterday I was the new girl at Darlington and totally overwhelmed by New York City. Now, looking out of Jolie's floor-to-ceiling windows at her view of the West Village, it felt different. Not exactly like home, but not a scary foreign place either. The trees down the streets were all bare by now, and dark fallen leaves blew in the wind.

Trent popped in *A Christmas Story* and we began a game of Trivial Pursuit.

"This movie reminds me of when I was ten. Only I didn't want a Red Ryder BB gun, although in retrospect it might have been a good gift, then I could have nipped Dad in the butt every time he annoyed me, but really I wanted a set of perm rods so I could give my golden retriever a perm." Trent turned toward me. "Perms were all the rage back then. I wrote to Santa, I even included a picture from my aunt Yvonne's beauty supply catalog. But my parents ignored all my requests and bought me a set of Matchbox cars."

"Trent," I said. "Where is your family? Do they live far away? Is that why you're here with us on Thanksgiving?"

Trent's mouth twitched slightly, and for a moment he looked sad. Then he sandwiched himself between me and Jolie on the couch, wrapping an arm around each of us.

"This is my family, sweetie," he said.

I nodded slowly. "Me too."

Jolie leaned over and gave Trent a soft kiss on the cheek, then got up and went into the kitchen.

I wanted to tell Trent that nothing was bad enough to keep you away from your family. That he needed to search deep into his heart and forgive whatever it was that made him sad and give his family a second chance, because as long as they were alive, there still was time for reconciliation. I wanted to tell him I wished my mom had the courage to ask for my forgiveness while she was alive and could explain herself. Because now I was caught in this purgatory of the unknown and it was pretty awful. But Trent was laughing at the Chinese waiters in the movie, singing, *Far a ra ra ra ra*, and I didn't want to break the mood. So I kept quiet.

"What's with her?" Trent said, nodding toward Jolie, who had returned to the kitchen and was peering into the oven.

I shrugged. "I don't know. She put the turkey in like three

hours ago, but she keeps opening and closing the oven and fiddling with the dials." Personally, I was preoccupied thinking about Owen. He had promised to call me tomorrow to finally have that third date.

"The light keeps going off," Jolie shouted from the kitchen. "The little red light. I turned it to 325 degrees, and the light went on. But then it went off. So I turned it up to 350 degrees, and the light came back on."

Trent and I looked at each other and bolted into the kitchen.

"You have it on 500 degrees!" Trent shouted.

"It was the only way the light would stay on," Jolie said, her voice shaky and shrill.

Trent extracted the steaming turkey from the oven.

"It's brown," Jolie said. "But it's supposed to be brown, right?"

Trent took a knife and attempted to slice a piece.

We all held our breath.

He sawed back and forth.

"Oh my God, it's like rubber!" Jolie said, putting her hand up to her eyes. She ran out of the room.

Trent called after her, "Come on, Jo. Who really wants to eat a bird anyway? They pluck their feathers with their own mouth."

We heard her bedroom door slam.

As soon as she was out of earshot, Trent and I burst out laughing.

"I bet if I threw this on the ground, it would bounce back up," Trent said.

"Poor Jolie," I said. "She really wanted to make a nice meal." I regained my composure and walked to Jolie's room.

"Come on," I said, sitting next to her on the bed. "There's so much food, we don't need a turkey."

"It's Thanksgiving! We're supposed to have turkey." She let out a string of expletives and I realized it had been a while since Jolie had cursed like a sailor, the way she did when I first moved in.

"Hey," I said. "I just realized it's been like a month since you've cursed. Great job!"

I truly was impressed, but Jolie took it for sarcasm.

"Well, that's just another thing I screwed up today," she said bitterly.

I exhaled, knowing it wasn't worth a rebuttal. I glanced over at her desk, picked up one of the invitations for Thanksgiving dinner, and tossed it in her lap. "Come on. Let's go."

When Jolie told Trent that we were going to a Thanksgiving party at the Tribeca loft of a very famous actress, he insisted on another outfit. Before we left, I was forced into a black satin bubble dress Jolie had bought for me. She said she'd wanted to save it and give it to me at Christmas but now was too perfect an occasion to wait. I looked at myself in the hallway mirror and couldn't help grinning wide. I looked amazing, my blond hair having grown to my shoulders and my highlights glowing in contrast to the elegant dark dress that showed off my knees.

We walked a few blocks down Perry Street, Jolie complaining that her stilettos kept lodging between the cobblestones. Jolie and I sat on the stoop in front of the mahogany double doors while Trent ran inside to change. Ten minutes later he emerged looking suave yet understated in a navy button-down and jeans. We hailed a cab and sped down the West Side Highway.

"I just want to know why you got invited and I didn't," Trent whined. "I mean, I do her hair just as often as you do her makeup."

The TV in the cab flashed. *Breaking news. The largest train crash in American history caused by a cell phone?* Jolie cringed and shut off the TV. My stomach tightened as I recalled that she discovered my parents' accident while in a cab.

The party was well under way by the time we arrived. Cocktail waitresses dressed in skimpy black uniforms passed out fancy finger foods and poured glasses of wine.

"Uh." Trent turned his nose up at the silver platter in front of him. "I'm so over sushi."

"Sushi?" I balked. "On Thanksgiving? Couldn't they at least have turkey kabobs or something?"

Jolie and Trent shuddered.

Trent made a beeline for the bar, and Jolie was surrounded by a circle of insanely tall and rail-thin women. They peppered Jolie with questions about whether she would be attending a photo shoot in Maui.

Jolie extended a hand in my direction. "This is my niece, Emily."

The models acknowledged me for a brief second, then resumed their Maui talk.

I decided to slip away. I wandered around the huge apartment, recognizing several celebrities from the tabloid magazines. There were also numerous non-celebrities walking around, but they all looked so styled and important, I felt completely out of place. Not to mention I was possibly the only person under the age of twenty.

Although I knew it was rude, I walked around the apartment looking for a quiet place. My parents would have been horrified at my bad manners, but I continued to scavenge. I walked down a hallway off the kitchen and found a door. I tried the knob. It was a bedroom, dark and silent. I debated. If I flipped the light switch, there was a possibility I would see some random couple in a compromising position sprawled out on the bed. I took my chances and found the light. To my delight, the room was vacant, and there was a TV.

I camped out on the floor, thinking that if I lay on the bed, that would really be crossing the line. I needed something to distract me from this first holiday without my parents. I found the remote. *It's a Wonderful Life* was on. I smiled and nestled my face against the side of the soft duvet that hung from the side of the bed. I watched the familiar story, trying to muster up some holiday spirit. As the credits were rolling across the screen, the bedroom door flung open and Trent peered in, flushed in the cheeks and a little wobbly on his feet.

"Emily? Is that you?" he whispered.

I peered up over the bed. "Yup."

He came in, shut the door behind him, and sat on the floor next to me. He placed a glass of red wine between his legs. He stroked the soft, beige duvet. "Nice linens," he said. Then he glanced up at the TV. "Are you bored?"

"No," I said. "Just wanted some time to myself."

He rolled his eyes with exaggeration. "I *know.* Some of these people are so hung up on themselves, it's like torture trying to converse with them. I just want to say, *Get over yourself.*"

I guessed Trent had spent the last hour or so in close proximity to the bar.

"But seriously," he continued. "I'm glad we have this time to ourselves because there is something I want to talk to you about."

"Okay," I said, clicking off the TV, thinking perhaps he had a new strategy for my hair.

Trent took a deep breath and placed a hand on my shoulder dramatically. "Emily. Sweet, innocent, rose-scented Emily."

Oh God. This was not going to be good.

He flung his arms out wide, as if addressing a crowd. "In life there are good bees and there are bad bees." He brought his hands together and cupped my chin. "And you, dear Emily, are the *beautiful flower.*" He paused, giving a philosophical look. "One of these days one of those buzzing bees is going to want to poke at your pollen . . ."

You've GOT to be kidding me!

"Trent!" I interrupted his monologue. "I'm not an IDIOT. I did attend sex ed in fifth grade, okay? Please stop, before I vomit."

"Well, it wasn't my idea," he said defensively. He raised his eyebrows as if to say, *You know who.*

"Aaargh," I groaned.

"She's just freaking out about that hot little number you've been spending time with."

I sighed. I didn't know who had less faith in me, Jolie or Georgia.

"I know, hon," Trent said. "Living with Jolie is a chore. I've started naming my wrinkles after her. Not that you can see any wrinkles, can you?" he asked, zooming in close to me.

I laughed.

"Ooh, I've got a great idea!" Trent said. "Let's go buy a pregnancy test and leave it in your trash can." He laughed devilishly.

"Trent!!"

"You're no fun. Okay, so promise me that your body is a temple and we can end this little conversation."

"Promise," I said.

"Ah, you *are* a good girl," he said, reaching up to hold on to the bed for support and hoisting himself up. "Come on, let's go home."

We walked back into the large loft area. Jolie was deep in conversation with a striking man with long, slicked-back hair. She circled the top of her wineglass with her index finger, smiling and laughing animatedly. The dark-skinned man leaned over, whispering something in her ear. Jolie flushed, dropped her head in embarrassment, and playfully pushed him away.

"Ew! Who's Rico Suave?" Trent said, gesturing toward Jolie's male companion. "Look at him—all that hardware on his belt! Throw a vest on him and he'd fit right in at a rodeo. Who does he think he is—John Wayne? And he's so over-styled. Anyone who uses that much hair gel gives me the creeps."

I jabbed Trent in the ribs. "Stop!"

Jolie was engrossed in their conversation, twirling her hair around her finger and biting her lip. I had never seen her this way before. She was smitten. I wondered if I wore my crush so obviously for the world to view.

We walked toward them. As we got closer, I heard the man speak in broken English.

Trent tapped the man on the arm. "Excuse me, the children's party next door is looking for their cowboy."

Jolie's eyes narrowed.

The man looked confused, trying to translate in his head.

Jolie shoved Trent away, taking the handsome man's arm. "Don't pay attention to him." She dug into her purse, pulling out her card. "Here," she said, scribbling on the back of the card. "My home number is on the back. My cell is on the front."

The man reached down, pulling his phone off his belt. "I put you in my phone right now," he said, examining the number on the card and tapping the digits on his phone. "*J-o-l-i-e.* Pretty name for a pretty girl."

Jolie's face glowed.

He leaned over and gave Jolie a kiss on the cheek. It was soft, and he lingered there just a second longer than you would expect. I thought I saw Jolie shiver. I wished I had a video camera to record and study how he made a simple gesture so sensual.

Trent elbowed Jolie.

"Okay," Jolie purred. "I have to go now."

Trent grabbed Jolie by the elbow and steered her back toward the door.

"Stop pushing me!" Jolie scowled.

"You're just mad because Rico Suave didn't give you *his* number," Trent said.

Jolie looked contemplative, thinking about Trent's comments. "Stop calling him Rico Suave! He's the highest-paid actor in Mexico!" Jolie said, looking back across the room at the handsome man.

"What, is he on a soap opera?! Wait! I recognize him, he's on that *Rhapsody in Rio*!" Trent started waving his hands around in imitation. *"Oh, Maria, I love you so!"*

Jolie rolled her eyes. "Get an atlas, brainiac. That's not Mexico."

"Maria! Maria! Don't leave me!" Trent danced around as we headed toward the elevator.

Jolie swatted Trent. "He's the *foundation* of Mexican cinema!"

Trent and I exploded in giggles as the doors opened in the lobby and we shuffled onto the street.

"Leave me alone," Jolie said, hailing another cab. But I could see she was grinning. As we headed home, the three of us sat in silence, listening to the static talk radio, and I realized we never did get to eat any Thanksgiving turkey.

chapter
twenty-five

THE BURNT TURKEY was still sitting in the roasting pan on the kitchen counter Friday morning, and casserole dishes cluttered the sink. Jolie scrubbed the dishes with a sponge in her hand, singing along with the radio. She turned and saw me.

"What's cooking, good looking?" She was awfully perky, especially after her disastrous attempt at cooking a Thanksgiving meal.

"Hey," I said, taking a towel and beginning to dry the dishes in the strainer. "Are you going shopping today?" It was, after all, Black Friday, the biggest shopping day of the year.

She smiled to herself, slowing down her scrubbing, as if daydreaming. I noticed she already was dressed, with makeup on. She turned to me, a serious look on her face now. "Did you want to go shopping? Because I sort of made plans, but I can cancel them—"

"No, no," I interrupted. "Don't cancel anything. I was just curious."

She relaxed her shoulders and the hint of a smile returned.

"In fact," I said. "I wanted to ask if I could go over to Owen's later."

"Owen's?" She contemplated. She nodded, but I don't really think she was paying attention. She seemed far off, dreaming of the sexy Mexican actor. I prayed that his handsome mug would continue to distract her so she wouldn't recall the events of my last rendezvous at Owen's house.

We finished the last of the pots and dishes in silence, each of us caught up in the anticipation of what the day would bring.

Four hours later, Jolie was sitting at the table, reading a magazine, her cell phone resting at her side, and I was channel surfing. Jolie picked up the cordless phone and scrolled through the caller ID. I wanted to tell her the phone hadn't rung all morning, but I was pretty sure she knew that.

An hour later, when the phone finally rang, we both sprang from our seats, Jolie beating me to the cordless.

"Hello?" she answered, plastering on a smile, as if we had a video phone. "Oh, sure," she said, her smile fading slightly. She walked over and handed the phone to me. She gave me a thumbs-up and I knew it was Owen. I found myself plastering on a smile too.

"Hi," I said, aiming for casual, not, *I've been sitting here breathlessly waiting for your call.*

"Happy day after Thanksgiving," Owen said. "I'm on the LIE right now in a butt-load of traffic."

"That sounds like fun."

"No, but I'm looking forward to some fun," he said, and I could visualize his flirtatious grin. "At this rate, I'll be home around three. Give me time to shower, whatever. Can you be here at four?"

Oh, please don't make me wait until four p.m.! "No problem," I said, and we hung up.

When I returned the phone to the kitchen, Jolie was examining her smeared reflection on the side of the toaster. She looked like she could use a distraction, so I asked her, "Want to help me find something to wear?"

"Absolutely."

As we fingered through the clothes in my closet, Jolie said, "I'm tired of useless makeup-ing."

"Huh?"

She pointed to a pair of jeans and sat on the bed. "You know, constant reapplication of lipstick with the delusional hope that the buzzer will ring and a gorgeous man will be waiting for you."

"Mexican party guy never called?"

She exhaled loudly. "Maybe he lost my number. Or maybe he was drunk and doesn't remember talking to me. I don't know. He didn't seem drunk. Do you think he was drunk?"

"Um, I don't think so," I said, feeling very twilight zone discussing with my pseudo-parent whether the hot Mexican actor from the party was or was not intoxicated. I wanted to gently point out that she clearly was abandoning her *look for the shy guy in the corner* theory. That in all likelihood she was setting herself up for a letdown from another player. But then I thought about my infatuation with Owen and that he certainly didn't fit the shy kid bill either. *Maybe it's in the genes,* I thought. Even Mom, with her shy guy husband, couldn't resist the charms of a golden boy.

Jolie pointed to a green cashmere scoop neck sweater. "Wear that," she said.

"Really?" I asked. "Even though I wear green every day at school?"

"Hey, if it works, don't fight it."

I smiled. "Thanks."

"So," Jolie said. "I trust there will be no incidents similar to your last visit with this guy."

Shoot. Why didn't that Mexican guy call and keep her thoughts elsewhere?

"I told you that was not going to happen again," I said firmly.

Jolie's expression looked serious, and I thought for sure I was about to get the lecture of a lifetime, but just as she opened her mouth, her cell phone rang. She glanced at the caller ID screen and brightened. "Hello?" she said sweetly as she walked out of my room.

THE DOORMAN SMILED AT ME knowingly, and I wondered if he remembered me. I'm sure he knew Owen's parents weren't home yet. I felt a flush of embarrassment but then reminded myself that Owen and I were just planning a nice quiet afternoon of getting to know each other better. Remember Trent's mantra: *My body is a temple.* Georgia would be so proud. Nothing is wrong with some kissing. A little kissing, a little fumbling around, then maybe I'd suggest a round of Scrabble.

I knocked on Owen's door, and immediately it swung open. I barely had time to notice how amazing he looked in his black hoodie sweatshirt because in a flash he grabbed my jacket at the waist and pulled me into the foyer.

His hands were in my hair, steering my face up, then he was kissing me. He kicked the door closed with his foot and pressed me up against the wall. He opened the buttons of my jacket with lightning speed, not even looking. He was too busy kissing, kissing, kissing me.

Where is all the fumbling?

Owen kissed with intent, and a bit of rough, excitement, and it made my tender jaw ache somewhat, just enough for me to pull back slightly. His lips moved away from my mouth and found my neck, where his little kisses sent sparks of electricity down my spine.

He's kissing my neck! I thought they only did that in movies and on Georgia's nutty soap. I certainly never saw my dad kiss my mom's neck. My eyes popped open. *Now is definitely not the time to start thinking about Mom and Dad. Oh my God, I bet they're watching my every move—hovering in a ghost-like presence in this enormous forty-foot ceiling.* At least with the Big Guy, I could hope he was distracted, pondering the political crisis in the Middle East or weeping about world famine, but now I couldn't lift the idea that my parents' eyes were everywhere.

My eyes stayed open as Owen kissed my earlobe. I needed to think about something other than my parents' voyeuristic opportunities. I examined the foyer. It looked exactly as I remembered it, with a mahogany table supporting an enormous vase of colorful flowers towering up. I tried to force my eyes closed, but I was transfixed, staring at a pair of pulpy centers of two gerber daisies leaning toward my head. Huge yellow flower eyes staring down at me like the eyes of God. Or my mother.

My body is a temple.

I gently pushed Owen away. "Now, that's what I call a hello!" I said playfully.

Owen smiled, took my hand, and led me into the living room. He sat down in the middle of the couch. I sat down, leaving a little cooling-off space between us.

He turned toward me with an expression I've seen on Georgia's face when she's about to nosedive into a piece of chocolate cake. While I was flattered to seem so . . . edible, I was also nervous at the direction this afternoon was taking. Everything was moving too quickly. Seventeen *said, Spend time getting to know your crush before making the decision to get physical.* The truth was, sometimes I felt like I didn't know Owen at all. I knew he was the captain of the swim team. He was an only child. He liked to travel. He liked waffles. That was definitely not enough. I pulled away, yanking my one leg up under the other.

"So," I said. "How was your Thanksgiving?"

He seemed suspended at a forty-five-degree angle, aiming for my lips, momentarily confused. "Um, boring. Typical. Ya know, family stuff." He straightened up. "And you?" he asked, not convincing me that he really wanted an answer.

I decided to answer anyway.

"Well, it was tough, I guess, being the first holiday without my parents." A lump stuck in my throat for a minute. It was so easy to talk about my parents with Anthony, why did I feel so self-conscious bringing it up with Owen?

"Uh-huh," he said with a small sigh.

"I didn't even eat turkey," I said, my eyes getting a little moist.

"Turkey's overrated," Owen said, leaning over and kissing me on the mouth. He kissed me more gently this time and suddenly, Thanksgiving was a distant memory. My body felt all chilled and on fire all at the same time. His hands slid onto my waist. The coldness of his hands startled me and I giggled like a schoolgirl. *Get a grip!*

Slowly, his hands started to slide over my stomach.

I hesitated, then grabbed his hands. "Owen," I whispered, shaking my head. "No."

"Oh, come on, please?" He groaned like a puppy.

Temptation crept over me. *My body doesn't HAVE to be a temple...*

His hands resumed their ascent.

I'm sure Owen wasn't accustomed to girls stopping him. Why would they? He's gorgeous! Who in their right mind would stop him? It wasn't that I wanted to stop him, necessarily, I needed to stop him. I wasn't exactly sure why. All I knew was that in the last several months, so much of me had been taken away: my parents, my home, my old life. How much more could I possibly give up without losing every fraction of the girl I was? But if I stopped him, would he lose interest in me and turn to the whole line of girls who certainly would not object to his rising hands?

"I'm sorry," I said, flustered. "But I don't think my parents would like it."

WHAT??!!

"We don't have to tell them," he said, kissing my ear.

"Sorry," I whispered again.

He dropped his head into the crook of my neck. He lay there for a second, like he was in pain, which actually, from what I read in *Seventeen*, might be true. Then he lifted himself back into a seated position on the couch.

Owen found the remote and flipped through the channels in silence. He pounded the remote buttons at lightning speed, not even stopping to see what program was on. *My God, he can't even commit to a channel—there's no way he's staying with me.*

"Look," I said. "*Seinfeld* is on."

He didn't respond, but he left it on that channel and set the remote down on the coffee table. He didn't laugh at any of the funny parts.

The air felt tense. He adjusted and readjusted his position on the couch.

"Oh," I said, reaching into my purse and retrieving the photo. "I kind of broke the frame in your bathroom the other night." I handed him the replacement frame.

Owen looked at the picture. He rolled his eyes. "Every year my mom makes me do volunteer work." He shook his head as if to say, *What a waste of time,* but I had studied that photo for hours and on his sunlit face was a genuine smile and unmistakable pride.

Owen's phone rang. He glanced at it, then flipped it open.

"E, wut up?" Owen said. "Yeah, yeah. She's here," he said, turning away from me slightly and lowering his voice. "No, man. Not exactly."

My face flamed. True, Owen could have been talking about anything, but I had the distinct feeling that I was the topic of his negative tone.

Suddenly, I knew why there were so many sad love songs. Being a girlfriend was hard.

"No way, really?" Owen's voice rose an octave. "Dude, that's perfect."

Well, at least *someone* was making Owen happy.

"Right. Cool. Later." He clicked the phone shut, then turned back toward me, smiling and visibly happier. "That was Ethan. His parents got in a fight and decided to take a makeup trip to some Biltmore place down in North Carolina."

"Oh, I read that they have a huge gingerbread house display every Christmas!" I interrupted.

He looked at me like I was crazy. "Okay. Whatever. Point is: they'll be gone for a week. So next weekend, party at Ethan's!" He leaned over and hugged me, his arms clenching me with enthusiasm. I pressed my chest against his and felt the joy of a hug. Just a hug—with no added intentions.

I decided to leave on a good note, while Owen was still pumped about the upcoming party. I faked an early curfew and left.

The minute I stepped out of the cab, I called Lindsey.

"I'm just so afraid he's going to dump me because I'm keeping things very PG-13, if you know what I mean," I explained.

"Well, if he dumps you for that reason, then he's not worth your time, is he?" Lindsey replied.

I would have expected reassurance of that nature from Georgia, but it was so nice to know that I had someone here, who knew Owen's status, who understood how hot he was and still validated my choice.

"Thanks, Lindsey," I said, clicking the phone shut and getting on the elevator.

When I opened the door to the apartment, all the lights were on, but Jolie was nowhere in sight. I dropped my purse on the counter and walked back toward my bedroom. A soft love song drifted from Jolie's room.

Gross. I could only imagine. *I guess Jolie doesn't have my willpower,* I thought with a chuckle.

I was about to walk into my room when Jolie's door opened and instead of my seeing two lovers entangled, Jolie emerged, puffy-eyed and makeup-less. She was dressed in dark jeans, a tight, white, button-down shirt, and had huge silver hoops in her ears and sky-high stilettos on her feet. She looked like she just came from a hot date, but her nose was red and she undoubtedly had been crying.

I turned toward her. "Hey, what's wrong?"

"Oh," she said, dabbing at her eyes. "Nothing. Really, I'm fine." She forced a smile. "How was Owen's? Want some hot cocoa?" She said this as if hot cocoa was the answer to all the world's problems.

"Sure," I said, following her into the kitchen and sitting at the table.

Jolie pulled out some mugs and rifled through the cabinets. "Want some marshmallows? I *love* marshmallows with hot cocoa."

"Okay, but if you're aiming for Suzy Sunshine, the tear-stained cheeks and Kleenex hanging from your nose are giving you away."

She dabbed her nose reflexively.

"I'm just kidding," I said. "But jeez, tell me what happened. Did hot party guy never show up?"

Jolie put the mugs down and sat across from me. She sighed. "He did. He showed up right on time."

"Well, what then? Did he bring his wife with him or something?"

Jolie laughed. Then her face crumpled and she covered her face in her hands. She looked so small and fragile, sniffing and dabbing at her eyes. "Your mom did it right," Jolie said. "She picked the right one."

My stomach clenched. "What do you mean?"

"I'm superficial, I know." Jolie sniffled. "It's my main flaw. I've always cared too much about good looks and money. Jill. Your mom." She shook her head slightly. "Your mom valued honesty and a good, solid companion. And at a young age, too. God! She was so smart! I've spent all these years following my heart to the charming and attractive men, living life like it's a fairy tale." Her eyes welled up again. "But then one day, I wake up and I'm thirty-eight, standing in a bar, listening to my Mexican Prince Charming feed me the same lines that used to make my knees go weak while he's staring at the butt of a slutty, twenty-year-old cocktail waitress. And it finally dawns on me: that to these kind of men, I am replaceable, a one-night stand." She dabbed at her eyes. "I've spent all these years being charmed but not loved. I just wish I had done it right a long time ago and found a true companion, like your mom did."

My mind was spinning. After reading those letters, who was to even say that Mom was happy with her choice of a companion? Perhaps Mom and Jolie were more alike than she realized.

"How do you know?" I said. "I mean, how do you know that Mom and Dad really were good companions? If they were, then why did she kiss someone else?"

Jolie looked at me like she was trying to read deep in the corners of my mind. Her eyes were so intense and then, in a move uncharacteristic of her, she took my hands and squeezed them. Without looking away, she said, "Your mother was happy, Emily. She was happy with your father, she was happy with her life, and most of all, she was happy with you."

chapter
twenty-six

AT SCHOOL ON MONDAY, no one was talking about Thanksgiving turkey. Everyone was talking about Ethan's upcoming party.

"Oh my God, Ethan's party, two years ago, was AMAZING," Andi said, dipping a celery stalk into her tub of low-fat ranch.

"It was out of control," Lindsey chimed, in setting her lunch tray down. "I swear, I think at one point five hundred people were there."

"I know," I said. "Owen told me."

"Speaking of Owen," Andi said. "Have you decided what you're going to get him for Christmas?"

Ugh. How to pick a gift for the guy who you've only actually gone out with three times? Not to mention, the guy who has everything? "No," I said. "I have no idea. Any suggestions?"

The three of us turned to look over at the guys' table.

Andi gave a little wave and smile in their direction. "All he wants for Christmas," she sang, "is YOU . . ."

My stomach flipped. Did she mean that in the literal sense? Had Owen spouted to Aidan that my friskiness was halting and borderline prudish? *Oh my God, can Owen be expecting my virginity wrapped up in a red bow as his stocking stuffer?*

"What are they doing?" Andi asked, eyeing the guys as they walked over toward the corner of the lunchroom, away from their usual table.

Lindsey turned toward me. "I think it's always a safe bet to get guys electronics. You know how men are all just little boys at heart. They love their toys."

I smiled at Lindsey.

"Seriously," Andi said, a little shrill. "What ARE they doing?"

Lindsey and I followed Andi's gaze across the room.

The guys huddled in a circle. Then Ethan emerged, walking solo toward a table in the corner of the cafeteria. There, sitting by herself, was Carly, eating a hamburger and reading a book.

"Who is he going to talk to?" Andi asked no one in particular, as if it was a crime for Ethan to talk to anyone outside our little circle of friends. "His *lab partner?*"

"Maybe they're talking about the project," I suggested.

Andi's shoulders relaxed a bit, but her eyes never left them.

Carly was so engrossed in her novel she didn't notice Ethan's presence until he tapped her on the shoulder and she nearly jumped out of her skin. Ethan laughed and then

Carly laughed, but she covered her mouth with her hand, as if embarrassed. He sat down next to her.

"What in the world?" Andi squinted toward them. "Look at her! Did she just offer him a fry? Oh my God, I think she just offered him a fry."

I wanted to say, *What's the big deal?* But I just looked on.

Ethan leaned over and whispered something in Carly's ear. A red flush rose in her cheeks, then with her big, brown eyes turned up toward him, she nodded yes.

Andi's eyes darted from Ethan back to the guys, who now were seated.

Ethan got up, gave Carly two friendly taps on the shoulder, then returned to his friends. They walked out to the patio, Ethan's head sticking up half a foot higher.

Andi grabbed her phone and frantically text messaged Aidan.

A few minutes later, Ethan, Aidan, and Owen walked over toward our table.

"What's up?" Aidan said, leaning over to peck Andi on the cheek.

"What was all that about?" Andi asked, nodding over toward Carly, who was once again engrossed in her book.

"What do you mean?" Aidan asked innocently, but with the slightest hint of a smile.

"Just chem stuff," Ethan said, then looked toward me. "Man, this project bites."

"Definitely." I looked into Ethan's eyes and wondered if he noticed all those times Carly stared at him in class. I wondered if he really talked about chemistry, or if he only went over there so his friends could laugh at how flustered she was around him.

After lunch, Owen and I were talking at my locker. He reached down and took my hand and I thought maybe he didn't mind a PG-13 relationship. Carly walked past us, heading in the opposite direction. She looked up for a second, a small smile directed toward me.

After she passed out of sight, Owen grinned. "Hey," he said to me. "Ethan invited Carly to his party."

"MY FAITH IS RESTORED in humankind," I said the next day in chemistry class.

"Yeah, well, I don't buy it," Anthony said, placing a row of test tubes on the lab bench.

"You don't buy it? What do you mean, *you don't buy it*? There's nothing to buy. It's a fact. Ethan invited Carly and she's accepted."

"Look," Anthony said. "I know you and Owen are all . . ." He made a manic sweeping hand gesture.

"What the heck does THAT mean?"

He sighed. "I know that you and Owen are *together*, and I'm not saying anything about him, okay? All I'm saying is that I know Ethan and I don't think the invitation is legit."

We both looked over at Carly.

"Looks like she's on your accessories bandwagon too," Anthony said.

"What?"

He reached over and fingered my mom's pearl necklace. "The pearls." He nodded toward Carly.

She had on a single-strand pearl necklace. Hmm.

"Don't tell me you haven't noticed," Anthony said, gesturing around the room.

I followed his hand and noticed five other girls wearing pearls. I wondered how long the girls had been wearing the pearls. Had they liked the look and decided to copy it? Or was it worthy of imitation only after I became Owen's girlfriend?

"Well," I said. "I think Ethan's invitation to Carly is legit. *You* just don't want to root for the underdog." I used a spatula to scoop up some of the yellow powder that was in a small bowl.

"I'm pulling for the underdog as much as anyone," he said, grabbing my hand. "Hey, do *not* pour that into the beaker." He pulled the beaker over to the other side of the lab bench. "Do you want to blow up the whole room? What's with you and explosions?"

"Oops," I said, laughing and spilling the yellow powder all over the bench.

"Jeez, you're a major hazard," Anthony teased.

Mrs. Klein announced it was time to clean up.

"Yeah, no joke," Anthony muttered under his breath, and pointed to the mess I had made.

"I bet you reflect every day on how lucky you are to have me as your lab partner," I joked.

Anthony rolled his eyes.

I used my hands to sweep the powder into a paper towel as Anthony cleaned up the test tubes and beakers.

The bell rang and the class filed out as Anthony and I were still jotting down our last few calculations. As we packed our notebooks into our backpacks, I noticed Carly was waiting just past our lab desk.

We had started to walk toward the door when Carly turned toward me and in a barely audible voice said, "Um, Emily, can I ask you something?"

Anthony and I exchanged glances.

"Sure," I said. "What's up?"

She darted a glance at Anthony, then said, "I'm not sure if you've heard . . ."

Oh, I bet I have, I thought.

"But Ethan asked me to come to his party on Friday."

I smiled brightly and faked surprise. "Wow, that's great, Carly!"

Carly's eyes widened and she grinned ear to ear. "I'm still in a little bit of shock."

We walked together down the hall. Anthony was just steps ahead of us, and I'm sure he was eavesdropping on our conversation.

"Um, I could be wrong," Carly said nervously. "But I think I heard you say that your aunt is a makeup artist?"

"Yeah, she is."

"Well, I guess I was wondering if you think there is any way . . ." Carly played with her hair for a minute. "I mean, I don't want to impose, but I was just wondering if there was any way I could maybe . . ."

"Of course!" I jumped in. "I was just going to ask if you

wanted to come over for some makeup tips. Jolie loves it when I bring people by to meet her." I grinned, trying to look encouraging and yet nonchalant.

"Oh, wow, really?" Carly exploded. "I mean, that would be so great. I could use some help. A lot of help, actually."

I smiled. "It'll be fun. Why don't we meet after class on Friday and you can just come home with me."

"Okay!" She didn't try to mask her enthusiasm.

I laughed. "Remember to bring something to change into."

She nodded. "Right. I can see myself forgetting that."

"This is my class," I said, pointing to my English classroom.

"Okay. See you!"

I watched her for a second, walking down the hall, blissful, and I prayed that I was right about Ethan's intentions and Anthony was wrong.

CutiepieG: Tell Anthony true love conquers all, even across the social hierarchy of high school! Look at Ricardo and Serena on *Rhapsody in Rio*. He's a wealthy neurosurgeon and she's a housekeeper with a weight problem! They've been together for two seasons!

Tennisfan500: I know, I want to believe it, but when I see them together in chem class, Ethan just doesn't seem that into her.

CutiepieG: Maybe he's just not a public display of affection kind of guy.

Tennisfan500: Maybe.

CutiepieG: Gotta run. Love ya.

Maybe Georgia was right. Maybe Ethan was the kind of person that looked beyond the exterior and found the good inside a person. Just because he was the school basketball star didn't mean that he couldn't look outside his circle of attractive, popular friends to find true love elsewhere. It was possible that he had an awakening, twenty years earlier than Jolie did, and realized, as totally cliché as it sounded, beauty was only skin deep.

I glanced in the mirror. There were so many girls at Darlington that were as pretty or prettier than I was. I had to believe that Ethan could like Carly, because it gave me hope that Owen really liked *me*.

chapter
twenty-seven

FRIDAY AFTERNOON, I met Carly in the lobby after school let out. She was holding a black duffel bag, staring out the glass front door.

"Hey!" I called out.

She spun around. "Hey!"

"I was going to walk—is that bag heavy?" I asked.

Carly slung the wide strap over her shoulder. "Nah, not at all. Let's go."

"Seriously, it's almost a mile. We can hail a cab." I started to wave my arm out toward the street.

Carly swatted my arm down. "Really, I'm fine. Besides, I could use the exercise."

Carly's implication of her weight made me uneasy. "Okay," I said.

We walked for a few minutes in silence, just rhythmic

inhales and exhales followed by small puffs of white steam coming from her mouth.

As we were approaching Father Demo Square at the corner of 6th and Carmine, Carly wiped the sweat off her forehead and smiled. "Man, that Anthony is a trip," she said.

"Anthony? Really? How so?"

"He's in my gym class, and I don't know, he's always just cracking everyone up."

The tiered fountain was bubbling and I thought maybe I heard her wrong. "Cracking everyone up?"

She nodded, smiling at some memory.

Hmm. Sure, Anthony teased me, but I had never seen him interacting with others that way. For some reason, I felt strangely jealous. I wanted to ask her to explain, for this idea intrigued me, but she seemed so winded.

"Here," I said, offering my hand. "My turn." I grabbed for her duffel bag.

"Thanks," she said, rubbing her shoulder. "That's really nice."

Now, back to Anthony . . .

"So what is it like living with your aunt?" Carly asked.

Oh, well. "It's different. I mean, she's cool. Fun. Stylish. But sometimes I just miss my parents." I started to pant. What did she have in that bag? A body?

"Of course you do," Carly said, breathing much easier now. "I miss my parents too—as a couple, I mean. They got divorced. That's why I moved."

"Oh, I didn't know. I'm sorry."

"Yeah, it sucks. Dad ran off with his secretary. I mean how stereotypical is that, right? I guess slutty secretary *Rebecca* must be a really good lay."

"Carly!" I laughed.

She cracked a smile. "I mean, God! My parents were happy! Dad goes and bangs some size-two whore and my whole world falls apart. No offense, you're probably a size two."

"None taken."

Carly peered in the window of Bleecker Street Records, and I was grateful to rest and catch my breath.

"Of course Mom thinks it's all *because* the whore's a size two. Like, just because she put on a few pounds, their marriage fell apart."

As we walked up to my apartment building, Carly stopped and stared out at the river. "Wow," she said. "This is amazing— all the shops, the trees, the river—what an awesome place to live."

I followed her gaze toward the dark water, and with the ripples of sun dancing on the waves, for the first time, the Hudson seemed to bounce instead of crash.

We walked into the lobby. The warm air engulfed me, and all at once I was sweating from the exertion. "What in the world do you have in here?" I asked, dumping the bag on the floor of the elevator with a loud plunk.

Carly reached over and took the bag. She grinned. "Shoes."

"Huh?"

"Well, I'm not a big fan of clothes because . . ." She gestured toward her body. "But I love shoes. I thought you could help me pick which pair to wear tonight."

The elevator door opened. "Jolie is going to love you. I think she mourns the fact that I prefer my Easy Spirit loafers to anything."

"Please tell me you did not just say *Easy Spirit*," Carly gasped.

I laughed. "I kind of have . . . restrictions about what shoes I'll wear. I have weird toes."

"Weird toes?" Carly asked.

"Oh, they're a sight," I said as I opened the apartment door.

Jolie was sitting on the couch, rubbing her toes, a pair of impossibly pointy black boots resting next to her. "Hey, girls. How was your day?"

We sat down on the couch beside her, taking off our jackets and dumping our school bags to the side. Introductions were made.

"Okay," I said to Carly. "Show us the goods."

Carly unzipped her black duffel bag and spilled about seven pairs of shoes onto the carpet.

Jolie reached down and grabbed a pair of boots. "Gorgeous," she muttered, flipping them slowly in her hands.

Jolie and Carly swooned over shoes while I fixed us all a snack. Once they decided that Carly should wear a pair of brick red heels to offset her totally black outfit, the three of us ventured into Jolie's office for some makeup.

As Carly sat down in the chair, my phone rang. It was Lindsey. I walked out into the hall.

"So, how's it going with Carly?" Lindsey asked.

"Good. She's nice. And funny," I said. We talked for a few minutes, then hung up.

I walked back toward Jolie's room. I could tell from the look on their faces that the conversation had drifted from jovial shoe talk to something on a more-serious level.

"Being thin is overrated," Jolie said while using a brush to work foundation onto Carly's forehead. "I work with celebrities that sacrifice everything to achieve a certain size. It's not worth it."

"That's easy for you to say because you're so skinny," Carly said.

"Look." Jolie pulled her brush away for a second. "Being thin does not equal being happy. I promise you that. You want to lose weight, fine. But do it to be healthy, not because you want to look like the girl on the cover of some magazine."

It was funny, because most of the time I saw Jolie fluttering around talking about makeup and gossip and attractive men. But as I stood there in the doorway, witnessing her tenderness and compassion, all I saw was my mother.

"Hel-lo!" The front door slammed. Footsteps followed, then Trent was at my side, reaching down and caressing my textured tights. "Very gorgeous. Very red carpet. So much going on with the texture. Love it." He walked behind me observing my short skirt. "Oh, that's problematic. What if you have to bend over? And don't think of putting your cell in those pockets; they'll hang lower than the hem." He looked past me into the office. "What's going on in here?" Trent's eyes roamed from me to Carly, then to Jolie. He walked into the room, a scrunched-up expression on his face. He extended a finger toward Carly. "What's going on here, love? You've got this long, Laura Ingalls hairdo, total black, mall-rat ensemble, but then you're rocking a pair of Christian Louboutin red, knotted patent leather slingbacks. You're sending so many messages I'm getting a migraine."

Carly looked down at her outfit. "I thought black was slimming."

Trent walked closer. "Well, monochromatic color palettes typically are a good choice."

Jolie looked over at Trent. "Carly and I were just talking about healthy ways to lose weight," she said, giving him a serious look.

Trent crossed the room and rested his hand on Carly's shoulder, locking eyes with her in the mirror. "Somewhere in there is a fabulous little body just dying to emerge. Well, honey, I've got the answer for you," Trent said, bending lower to Carly's ear. "RAUL."

"Raul?" I asked. "What's Raul?"

"Not what, WHO," Trent said, looking at me. "Raul is my personal trainer."

"Really?" Carly asked, obviously interested.

"Oh, sweetie, the man's a genius. Look at me," he said, gesturing toward his broad shoulders and tight abs.

"Yeah," Carly said. "But I'm sure you had like five pounds to lose. Anyone can be a genius if they have good material to mold."

"Ooh, aren't you a doll?" Trent said, tapping Carly's hand. "I know. It's a crime I'm not skinnier with all the exercise I do."

"Waving a blow dryer around does not constitute a work-out," Jolie said.

"Try fixing some of these models with their foot-long extensions—it's quite a bicep challenge." Trent turned back toward Carly. "But the truth is, before Raul, I was soooo untoned. Tell them, Jolie: *flab-a-lab*."

Carly and I laughed.

"You've gotta see it to believe it," Trent said. "You want to come to a session with me?"

Carly's head whipped around toward Trent. "Oh my God, yes."

"Great," Trent said. "Jolie, give her my digits. I'll call you from the tree stand in an hour. Gotta pick out the perfect one!" And with that, he was gone.

Carly was beaming so much I thought her glasses might pop off of her face. Trent had appeared and promised to turn her life around like he was her fairy godmother or something.

And for the first time, I envied Carly.

chapter
twenty-eight

AS I WAS DOUBLE-CHECKING Ethan's apartment number, I saw Lindsey emerge from a taxi. She paid the cabbie and waved wildly, running toward us.

"Hey!" Lindsey yelled, leaning in to give me a hug. "You look so pretty! Ooh, awesome tights! Love the texture!" Lindsey was dressed in an adorable deep blue shift dress with a white wool coat, and I noticed her legs were bare despite the cold.

"Have you guys met?" I asked, turning toward Carly. "This is Lindsey."

Lindsey smiled, shaking her dark tousled hair. "Hey, great shoes."

"Thanks. I got them on sale last week." Carly beamed. Her face really did look sophisticated with Jolie's makeover. Her eyes looked brighter than ever, even behind her glasses—which Jolie had insisted she wear.

"Nice," Lindsey said, walking toward the doorman, who was giving us the once-over with an acerbic look.

The mirrored elevator doors opened and a group of scantily clad girls stumbled out, smelling of smoke and stale beer. They had their arms slung over each other's shoulders and were laughing loudly.

"Looks like the party is well under way," Lindsey said, walking into the elevator.

I looked over at Carly. She was nervously tapping her hands against her legs.

"You okay?" I asked her.

Carly nodded but looked like she was about to throw up.

"It's just a party," I said. "It's fun. Don't worry! Remember, Ethan wanted you here."

Carly inhaled and seemed to relax a little.

Lindsey smiled at Carly in the mirrored elevator door.

As we walked into the hall, the reverberations of the loud music shook the floor.

The door to Ethan's apartment was propped open by two unfamiliar people leaning against the door, kissing.

"Get a room," Lindsey said, pushing past the couple.

The girl, without unlocking her lips, pointed up toward mistletoe hanging above the doorjamb.

"Since when does mistletoe involve the exchange of bodily fluids?" Lindsey scowled.

Carly took my arm. "I think I need to find a bathroom."

"Are you okay?" I asked, worried.

"It's just nerves," Carly answered. "Sometimes I get an upset stomach."

"Okay," Lindsey said, taking Carly's hand and steering her toward a door against the far wall. "You'll be fine. Just take a few deep breaths. Emily and I will be right out here when you're done."

Carly slid into the bathroom.

"She doesn't look good. Her face is practically green," Lindsey said.

"I think she's really worried about making a good impression for Ethan," I said.

"Well," Lindsey said, pushing past the mobs of people huddled in the living room. "If she pukes, it's total social suicide."

I grimaced, knowing it was semi-true. I looked across the living room into the kitchen, where I saw Owen, Ethan, and Aidan flipping coins into cups. I waved my hand in the air and Owen saw me. He smiled his thousand-watt smile and waved me over.

"He's so hot," a random girl said to me.

Lindsey and I turned to look at the girl, who had her chestnut hair pulled into two ponytails.

She continued. "I mean Owen is like a god. How did you get him?" She pulled her one ponytail around to her mouth and chewed on her hair.

Lindsey gave me a look and mouthed, *Whatever.* We left the ponytail girl without answering and walked toward the kitchen. I looked back over my shoulder. She was still watching us, chewing her hair. So, I thought, to the outside world it seemed outrageous that Owen could like me. My spirits slumped. I followed Lindsey into the kitchen.

Owen pulled me toward him, leaning down to kiss me.

"Check you out," he said, sliding his hands over my textured thighs.

The ponytailed girl from the living room watched intently.

I met her eye and reached up to give Owen another kiss. *There,* I telepathically told the ponytail girl, *I am enough.*

Owen shoved a blue plastic cup in my face. "Drink?"

"No, I'm good," I said, watching Aidan walk across the room with a blue cup in each hand, foam overflowing at the tops. He crossed the kitchen to a long table and plopped a cup down in front of Andi. She waved over his shoulder at me.

"Hey, girl!" Andi said. "Have a seat!"

"Oh, I'm waiting for Carly. She's in the bathroom," I said.

I saw an unidentifiable look pass across Andi's face. Her eyes darted to the left, then back to the table. She looked down and massaged her cuticles. "Okay," she said softly, not making eye contact with me.

I followed her glance to the far left corner of the kitchen. There, propped up against the black granite countertop, was a large, white, dry-erase board. It was clearly supposed to be hidden by a cabinet door, but someone had pushed the door aside so you could see the whole thing. Across the board a grid was drawn in navy blue marker. Down the left side about fifteen guys' names were written. Dollar amounts were quoted in the next margin. It was obviously some kind of a bet. Initially I figured it was a sports bet like the football bets Owen always talked about. But then my heart stopped when I saw what was printed across the top of the board in big, block letters: CARLY.

The writing in the right margin was smaller and not legible, so I walked closer to the board. Andi's arm shot out and grabbed my sleeve. I yanked my arm away, my heart picking up speed as I approached. I could feel Andi's eyes following me. I pushed past a burly guy shuffling a deck of cards on the counter.

"Hey, watch it!" he growled.

I ignored him, squeezing in closer to the counter. My stomach turned and horror rose in my chest. I saw what was written beneath Carly's name: *Will the cow give Ethan a ride?*

Across from each guy's name and dollar amount, a prediction was made. How far could Ethan get Carly to go?

Dave—$500.—Kiss and run (for your life!)

Chris—$500.—Naked, above the belt

Ethan—$750.—All the way, baby, with her tent-size underwear balled up on the floor

The list went on and on.

I stood there frozen, trying to comprehend such cruelty.

Just then, I saw the bathroom door open down the hall and Carly emerged, rosy and smiling. I felt the air stir in the kitchen as all the guys noticed her too.

"It's go time," I heard someone say.

A blur of Owen's navy shirt swirled past me.

My heart was beating so fast I was sure it was popping in and out of my chest like in a cartoon. I looked over at Owen. He was staring in Carly's direction, patting Ethan on the shoulder.

Ethan grabbed a cup. "Better fill this up," he said.

"Maybe not, dude." Aidan laughed. "She might just be willing."

Ethan shuddered. "I meant for *me*. I need the drink, moron."

They laughed.

I scanned the room, frantically searching for Lindsey. I spotted her talking to a girl from her homeroom. I pushed through the circle of guys toward her. Owen grabbed my arm, but I pushed his hand away, darting toward Lindsey.

Andi chased after me. "Em, it's just a joke."

I whipped around to face her. "A joke?" I said, my voice rising.

"Shhh," Andi said, holding her manicured finger up to her mouth.

I stared at her in disbelief. "You think this is *funny*?"

Lindsey came over. "Hey, what's going on?" she asked, eyes darting back and forth between me and Andi.

"They," I said, pointing toward the guys. "They are getting ready to humiliate Carly."

Andi was quiet, looking across the room toward Aidan.

I grabbed Lindsey's hand and pulled her across the room to the bet board.

She stood there, jaw dropped. "Oh my God," she whispered. "We have to get Carly out of here."

Our eyes shot back toward the living room. Carly was attempting to walk into the kitchen but was stuck behind the kissing couple who had migrated from the front door.

I turned toward Andi.

She looked over toward Aidan, then back toward us.

I raised my eyebrows as if to say, *Are you coming?*

But she didn't move.

So Lindsey and I turned and left Andi standing in the kitchen. We shoved our way into the living room.

"Quick," I said. "Whip up some tears."

"Huh?" Lindsey asked.

"Just do it!" I commanded as we pushed the slobbering couple out of the way.

Carly saw us and lit up. "I was wondering where you guys were!"

I grabbed Carly's arm and spun her around, away from the kitchen. "We've gotta go."

"What?" Carly said, dumbfounded. "But we just got here."

I jabbed Lindsey. She sniffled.

"Crisis," I whispered. "Lindsey just saw her boyfriend kissing another girl."

"You have a boyfriend?" Carly asked Lindsey.

"Um—well," Lindsey stammered.

I yanked both of their arms toward the door. "COME ON!"

I know I heard footsteps approaching. I know I heard protests from the kitchen. I know I heard Owen calling my name. But I didn't stop. I opened the apartment door, propped it with my foot, and pushed Carly and Lindsey out into the hallway.

"Um, maybe I should just say goodbye to Ethan," Carly said. "He doesn't even know that I came."

Lindsey flared her nostrils, wrinkled her forehead, and quivered her lip. "I can't believe that jerk! And he just told me he loved me!" She let her head fall into her hands. "Ooh, I thought I loved him!"

Carly patted her back but looked longingly at the door.

"Tell you what," I said. "I'll run inside and tell Ethan what happened and that we have to go. Okay? You stay here with Lindsey; I really don't want her to be alone."

"Ooooooooh. Aaaaaah," Lindsey wailed into her hands.

I opened the door a sliver and squeezed in, not wanting Carly to get any glimpse of inside. I decided I would find Owen and tell him that I was really upset that he participated in this joke and that we would have to talk about it tomorrow. I started to walk toward the kitchen, then froze.

I saw the back of Owen's blond hair and his shoulder propped against the wall. With his left hand he twirled the chestnut-colored ponytail of the girl we saw earlier. Her hands were wrapped around his waist. As she threw her head back and laughed, Owen leaned in closer, almost touching her neck with his nose.

I stood there, watching my boyfriend fall all over some other girl. *I guess I wasn't enough*, I thought miserably, a well of tears filling my eyes. Then Jolie's words rang in my ears: *To those kind of men, you are replaceable.*

I whipped around and walked out the door.

Lindsey and Carly were squatting down on the floor.

"It's just that . . . I trusted him." Lindsey fake-sniffled as Carly patted her back.

"Okay," I said. "Let's go."

They got up and we took the elevator downstairs and hailed a cab home.

"**WE WISH YOU** A MERRY CHRISTMAS, WE WISH YOU A MERRY CHRISTMAS, WE WISH YOU A MERRY CHRISTMAS AND A HAPPY NEW YEAR." Jolie and Trent were singing at the top of their lungs, dancing around an enormous evergreen whose limbs were bending at the ceiling and protruding into the fireplace.

"Oh, Emily, you scared me," Jolie said, dropping an ornament onto the carpet.

"Sorry. Hi. Wow, looks like we had a visit from some elves. Is it me or is it still only December 5th?" I said, looking around at the huge, retro colored lights strung across the door frame.

"Don't knock the spirit, sugar. It's important to be ahead of the curve with one's Christmas planning," Trent said, laying a long string of red beads around my neck.

"Why are you home so early?" Jolie asked while placing a silver ornament on the tree. "I thought this party was *going to be huge.* Not that I was eavesdropping or anything."

"Oh, it wasn't that great," I said, and took off my coat. I headed to my room to call Georgia, ignoring their questioning expressions.

"Please tell me you're not locked up in a bathroom, ready to puke again," Georgia said as soon as she answered the phone.

I opened my mouth and the entire day's events just spilled out of me, starting with getting ready with Carly and ending with our fake crisis escape route.

"Wow." That was all Georgia said. And not many things render Georgia speechless.

"I feel like such an idiot," I said, feeling the tears prick the corners of my eyes.

"Why do *you* feel like an idiot? Because Owen was hitting on another girl?"

"I just don't understand. Five minutes earlier he was all

over me." I gurgled on my tears again. "I just thought he might actually like me."

Georgia sighed.

"And then the bet—the things he wrote—I guess I didn't know him at all."

It was quiet for a moment, then Georgia spoke. "Remember that summer when you and I decided we were going to bake a blackberry pie?" She said randomly.

"Uh-huh," I said, wondering how a pie would relate to my current crisis.

"And remember how my mom kept telling us to wait, that the blackberry trees weren't ripe yet, but I insisted they looked so plump and juicy?"

"Yeah."

"And then my mom in her snide little way said that if the deer weren't eating them yet, we really shouldn't . . ."

"Georgia, is there a point to this little trip down memory lane?"

She exhaled with exaggerated annoyance. "Remember how you popped a few blackberries in your mouth?"

"I do."

"And as much as it pains me to admit my mother was right, just because the berries looked perfect on the outside didn't mean they were perfect on the inside."

God, why did Georgia have to be so insightful?

I LAY IN BED later that night, thinking about how Lindsey hadn't hesitated to abandon the party simply because she wanted to help me protect Carly—someone who Lindsey barely knew. But Andi, on the other hand, torn between her loyalties, ultimately chose her boyfriend. And Carly gave up all chances of romance to comfort Lindsey, a virtual stranger.

How well do we really know anyone?

I had always assumed that Jolie was single and career-minded by choice, not because she repeatedly ended up with the wrong guy. And given Trent's focus on fashion and flair for drama, I was completely unprepared to see the softer, kinder side of him. Maybe I'd spent my whole life failing to see people as they really were. After all, Mom's letters and picture revealed a side of her I never thought existed. I spent every day of sixteen years with them, but did I ever really know my parents?

I thought back to the day on the cold, concrete steps of the Metropolitan Museum, lost in my anonymity. Maybe we were all just strangers, I thought, passing each other by but seldom taking the time to truly understand each other.

chapter twenty-nine

THE REVENGE OF MY MOUTH returned the next morning.

I glanced over at my unused night guard lying on the dresser. *I'm such an idiot.*

I gently pried my locked jaws open to slide some Advil down the back of my throat, then ambled out into the kitchen.

Jolie was standing in front of a frying pan. She turned toward me with a spatula in her hand. "Look! I'm making a healthy twist on the Egg McMuffin!"

I stared down at the frying eggs, turkey bacon, and fat-free cheese in the pan and at the plate of toasted whole wheat English muffins.

She scooped up the eggs and turkey bacon and cheese and layered them into a sandwich on the muffins.

"I didn't even break the yolk," Jolie said triumphantly.

I sat down at the kitchen table. Why did Jolie have to have her first successful attempt in the kitchen on a day I couldn't open my mouth more than an inch wide? I forced a smile. "Mmmm. Looks great." I took the heel of my hand and squeezed the sandwich down as flat as a pancake. Yellow egg yolk oozed out the sides of the muffin.

Jolie watched with a crestfallen expression.

I continued as if everything was normal. I broke a tiny sliver of the sandwich, slanted my head to the side, and gently slid the food between my lips. I swear my jaw creaked.

"Okay," Jolie said abruptly. "What's going on?"

"What?" I faked ignorance. "This is so delicious." Too bad my eyes were welling up.

"First you come home from your big party after like ten minutes," Jolie said. "Then you lock yourself in your room on the phone all night. And now you're acting all strange and robot-like."

"No biggie. My jaw is hurting again this morning. Just a little," I said, trying to act nonchalant.

"Have you been wearing your night guard?"

"Well, *most* of the time."

Jolie's lips straightened into a thin line.

"Don't worry about it," I said. "It hasn't been bothering me at all. I had a bad night. Bad night's sleep, I mean. I might have ground my teeth a little."

Jolie stared at me.

"I swear. I—I'm fine," I stammered.

"Exactly what happened last night that made you stressed

enough to grind your teeth again?" Jolie leaned forward on the table, inching closer to me.

"Nothing."

"Spill!" Jolie commanded.

So I spilled literally and figuratively. "It's just the kids here are awful," I started, tears already rolling down my cheeks as I told her all the details of the joke and how Lindsey and I abandoned the party to save Carly from humiliation. Jolie listened without interruption. I purposefully left out any details about Owen, particularly finding him in an embrace with the pony-tail girl.

Apparently, Jolie noted his absence. "So, where was Owen while all this was going on?" she inquired.

I reached over and picked up the top bun from the muffin sandwich. I started tearing it into small pieces, avoiding the question.

"He was in on it. The joke," Jolie surmised.

I picked my eyes up off the muffin and looked into her pale eyes.

"Look," Jolie said. "God knows I'm not one to preach, but I've spent my last day waiting for a sexy Mexican actor to call. I just hate to see you make the same mistakes I've made." She paused, threw her hands up in the air. "I know, you're sixteen! All I'm going to say is when you lie down with dogs, you get fleas. You know what I mean?"

What?

"What I'm saying is, before you go spending all your time with this guy and his friends, think about the type of person he is. You can tell a lot about someone by the company they keep. And if he wouldn't flinch about hurting sweet Carly, what makes you think he wouldn't hurt you?"

I sighed. This I understood.

As if on cue, my cell phone rang. I picked it up from the kitchen counter and glanced at the caller ID. It was Owen. I laid it down on the table, unanswered. Jolie saw his name flash on my screen. She reached over and patted my hand, then gave me a half smile.

After three unanswered phone calls from Owen, when I heard a knock at the door, I assumed it was him. I imagined him distraught, begging for forgiveness.

Emily, I was such a child. A wicked, immature child. Please don't walk out on me. I can't LIVE without you.

I would let him grovel. Perhaps I'd invite Jolie to witness his newfound maturity and humility. Of course he had made mistakes. A mistake to hurt Carly, but a bigger mistake to risk losing me. I fluffed my hair and opened the door.

"Hi," Carly said from behind a fuzzy black scarf. She unwound the wrap and entered. She took off her gloves, unzipped her coat, and placed them on the couch before I could formulate a thought.

"When I got home, I realized I left my shoe bag," Carly said, then pointed to her black duffel bag tucked into the corner of the living room.

"Oh, right. Of course, sit down." I went over to the corner and retrieved the bag.

Jolie walked into the living room holding a plate with the

uneaten egg sandwich. "Hungry?" she asked Carly. "I made it myself."

Carly eyed the plate for a moment, then shook her head. "Nah, I'm meeting Trent at the gym in an hour. But it looks really good."

Jolie beamed, returned to the kitchen, and started washing dishes.

Carly and I sat on the couch in silence for a minute, both of us staring at the sparkling lights on the Christmas tree.

"Wow, I'm pretty sure that wasn't here last night," Carly said, gesturing toward the tree.

"Yeah, Trent and Jolie decorated last night."

Last night. The words hung in the air.

Carly leaned forward, looking toward the kitchen to see if Jolie could see us, then relaxed back into the white leather couch. She cleared her throat. "I know what you did for me." Her voice cracked. "Last night. I know."

How could she know? Carly didn't exactly have many friends. Who did she know well enough to converse with between ten p.m. Friday night and eleven a.m. this morning that could fill her in on all the gory details of the unexecuted joke? I suddenly realized that Carly was crying, her head downcast and hands at her eyes. *Should I put my arm around her? What should I say?*

"I'm sorry," I said. *No, I hated it when people kept apologizing to me after my parents died. After all my grief counseling, shouldn't I know how to comfort someone?*

"It's not a big deal," I said. *Lovely, downplay her feelings. I really suck at this.*

I handed Carly a tissue and she dabbed at her eyes.

"Wh-what was I thinking?" she stammered. "That he could actually like me?" She gestured at herself. "Like *this*?"

I wanted to tell her that I felt the same way about Owen. I wanted to tell her that thirty seconds after I left the party, my boyfriend was on the verge of a hookup with another girl. But I didn't want to be a topper—one of those people who competes for the worst life.

I took a breath and tried again. "Ethan's a jackass."

Carly sniffled.

The water in the kitchen turned off.

Jolie rounded the corner, a look of concern on her face. She came over and sat on the coffee table facing us. "Hey, girl," she said to Carly. "You're crying all your mascara off."

Carly reflexively touched her eyes.

"But I'm pretty sure I've got a tube of brown-black lengthening mascara with your name on it." Jolie pulled her petite legs up onto the glass coffee table and sat cross-legged across from us. She touched Carly's hand. "I know, honey, it's so hard when someone crushes you. I've spent half my life trying to figure out why someone doesn't like me or what I could do to *make* someone like me." She looked toward me. "Your mom—she was amazing. She never let other people's opinions faze her. She just strove to be herself—be her best. I remember one day I cried to her about a guy who was particularly critical. She asked me, was I looking for happiness with myself or acceptance from others? Because if I spent a lifetime looking for acceptance, I'd never be happy."

Carly nodded, then turned toward me. "Your mom sounds like she was pretty amazing."

A lump formed in the back of my throat. "She was." I sniffed, the anger I'd been carrying around about the apology melting just a little. "She was."

chapter thirty

I SPENT THE NEXT WEEK avoiding Owen at all costs. Andi and Lindsey helped, even getting passes to take me out to lunch off-campus on Thursday. I just couldn't deal with talking to him. I wasn't sure if we'd ever really been a couple at all, if I was right to expect anything better. All I knew was that it hurt to even look at him. So most of the week went by in a blur of tiles as I stared at the hall floors hurrying from class to class, trying to focus for once on schoolwork. The semester was almost over and people were starting to cram for finals anyway.

Anthony arrived at Jolie's apartment at noon the next Sunday to work on our final lab report, which was supposed to be an analysis of everything we'd done the last two months. He was all windblown with rosy cheeks and a red nose.

"You look like you're freezing," I said.

"Nah," he said, taking off a black wool cap with an NY Giants emblem stitched across the top. "I love this weather. They say it might snow this week!"

"I can't believe it's only eleven more days until Christmas,"

I said as we took our normal seats at the kitchen table, spreading our notebooks and papers out between us.

"And only a week of actual school left before break starts," he reminded me.

It was strange to think that this would be the last time Anthony and I would hover over our calculations and crunch numbers. Chemistry Sundays had become a habit, something familiar and comfortable, like slipping into an old pair of pajamas at night. Even though I totally hated the actual work, I liked knowing every Sunday was devoted to this particular project.

My cell phone beeped. I glanced down at the text: 12 HOURS ON A PLANE WITH MY PARENTS! DAD ALREADY SPILLED PEANUTS ON THE STEWARDESS! It was all caps like Georgia was screaming. I laughed.

"Georgia's on her way to a Hawaiian cruise," I told Anthony. "Her family's Jewish and they always take vacations the week *before* Christmas."

"Hey," Anthony said. "Is your jaw hurting again?"

I realized I was unconsciously massaging my lower jawbone. "Oh, not really," I said, taking my hand down.

Jolie appeared, hair up in a ponytail with a bandanna headband and workout clothes on. She smiled at Anthony. "Don't you know that you're not allowed in this house if you don't bring goods from the bakery?"

Anthony reached down into his bag and pulled out a familiar white cardboard box tied with a string. He handed it to Jolie. "For you: a thousand calories."

"Score," she said, taking the box into the kitchen.

Anthony laughed. "Hey, how was the big party at Ethan's last weekend?" he asked me.

Jolie breezed through, her mouth full. "I'm off to the gym. Work hard. See you later."

"You're going to need an extra hour on the treadmill," Anthony called after her.

"It's so worth it," Jolie said, closing the door behind her.

Anthony looked back toward me. "So, did true love conquer all? Did Ethan and Carly hook up? Did fireworks blast, soft music play, and pink rain fall from the sky?"

He was being sarcastic, but I realized that he had no idea what happened. How was it possible that Carly, a student at Darlington for a mere two months, had the connections to obtain a full report down to every horrific detail in a matter of hours but Anthony, who had attended school with these people for his entire academic career, had no outlet for gossip even after an entire *week* of school had passed since the party? I remembered seeing him with his neighborhood friends and thinking how he had his own private world outside of the small, cliquish Darlington universe.

"Well, I guess you can gloat," I said. "You were right."

He looked intrigued.

I told him the whole story.

He didn't say anything, but I worried that he was judging me. That he was thinking: *These are your friends, your boyfriend.* I wanted to defend myself, to say something, but I couldn't find the right words. So we both just sat there in silence for an eternity staring across the living room at the twinkling colored Christmas lights.

Anthony was the first to speak. "Well, that sucks. For Carly, I mean." Then he pushed his paper over toward me. "So I figured out that part three of the compound mixture must contain mercury."

I let him show me his calculations and conclusions, but as usual, my mind was miles away.

LATER THAT NIGHT I called Owen. I told him that I wanted to break up. I couldn't face another week of avoiding him and saying nothing. As much as I was worried what would happen at school once we were no longer a couple, I just couldn't see myself dating someone who could be so mean to a girl simply because she was overweight.

"What's up?" Owen asked when he picked up the phone, as though nothing had happened.

"Hey, Owen," I said, pausing slightly and wandering around my bedroom. Finally I sat down on the edge of the bed and took a breath. "So I've been thinking. About how we've been sort of hanging out and stuff. And I think that it's time for me to, um, move on."

I heard him sigh. "Is this like a breakup call or something?"

"I guess so. I mean, yeah. It is." I felt awful and relieved at the same time.

I waited for him to say he was foolish, or sorry, or *something*, but all he said was, "Are you sure? Because I thought we had something good going."

"I'm pretty sure. I've done some thinking, and—"

"Hold up, Emily? I have a call waiting, can you give me a sec?"

"It's okay, just go ahead and take it. See you in school!"

And then I hung up, after the shortest breakup conversation in history.

I put in an immediate call to Lindsey.

"I THOUGHT WE HAD SOMETHING GOOD GOING? Are you kidding me? What a moron," Lindsey said.

"I know, right?"

"Are you okay with it?" she asked.

I thought about what it would be like to not have him waiting at my locker. What it would be like if I wasn't invited to all the best parties or how I would feel if I saw Owen walking hand in hand with the ponytail girl. "I don't know," I said honestly. "I just don't know."

chapter
thirty-one

TO MY SURPRISE, Owen was standing at my locker first thing Monday morning. There also was a circle of strategically placed gossipy girls, including Sammy Greensboro and Vera Stewart, at surrounding lockers, ears perked and waiting.

"Hey," Owen said.

"Hi," I said, going right for the combination dial, trying to avoid his ocean green eyes.

He leaned his head against the locker next to mine, finding my eyes. "What's this all about, Em? We barely even had a chance, ya know?"

His eyes were so soft. I felt myself wavering. I didn't answer, just searched for my history book.

"Look, if this is about Tara . . ."

I whipped my head around. "Who's Tara?"

Owen's cheeks flushed. He swept his hand through his hair, massaging his scalp.

"Oh," I said curtly. "I guess that's the girl with the ponytail from the party?"

"It wasn't a big deal," Owen said.

Heat rose in my cheeks. "Was I just a challenge? The new girl—someone totally different than the norm?" I slammed my locker shut. "It doesn't even matter. All I know is I wasn't worth being faithful to."

The hallway was so quiet I heard my loafers clomp as I walked toward my homeroom. I opened the door, crossed the room, took my seat, and planted my head straight down on the desk.

"LISTEN, I KNOW things have been kinda tricky with Owen lately, Em," Andi said at lunch later, interrupting my conversation with Lindsey about our Christmas plans. "But I really think you should still give him a chance to apologize and make things work. I mean, a million girls would jump at the chance to date Owen. Would you really want to throw that away?"

"I don't know, I—" I began.

But Andi forged on. "Think about what he's done for your popularity in this school."

I looked across the lunchroom at the fireplace. "It just isn't worth it to me." I didn't mean it to come out harsh, I just wanted to be honest.

But Andi shrugged, got up, turned, and walked across the lunchroom. I watched her exit through the patio doors, shiver from the cold, and wrap her arms around Aidan from behind. He turned and gave her a kiss. For Andi, life without her boyfriend and popularity was unimaginable.

I stared up at the festive silver bells strung across the ceiling. Without looking down, I whispered, "Why does a breakup never just involve the two who are doing the breaking?"

"I don't know," Lindsey said, following my gaze upward. "Silver bells, silver bells," she sang softly. "Soon it will be Christmas Day."

WHEN I SAT DOWN in chemistry class, Anthony handed me a thick stack of papers.

"You retyped our report?" I asked. "Why? I had my copy done."

He gave me a sympathetic smile, something completely unfamiliar to his usual teasing nature. Obviously, he had heard about the breakup. "I didn't change anything," he said. "Just, ya know, tidied it up a bit."

I flipped through the pages, feeling guilty that I had contributed so little to our partnership.

As if he could read my mind, Anthony said, "You've kept things exciting."

I stuffed my copies back into my backpack and passed the newly typed report forward. Anthony tapped me on the arm and pointed his chin toward the back of the room. "Guess she's not too heartbroken, huh?"

"What?" I turned my head. At the back lab table Carly and Ethan were smiling at each other. Carly whispered something in Ethan's ear and he burst out laughing. Mrs. Klein gave him an evil look, so he covered his mouth, but his shoulders were still shaking. Carly smirked at him playfully and handed their reports forward.

Does she have no pride?!!!! I wanted to march over there and smack her on the head. Her humiliation had prompted me to break up with my boyfriend, and here she was, making jokes with her tormentor! All class I was fidgety. I kept stealing glances toward Carly but never could catch her eye. I decided to wait for her after class.

When Carly walked into the hall, I grabbed her arm. "Hey," I said.

"Oh, hi!" Carly said.

Ethan came from behind, tapped Carly on the shoulder, then flashed her a peace sign as he walked on down the hallway. She smiled toward him, holding her fingers into the same V shape.

I stared at her, dumbfounded. *"What was THAT?* I guess everything's *peaceful* between you guys?" My voice was shrill.

Carly started to head down the hall, so I walked with her, even though my next class was in the opposite direction.

"I met Ethan at the library on Sunday so we could finish our chem reports," Carly said.

"Uh-huh," I said, waiting for more.

"Well, we had a long talk. I told him how upset I was. He said he was sorry for hurting me, and I forgave him."

"He said he was sorry, and you forgave him. That's it? You're going to let him off that easily? After *humiliating* you?" I couldn't believe what I was hearing.

Carly stopped in front of her English lit classroom. "Yes, it was humiliating," Carly said calmly. "But you know what? I'm glad it happened."

I gave her a crazy look. "What?"

"That night my mom and I sat on the couch eating Doritos and talking about how men will never love us. My destiny, I thought, was to be fat and alone. But the next morning I was at the gym with Trent and I had a total meltdown. And Trent said something that really stuck with me. It wasn't about my weight. If I walk around thinking I'm not worthy of love and respect, I'll never get it. When I'm happy with myself, no one will ever be able to shatter me emotionally again."

"TRENT said that?" I thought about how Trent had been so supportive to Carly. It's funny how just because Trent was eccentric and always cracking jokes, he always surprised me when he showed signs of compassion. But this wasn't the first time I had seen his acts of kindness.

Carly laughed. "Yeah, I know. But I think spending so much time with women has given him some insight into our insecurities. So after the gym, I called my counselor and scheduled an emergency session. He said this was a perfect opportunity for me to learn how to forgive." Carly averted her eyes momentarily. "I guess I still haven't forgiven my father for leaving. So, according to my counselor, this whole thing with Ethan is a *stepping stone for my personal growth*." She made air quotes and rolled her eyes.

"Man, where do they come up with this stuff?"

"I know. But I just decided—you know what? The man might have a point. So I decided to confront Ethan, and it was so freeing."

I smirked. "So what exactly did you say to Ethan on Sunday?"

The bell rang. Locker doors slammed shut and people from the hallway raced into their classrooms.

Carly smiled. "I told Ethan he was an ass."

I laughed.

"I told him that just because he was graced with over six feet of height and long lean muscles, it did not give him the right to put down someone less genetically gifted. Then I told him he was an idiot and totally incapable of passing our chemistry lab without me so he better get down on his knees and beg for forgiveness."

I laughed. "So did he?"

"Apologize? Yeah, he did. And he was pretty nice about it."

I smiled. "Well, I'm glad you feel better about it."

"Yeah, I mean, don't think I still don't have moments where I visualize Ethan's skull crashing into a metal basketball hoop." Carly smiled and swung her purse over her shoulder. "Hey, and thanks—for Friday night and Saturday—well, thanks for everything." She opened the classroom door and disappeared within.

I EXPECTED A SEVERE REPRIMAND or at the very least a little *tsk-tsk* from Dr. Reeves. But he was all smiles, humming Christmas carols and talking snow.

"I remember back when I was a little boy up in Vermont, every Christmas was white," Dr. Reeves said with nostalgia. He massaged my jaws, prodded at my teeth. "This is going to make you feel a whole lot better, hon." He handed me a case, rattling the retainer inside. He smiled. "But it only helps if you wear it."

"Okay," I said, taking the case. "I promise."

He extended his hand to me. "Now where's that pretty little aunt of yours?"

Hmm. "In the waiting room," I said.

"I'd just like to talk to her about some follow-up appointments," Dr. Reeves said, following me out of the exam room.

Jolie sat in a deep leather chair reading *InStyle*. She saw us approaching and stood up.

Dr. Reeves shook her hand, and I noticed he remembered her name.

They talked about my new night guard and follow-up appointments. Then the conversation turned to the holidays, the weather, tourists flooding the city. Dr. Reeves smiled a lot and Jolie played with her hair. They didn't seem to notice me or the mounting number of patients filling up the waiting room.

I excused myself and went to the bathroom.

When I returned, Dr. Reeves was gone.

"I wonder if he's that friendly with all of his patients' aunts," I said playfully.

Jolie didn't say anything, but she smiled, biting her lips a little.

We got into a cab and Jolie gave the driver our address.

"You know," Jolie said suddenly. "It's time."

"Time?" I asked.

"Time to move on. I'm at a place now where I'm not looking just for intensity and romance. I want to live with an everyday contentment. It's time to forgive all those jerks from before—forget all the hurt and give the shy kid an honest try."

"Oh my God, the dentist asked you out!" I exclaimed.

She smiled wistfully out the cab's dirty window. "The dentist asked me out."

THAT NIGHT I COULDN'T get the idea of forgiveness out of my mind. Carly, who was so willing to forgive and forget—even to bond—with the person who humiliated her, and Jolie deciding to let go of a lifetime of disappointing relationship failures. I couldn't help but realize that there was one blatant person who had not yet rendered forgiveness. That person was me.

chapter
thirty-two

IT WAS A SNOWY SATURDAY NIGHT when I found the answer I had spent months searching for. The ironic thing is, on that night, I wasn't searching for answers. When Jolie said she knew nothing about the apology, that the letters were insignificant, I believed her. Or maybe it was just what I wanted to believe. So I thought there was nothing left to hide. All I was looking for was a roll of Scotch tape to wrap Jolie's Christmas gift.

I was bundled in red plaid pajamas, my nightstand lamp burning as a flurry of snow trickled down and painted the Manhattan landscape white. Jolie had put on a brick red ball gown, twirled in a circle like a princess, and left for her fancy work party, which was held every year at some mansion on Long Island. Once she was gone, I pulled the small jewelry box out from my dresser drawer and dangled the necklace from my finger. It was a delicate silver chain with a charm in the shape of a lipstick tube. In my mind, I thought this could be a new beginning for me and Jolie. Maybe we could finally put the past behind us and accept that the apology would remain unsolved. Lipstick could be seen for what it was—makeup—not the instrument used to scrawl my mother's final words.

I laid the jewelry box on a sheet of silver wrapping paper and got up to search for the tape. I found none in the kitchen or living room, so I ventured back to Jolie's office. I rummaged through the large writing desk. The top two drawers contained bills and paperwork. The bottom drawer was locked. I'm not a nosy person. I respect privacy. But for some reason my heart started racing and I kept thinking about the hidden manila envelope filled with the letters from "D." Could there be something else to hide? I scavenged through the top drawer until I found a key and shoved it in the lock.

Diaries. Black-and-white-speckled composition notebooks and although I had never seen them before, I just *knew* in my heart that they were my mother's. I reached in and opened the first one. I drew in my breath as I saw my mother's slanted left-handed cursive. Something in me snapped.

I grabbed the books, clutched them to my chest, and raced off to my bedroom. As I skimmed through the black-inked pages, I had the strongest feeling of déjà vu. It was a feeling of fear deep in the pit of my stomach I had only experienced once before, on a summer trip to Hershey Park. On that day I was strapped into the hot, black seat of the Storm Runner roller coaster. As the coaster started its wobbly ascent, my legs dangled in the still summer air and my heart quickened to a steady beat. With the slow rickety buildup of suspense, my stomach clenched and my breath shortened until the coaster suddenly reached the peak, tilted slightly forward, then sat motionless for what seemed like an eternity. I teetered eighteen stories high in the air with the seamless blue sky fading into to the miles of green Pennsylvania landscape. My head spun with anticipation and fear. I knew that I couldn't stay at the top forever, because just like Newton says, all things that go up must come down.

That's how I felt on that blustery Saturday night as I flipped each scribbled page of Mom's diaries. Suspended. Caught between the *before* and *after*.

And just like on that roller-coaster ride so many years ago, I came crashing down.

Words filled my eyes.

Terrible words, like: *Affair . . . Daniel . . . Guilt . . . Guilt . . . Guilt.*

And just when I thought I wanted to cover my eyes and bury my head, it got worse: *Pregnant . . . Not sure . . . I count the days . . . I think it's Daniel's . . . I can't tell Mark . . .*

LIFE IS DEEPLY UNFAIR. It took real talent to make my life even more tragic. But there I was, not just an orphan, but a bastard child. I was so mad at my mother. I was angry at Jolie. I had no idea how to process this new information. I had a hard enough time with death. Now, to discover my mother forever questioned my paternity—it made dead parents seem positively trivial.

I wanted to call Georgia, but she was on a ship in Hawaii.

I wanted to call Lindsey, but she was at her grandmother's house in Westchester.

I wanted to pick up my phone and speed dial the Big Guy and have a conference call with him and my mother. I'd like to tell them both: *This is so not fair.*

Instead, I picked up the lipstick necklace and with all my strength yanked the chain until the clasp gave way and popped open. The lipstick charm flung off the necklace and bounced against the bedroom wall with a *ping*. I cried hysterically as I grabbed a pair of tweezers off my bathroom counter. I picked up the charm off the floor and with the tweezers I dug and ground until the little round diamond at the base of the tube was flung out of its setting. Then I collapsed into a puddle and cried.

I woke up in the middle of the night, disoriented, sleeping on the floor. I was eye level with the stack of twelve unused canvases, and I thought about my dad and his ten pairs of sunglasses. I wondered if hording was inherited or a learned habit.

I turned on the light and walked over to my bookcase. I examined a photograph of my dad. I didn't have his strong jaw, his golden brown eyes, or his slightly crooked nose.

I thought back to biology class. We learned that earlobes reveal a lot about genetics. Some people have lobes that dangle, while others have lobes that attach directly to the jawline. I turned on my desk lamp and squinted at the picture, bringing it closer to my face. I still couldn't make out whether his earlobes dangled like mine. Why had I never paid attention to my dad's earlobes?! I threw the picture on the ground. My mom's mega-smile beamed at me from the carpet. *How could she smile?! Knowing she was a cheater and a liar! How dare she put on a Carol Brady perfect mother image for sixteen years when deep down she was an evil, evil woman.*

The guilt shot through me instantly. My mom was always so good to me.

How can you be so mad at someone you love?

I took the picture of my parents and tore it straight down the middle, separating my parents from their embrace. *There,* I thought, *you don't deserve to be in his arms.* I took my mom's side of the picture and tore it in half. I tore those pieces in half again, dropping the torn remains of my mother's face on the carpet like a cloud of confetti. Then I fell on the beige carpet, buried my face in the remains of my photograph, and cried.

The next morning there was a chipper message on the answering machine. *Just wanted to let you know I'm staying the night here in one of the guest rooms. The party was great. Be home tomorrow!*

The sound of her voice, so carefree and guiltless, drove a stake through my heart. I turned and ran down the hall to her office. I headed straight for the vanity and started grabbing anything I could find. I threw pots of blush and powder, the fine debris puffing up into the air. I smashed bottles of liquid foundation, staining the carpet different shades of flesh. Finally I took every single tube of lipstick and pelted them out the window, not caring if there were pedestrians below.

An hour later, I walked to the living room, leaving her studio in disarray. I planted myself on the couch and flipped around the stations on the TV. *When Harry Met Sally* was playing on a movie channel. I pulled the afghan up to my neck. I watched Harry and Sally fumble through years of friendship and fights. It was hard to believe it wasn't so long ago when Jolie, Trent, Lindsey, and I watched this movie, laughing and dissecting the wardrobe and hair choices. That was back when my life was just about death and dying, I thought sarcastically. I remembered that day Anthony and I sat in the park and talked about the movie. I had just read the card about Mom's first date with "D"—Daniel, I now knew. Anthony had cautioned me against searching for answers. It's almost like he knew there was a secret destined to destroy me. He wanted to spare me.

I watched the dramatic climax of the movie, when Harry had an epiphany and suddenly realized that he loved Sally. He dashed through the streets of New York on New Year's Eve to find her so he could profess his true love.

For some reason, my mind kept returning to that day at the park. And Anthony. And all those times he talked to me about my parents and my grief. Truthfully, lying on the couch in that moment of despair, I wanted nothing more than to cry on his shoulder. I thought about how he was funny and smart. And I never felt nervous or uncomfortable around him. And how on our first chemistry Sunday the attraction was there, but in my delirious, post-traumatic-stress rampage, I pushed it, and him, away. And then we became friends. Friends. And in the constant melodrama of my life, I'm sure it happened slowly, but suddenly, with all the emotions raging in my head, I was bursting with revelation: I didn't want to just be friends with Anthony. I wanted it to be him that comforted me about my mother's apology. I wanted it to be him that held me and stroked my hair. I wanted him to help me with this new information. I wanted Anthony to help me find my father.

I tossed the afghan to the floor. Sure, my life was in shambles. Yes, my mother had lied to me and my father. Jolie had lied to me. It was quite possible my biological father didn't even know I existed. Things were awful in my life, but maybe, just maybe, if I acted before I lost my nerve, I could make *something* right. I couldn't pass up this opportunity to let Anthony know how I truly felt. I quickly smoothed my hair into a ponytail and slid some sheer lip gloss on my lips. I grabbed my jacket and purse and headed out the door. Just like Harry, I would dash through the streets of New York to profess my love.

Swarms of people hovered in the subway car. I stood pressed between an Indian woman dressed in a sari and a model-thin tall woman dressed in jeans. We swayed back and forth with the movement of the cars. Should I tell Anthony about my mother's diaries first or jump right to the part about how I felt about him? How would I profess my feelings? I could swipe Harry's line: *When you figure out you want to spend the rest of your life with someone, you want the rest of your life to start as soon as possible.* But I figured Anthony would probably bust me for plagiarism.

I got off and silently congratulated myself for remembering his stop without the aid of MapQuest or a phone call. I pulled my scarf tight around my neck. I walked past the deserted park and turned right down Anthony's street. The rows of brownstones were decorated with white lights and Christmas wreaths. Three rows of children stood on a stoop and sang Christmas carols to an elderly woman at her door. And that moment of Norman Rockwell holiday perfection gave me a lump in my throat. Maybe the holidays could be right again. Anthony would help me find the joy again.

A green wreath hung on the front door of Anthony's brownstone. Faux candles burned white light in the windows, and a string of colored lights spiraled down the front railing. I took a deep breath of the cold air and climbed the front stoop. I was about to knock on the door when through the sheer curtains, I saw two figures walk by. I leaned over to the left, bracing my hand on the flower box, and peered in through the crack of the curtains. It was Anthony, standing next to the fireplace and talking to someone who was sitting on the couch. His dark hair was rumpled and his hands were shoved in his jean pockets. My eyes filled at the sight of him. *Yes, Anthony! You've been right in front of me all along!*

Anthony took his hands out of his pockets and made a gesture as if to call the person on the couch over to him. A muffled voice spoke. I leaned closer to the window. I heard laughter. Suddenly, from the far right of the room, a figure came into view. Long, dark hair. Hourglass figure. A long, slender hand with red-polished nails coming forward to touch Anthony's face. Adrienne.

My hand slipped from the window box into the damp soil and crushed the pinecones. Oh my God. Adrienne leaned over and Anthony hugged her. *Oh my God.* His arms were around her tight blue sweater. He rested his chin on her shoulder. Her hair cascaded around his face. I flung my hand out of the black dirt, bolted down the steps, and ran as fast as I could down the street. My lungs burned as I drew in breaths of bitter air. I made it all the way to the park, then collapsed onto an empty bench. And my poor naive heart shattered into a million little pieces and trickled to the ground like the falling snow.

Why? Why is this happening? All the months of redirecting my energy to a new location, a new look, a new social status all to find myself back where I started: *alone. With no parents. No boyfriend. No happiness.*

I looked around at the people walking by. A woman chatted on her cell phone. *Yeah, I can be in Midtown by eight p.m. . . .* she said. I spun my head around to take in my setting. *Oh my God.* I was in *Brooklyn*? What had I done? Twenty-four hours ago I found out my whole life had been a lie and I ran off to *Anthony*??!! What was wrong with me? Anthony could fix my chemistry labs, but this—my parents' death, the apology, the discovery—this was *irreparable.* The weight of that revelation washed over me and I buried my head in my hands and cried.

I will never know, I thought. *I will never know my true father.*

Darkness enveloped me and the snowy air turned frigid as I sat there, shivering, utterly alone.

chapter
thirty two

I DON'T KNOW HOW LONG I sat on that park bench that night like a statue, but the chill got so deep into my bones I was forcibly shaking before I finally looked at my cell phone and saw fourteen missed calls from Jolie. I answered her next call. When I told her that I was in Brooklyn and needed a ride home, she asked no questions other than if I was okay. She said to stay warm and she'd be there in a heartbeat.

An indigo blue BMW pulled up to the curb. The driver's door opened and Jolie stepped out looking beautiful but frantic.

"Whose car is that?" I asked, expecting her to be in Trent's car. My legs had fallen asleep and pins and needles shot up from my feet as I stood.

Jolie offered me her hand for support. "It's Jacob's car."

"Jacob?"

"Reeves. Dr. Reeves." She opened the passenger door lock with a click of the key chain.

I sat in the warm car and shut the door.

Jolie walked around and got in the driver's side. She smiled. "He was making me dinner." Her smile faded. "*Us* dinner. He was making *us* dinner, but you didn't answer your cell. I called like fifty times. I was so worried."

"Sorry," I said flatly, looking out the window.

We were both quiet as Jolie put the car in drive and pulled away from the curb. We were across the Brooklyn Bridge and into the throes of Manhattan traffic when Jolie finally spoke. She didn't face me but kept her eye on the car in front of us. "You read them, didn't you?"

I sat there, numb.

"I came home and found my studio in shambles, the torn picture on your carpet, and now this," she said, extending her hand back behind her shoulder, as if to say, *picking you up in Brooklyn.*

I let her tally up my erratic behavior without defense.

She parked the car across the street from our apartment, turned, and looked at me, her lip quivering. "I'm sorry," she whispered, barely audible.

I looked at the huge towering building and thought about how we had parked in that exact spot three months ago. I wondered if on that day, Jolie had already read the diaries. If she had already planned to hide them. If she had calculated her deception.

I squeezed my hands into fists and exploded. "How could you DO THIS to me?!" I shrieked. I felt my chest cave in. I started to hyperventilate. "HOW COULD YOU LIE TO ME ALL THIS TIME?"

"I don't know! I don't know! God, what did I do?" She laid her forehead on the steering wheel and cried.

My chest was heaving up and down, my lungs burning, my eyes swelling, my heart breaking over and over again.

After a long time, Jolie turned toward me and softly whispered, "I'm sorry."

We walked into the apartment in silence. I collapsed onto the couch, still in my coat, and pulled the blanket over me. "All this time," I said. "You knew all this time and didn't tell me."

"I didn't know what to do," she said. "I could barely keep it together and you . . ." She looked over at me. "You were comatose on the couch shoving donuts in your mouth. I didn't think you could deal with *this* too. It wasn't just me; my psychologist thought you weren't ready to know. Maybe you didn't *want* to know."

"You talk to a shrink about me?"

"Of course I talk to a shrink about you!" Jolie exclaimed. "This is not exactly easy territory for me, Emily. I'm doing the best I can." Jolie took off her coat and gloves, then took one of the kitchen chairs over toward the cabinets. She climbed onto the chair and opened a top cabinet. She rifled around, then pulled down a spiral-bound notebook. She carefully tucked the notebook under her arm and hopped to the ground. She came back to the table and opened the book. The lined page was covered with Jolie's scratchy handwriting.

She scanned her notes. "Dr. Stiltson had this really interesting take on secrets. She said secrets are like stars. They blaze inside the heart and ultimately could be explosive. But there are two types of secrets. Small secrets, like small stars, will burn out. With time and space they lose their importance and simply vanish. No harm done. But big secrets, like massive stars, with time and constant fear grow stronger, creating a gravitational pull that eventually . . ." Jolie squinted closer to her paper. "When they get so big, they become a black hole."

"Okay, wait," I said. "Are you reading *notes*? You took notes at the shrink's?"

Jolie looked down at her page, then back at me, and suddenly with great release, we started to laugh. "Cut me some slack," Jolie said. "I was never very good at school."

The tears were spilling down our cheeks as we cackled. *Laughter through tears,* those are the kind of movies my mom loved, I remembered telling Anthony.

Jolie became serious again. "Dr. Stiltson really made a lot of sense. It helped me and I thought that maybe it would help you—understand—why your mother did what she did. Your mother was a good person," she said, her voice shaky. "She made a mistake. One mistake. And that secret haunted her like a black hole for the rest of her life. But she tortured herself and remained quiet because that's what she thought was best for you. And for your father. If anything, I think her silence shows how much she really loved you. She let that secret burn slowly in her heart for years. I mean, I get it now. I get why your mom went so overboard taking care of you and your dad so selflessly, because in her heart she was always trying to forgive herself."

The knot in my stomach tightened.

"We'll never know what was going through your mom's mind when that plane was going down and why she suddenly felt the need to beg for forgiveness. We have to accept that we will never understand why she did that. But Emily, we *can* understand how sorry she was and how that one mistake doesn't change the fact that your mother was a good and loving person."

Jolie closed her notebook and placed it on the coffee table. She looked at me, her green eyes watery and sad. "If you want to be mad at me, okay, be mad at me. But please don't be mad at your mother."

My lip quivered. "What do I do now? How can I go on knowing that my biological father might just be roaming around and all I have is a first name?"

"She never confirmed her suspicion," Jolie said. "She never knew for sure."

I looked out the window into the night sky. The snow was still sprinkling down, blanketing the city in a new, fresh landscape.

"That's why I kept the letters," Jolie finally said, following my gaze. "There's a return address."

LATER, IN BED, I stared out the window at the stars in the sky. Stars and secrets and mistakes, I thought. One mistake. My mom made one mistake. Jolie kept insisting that one mistake shouldn't change my view of Mom, but as I stared out at the Big Dipper, my mind kept spinning. How did that one mistake change who I was, both biologically and emotionally? Did it change nothing, or did it change everything?

chapter
thirty-three

ON CHRISTMAS EVE DAY, the snow was still falling and the entire city was consumed with the idea of a white Christmas.

"Are you ready?" Jolie asked, chugging from her Starbucks cup.

"I think so." I zipped up my coat and wrapped a scarf around my mouth. It was cold out, I thought, but maybe it would also be nice to be partially hidden.

We hailed a cab and I announced to the driver the address from the envelope that I had stared at and memorized for the last fourteen hours.

We took Lexington Avenue all the way up to the Upper East Side. I tried to let the elaborately decorated window displays distract me, but to no avail. My mind was spinning. What would he look like? What would he say? We slowed down to an apartment building near Lenox Hill Hospital and I wondered briefly if he was a doctor.

The woman who answered the door had a parrot sitting on her shoulder, a thick European accent, and absolutely no idea who had lived in the apartment before she did.

Neither did any of the neighbors.

"There's got to be some kind of website that looks back at address history," Jolie said on the cab ride home, but I was miles away, wondering how I could go on with such a permanent void.

Back at the apartment, Jolie handed me a chocolate donut and I sank back into the couch. *Christmas Vacation* was on TV, and when I couldn't take any more zany Chevy Chase, I reached for the remote, accidentally knocking the gray ashtray off the coffee table. I bent down to pick it up, and feeling the smooth ceramic made me recall the day I ran off to the Metropolitan Museum of Art. The day I searched for Mom's gallery to somehow be closer to her. I turned the cold ashtray in my hands, remembering the gallery. The spiral staircase, the diamond-patterned floor, the handsome man with the cleft chin stopping in front of me. *I'm sorry. I thought I recognized you.*

People always said I looked like my mother.

All at once I dropped the ashtray to the table, sending it clattering, and ran to my closet. I ransacked through my boxes until I found the photo of Mom and "D" at the Statue of Liberty.

Thick wavy brown hair, handsome face, and a cleft chin.

I tore out of the apartment and hailed a cab. I knew it was Christmas Eve and the chance of him being there was slim, but I couldn't wait another second. I had to go.

As we slowed down near 86th Street, I saw the light in the gallery was on.

Oh my God. Someone is in there.

I had the cabdriver pull over across the street. I got out and tried to collect my thoughts. I leaned against the cold metal cart of a pretzel vendor.

"Pretzel?" the vendor asked.

I shook my head. "No, thank you. I'm just . . ." I pointed across the street toward the art gallery. The door opened.

"Oh my God!" I gasped.

"What?" The pretzel vendor looked panicked.

I continued to point. "I'm not going to make a scene, I promise."

"Okay." The pretzel vendor nodded. "Here," he said kindly. "Lean under the umbrella so the snow doesn't get you wet."

"Thanks. Look at him!" I kept pointing. He was wearing a camel-colored overcoat and had his arm around a young pretty woman. "He probably makes a habit of seducing the young women who work with him. He ruins lives!"

"Sure, he does," the pretzel vendor said.

"What a player!" I growled.

"Scum," the pretzel vendor said.

"I mean, look at his hair! It's so suave you just *know* he uses a blow dryer!"

"Absolutely." The pretzel vendor handed me a pretzel.

I tore off a piece and ate it. As the chunks of salt hit my lips, I felt relief. This man, this *Daniel*, who was locking up the gallery door and going to spend Christmas Eve with his pretty girlfriend, there was no way he could be my father.

The woman leaned over and said something in Daniel's ear. And Daniel threw his head back and laughed so loudly the pretzel vendor looked up toward the sky. Looked, I was sure, for a flock of geese honking by.

And I knew.

Suddenly, I was racing across the street, the pretzel flying out of my hands, skidding on piles of slush. I marched up the steps of the gallery, one finger pointed in accusation, the other frantically pushing up my nonexistent glasses, trying to clear my tear-blurred vision.

"YOU ARE DANIEL!" I shouted.

He stopped, his arm slowly dropping from the pretty woman's shoulder.

The woman instinctively reached into her purse, clutched her cell phone. "Daniel?" she asked.

Daniel was stone still, a statue collecting snow on his sculpted hair. Then slowly he hunched down, extended his hand toward my face. He looked like he wanted to touch my cheek, but instead he opted to pull his hand back and cover his mouth. "My God," he whispered through his leather gloves. "My God."

You could see the comprehension cross his face, and I realized he hadn't known that I existed. He sat down on the wet, concrete steps.

The pretty woman looked back and forth between us. "What is going on?"

But Daniel ignored her, staring so intently at my face I wanted to pull the scarf up over my eyes.

"Jill," Daniel said softly. *My mother's name.*

I started to cry. "You'll never be my *true* father," I said.

The pretty woman slowly dropped her cell phone back into her purse.

Daniel pushed on his knees and returned to a standing position. "I suppose you're right," he said. "But I was never given a chance to be."

My heart was thumping, and I didn't know what to say. This was not at all what I expected. He was supposed to be a player—he was supposed to brush me aside and say I wasn't entitled to anything from him. "My father was a good man," I finally said.

Daniel nodded. "Yes. I'm sure he is." Then Daniel stopped, noting my verb tense. "Oh," he whispered. "And your mother?"

I couldn't answer; my lip just trembled.

Daniel nodded, his eyes shifting down. "I see." He reached into his wallet.

"I don't need your money," I started, but he extended his business card.

"Now you know where to find me," he said. "If you ever want to." He smiled a handsome but also kind smile. "No obligations."

I took the card, turned, and bolted down the steps and across the street, only turning back once to see Daniel still standing in front of the gallery, watching me leave.

chapter thirty-four

THE FREEZING TEMPERATURES plummeted further and much to the delight of everyone, the snow remained on the ground for Christmas Day. While there were no active snow-flakes falling, the mounds of white ornamentation lining the street were enough for the city to declare it *a white Christmas*.

As I fumbled out of bed into the living room, I was not surprised to see an insane number of beautifully wrapped gifts under the tree. I plopped down on the couch and watched Jolie scuttle around setting china on the table.

Jolie disappeared into the kitchen. "I'm making a turkey," she called. Her head appeared from behind the wall. "I've done some research." She grinned. "This time I'm going to get it right."

"We'll see," I teased.

The phone rang. "Hey. Merry Christmas!" It was Anthony.

My stomach flipped. I recalled my frantic rush to him for

comfort, friendship, and love. Of course, he didn't know of my manic attempt, but still, everything felt different. In my mind, I had crossed some invisible line. Could our relationship still be easy and comfortable now that visions of Anthony and Adrienne's embrace scrolled through my mind?

"Merry Christmas," I said, feeling embarrassed and exposed like he could read my thoughts.

"What's wrong?" he asked. "You don't sound like yourself. Are you sick?"

I didn't want to say anything, but suddenly there was a feeling deep in my gut, not unlike right before you throw up. I felt it rumble deep within me like an avalanche, then the words spilled out of my mouth without control. "I know my mother's secret," I said, voice quivering. "I know why she apologized." I started to cry.

"What was she apologizing for?" Anthony asked calmly.

I told him everything through hiccups and sobs, including my journey uptown to meet my father. "On the one hand, I feel relieved to finally understand." I sniffed. "I don't know; it's just so hard to accept."

"And you've known about this for two days? Why didn't you tell me? I could have gone with you to meet him. Given you support."

And before I could stop myself, I said, "I tried."

"Huh?"

"I tried to go over to your house Sunday afternoon, but when I got there . . ." I started to cry again. "You were . . . busy."

"Busy? What are you talking about?" Anthony sounded genuinely confused.

"Busy hooking up with that girl—Adrienne—you know the one with the really curvy butt and the long dark hair," I said.

Anthony laughed. "What the hell are you talking about?"

"I saw you. Through the curtains. I wasn't spying or anything, I swear, it's just that when I was about to knock on your door, something caught my eye through the window—it was probably Adrienne and her big swaying hips. And I saw the two of you. Hugging and groping and God knows what else. So I wasn't going to interrupt your little lovefest with my problems." I started to cry again.

"Good God," Anthony said, sighing. "Okay, calm down. First of all, there was no *lovefest*. Adrienne's my cousin. She has a thing for my friend Bobby. And he had just blown her off—or at least that's what she thought. Listen, stop crying, Em, it's going to be okay. I really wish you would have just come in. I could have talked to you about all this. You shouldn't have to deal with this alone."

Suddenly, I was horrified at my raw vulnerability. Anthony knew that when I found out this news, I went running to him before anyone else. He probably thought I had no friends or worse, that I was totally in love with him. "I have Georgia," I said defensively.

"She's in Hawaii. Come on, give me some credit. I do listen to you, even when you ramble."

I found myself smiling through the tears.

"What can I do?" Anthony asked. "How can I help?"

"Thanks," I said. "I don't think there's much anyone can do." We hung up.

When I walked back into the living room, Lindsey had just

arrived. She took off her coat and greeted Jolie and Trent, who had also arrived while I was on the phone.

Lindsey ran over holding a new necklace out for me to admire. "Look! My parents must have really felt bad about being gone—they left this with my grandmother." She held out a huge diamond pendant that hung gracefully from a silver chain.

"Wow! That's beautiful!" I gushed.

Trent and Jolie hovered over to see.

"Girl, that might just sparkle more than you do!" Trent said. He leaned in closer. "Ooh, Cartier!"

A blaring fire alarm sounded from the kitchen.

"Damn it!" Jolie yelled, racing toward the smoke clouds.

Trent shook his head and mouthed: *HOPE-LESS.*

We giggled.

Jolie reappeared looking relieved. "No big deal. Luckily I bought extras just in case."

Extras of what, we'll never know, because just then the door-man buzzed, sending up another guest. Then, before we could move, the door swung open and in walked Dr. Reeves wrapped in a long cashmere coat and scarf. He removed his coat, placing it over the back of a chair. He was wearing dark jeans pressed with a crease down the middle and a white button-down shirt. He was handsome. Maybe not movie star glamour like Jolie's beaus of the past, but handsome in a way to fluster a crowd of PTA moms.

"Hi, guys!" Dr. Reeves said casually. He walked over to Jolie and gave her a peck on the cheek. Jolie smiled and her cheeks reddened slightly.

Dr. Reeves extended his hand and introduced himself as Jacob to Lindsey and Trent. He patted my back with familiarity and said, "How are the choppers, kiddo?"

I nodded. "Doing good, thanks." There was something odd about seeing Dr. Reeves outside of his office without the hum of painful equipment in the background. But it was nice too, because in some way totally unexpected he reminded me of my father. Certainly my father didn't have his suave nature or his fancy wardrobe, but they were both easygoing and exuded a certain comfort. And I was glad for Jolie to finally have that.

Trent pulled out Scrabble, and he and Jacob started a game while Lindsey and I went to help Jolie in the kitchen.

We leaned over Jolie's shoulder. She was using a wooden spoon to fish out flakes of black burnt char from a lumpy substance I could only guess was stuffing.

"It'll be okay," Jolie said, talking more to herself than us.

Surprisingly, the turkey didn't look half bad. At least it didn't look so dehydrated and crusty like last time. I had started to wash the lettuce for the salad when again, there was a buzz. The doorman announced two more visitors. We all looked around at each other dumbfounded.

Jolie leaned her head out into the living room and glared at Trent. "If you ordered Chinese, I will kill you!"

We all laughed. Jolie opened the door, and no one was more shocked than me to see Anthony, familiar NY Giants hat on his head and several white boxes in his hand. Behind him, a woman who had to be his mother was holding a large bag in one hand and a huge centerpiece of festive flowers in the other. Jolie ushered them in, taking the bag from Mrs. Rucelli's hands.

Anthony reached for the flowers and put them in the center of the kitchen table. "See, Ma, I told you they wouldn't have flowers."

Mrs. Rucelli smacked Anthony on his head and spouted something in Italian. She turned to Jolie. "My boy," she said with her heavy accent. "He have no manners. These," she said gesturing to the arrangement, "are for you."

Jolie smiled. "Thank you so much. I didn't know you were coming," she said, shooting me a look. "But please, make yourself comfortable."

Mrs. Rucelli took off her coat. "My boy tells me you need a little help around the food. Me," she said, pointing to her enormous body. "I love food. So, we make a go together, no?"

Jolie smiled, shaking a finger at Anthony. "You talking trash about me?" she teased.

Anthony set the white cardboard boxes down on the table. "Not me," he said, hiding his finger and pointing over at me.

"I SEE THAT!" I said, walking over toward him.

Anthony stood there in his pressed khaki pants and navy blue hoodie. The outfit was so mismatched it just reeked of a battle between him and his mother. She won the bottom half, he won the top. My heart raced when I looked at him. Part of me wanted to run to him and hug him, but an equally persuasive part of me wanted to escape to my room and lock the door. We stood there motionless. Then Anthony casually reached over and gave me a hug. "Merry Christmas, Em," he whispered in my ear.

My eyes filled up, and I reached around to blot them with my sleeve. Lindsey met my glance and smiled. I pulled away and took Anthony by the arm to introduce him to Trent and Jacob.

Lindsey sat on the couch between Trent and Jacob. Anthony and I sat on the floor on the opposite side of the coffee table. Lindsey pulled out two more Scrabble wells and placed them in front of us.

Trent stood up and with a dramatic sweep of his arm flung all the tiles off the board back into the box. "Good, let's start over," he said, crossing out his and Jacob's tallies.

"Look out for the sore loser," Jacob said, laughing.

"Pu-lease! You were using all your fancy dental jargon," Trent said.

"Jargon?! I used the word *clean*!" Jacob laughed. He turned to us. "He's just mad because I was up by fifty points."

I watched Anthony pass out tiles and Lindsey offer to keep score as Trent and Jacob argued whether *schmooze* was a word. There was the sound of a food processor humming in the kitchen followed by laughter. Jolie popped out from the kitchen wiping her hands on Mom's retro apron and turned on the radio.

Christmas music filled the apartment. *Have a holly jolly Christmas. It's the best time of the year.*

I thought about years of Christmas holidays celebrated on Arbor Way with my parents. The cornucopia of holiday cheer, with stuffed stockings draped on the mantel and happiness in our hearts. I allowed a few scribbled lines in an old diary to somehow erase all my solid family memories. But in my heart, I knew it didn't have to. I could still hold on to that family image carved into my mind before the plane crash, before the diaries. But now, with my parents gone, could Christmas ever be the same?

As I sat there, watching Lindsey tease Trent about a misspelled Scrabble word, I leaned slightly against Anthony and he didn't back away. He stayed there, firm, like a rock of strength. And suddenly, it occurred to me: Christmas was no longer about model families and decorated trees and perfect turkey dinners. That holiday became a symbol of change. It was about crawling out from under the wreckage and rebuilding after disaster—making new memories and new families with people who fill our voids and make us laugh. Because as my sports-obsessed shrink once said: *The game must go on.*

Anthony laid down five tiles to spell the word *crazy.* He put his arm around me. "You're the definition, Em."

We all laughed.

Jolie and Mrs. Rucelli appeared from the kitchen and said that in about one hour, a *homemade* Christmas meal would be served.

"Oh, thank God. My Christmas prayers have been answered," Trent said.

And we all laughed. Even Jolie.

AFTER EVERYONE HAD LEFT, I gave Jolie her present.

When she pulled the lipstick necklace out of the box, she started to cry.

"The clasp is broken, but the jeweler said he would replace it. And I used Krazy Glue to glue the diamond back in, so that's why it's not so sparkly, but it is real."

Jolie held the chain up to her neck. "I want to put it on,

but . . ." She looked down at the broken clasp and started to laugh. Soon we were both laughing and I was telling her about my night of destruction.

"I have something for you too," Jolie said.

I gestured to the mountain of gifts under the tree. "I think I have enough."

She shook her head. "Wait here." She returned with a box covered in plain brown paper.

"It's okay to be hurt," Jolie said. "It's okay to be confused. This grief will always be a part of who you are. But one day you'll wake up and realize you didn't dream about the plane crash or think about the apology. And you'll know that you've started to heal." She handed me the box. Across the paper, written with a thick, black Sharpie, it read: *These have always belonged to you.*

Jolie smiled at me. "It's your decision what to do with this information."

Inside were my mother's diaries.

EPILOGUE

"NOW *THAT* was some New Year's Eve party," Georgia said, lying in her sleeping bag on my bedroom floor.

"That's how we do it in the city," Lindsey said, grabbing the pillow from under Carly's head.

"Still sleeping!" Carly bellowed.

"I'm still a little surprised I was invited," I said.

"Why?" Lindsey asked, sitting up. "People like you for you—not just because you were half of a wonder couple."

I smiled and tried not to look too surprised.

"Even Andi," Lindsey said, somehow reading my insecurities.

"I can't believe it's a new year," Carly said, climbing up to sit next to me on the bed.

"It's going to be a better year," Lindsey said, stealing a glance at the diaries stacked up on my desk.

"I hope," I said softly, thinking I was lucky to have such good friends help me through my crisis.

"No *hoping* about it," Georgia said. "I have *confirmation*."

"Oh, jeez," I mumbled.

Georgia stood up as if addressing a crowd. "After Sister Ginger..." She looked at Lindsey and Carly. "That's my psychic. After she finished telling me that I *should* mail my evil twin sister story line pitch to the *Rhapsody in Rio* writing department, I asked her if she could do a tarot card reading for Emily."

I rolled my eyes.

"Interesting!" Carly said.

"Very!" Georgia exclaimed as she unzipped her suitcase and pulled out a piece of paper. "Sister Ginger's tarot card reading for Emily Carson." She dramatically extended her arm. "High Priestess, Strength, the Lovers. *All upright.*"

Lindsey and Carly looked at me for interpretation.

I shrugged. "I don't know what she's talking about!"

Georgia opened her eyes wide. "High Priestess means secret knowledge. Strength means courage. Lovers means harmony and union. Sister Ginger's interpretation? Emily's heart understands, Emily's heart mends, Emily's heart loves. LOVES, Emily, LOVES. There's romance in your future!"

Lindsey and Carly clapped, and we all laughed.

AFTER CARLY AND LINDSEY left that morning, Georgia and I hugged goodbye and promised to see each other for spring break. Then she took a cab to Penn Station and the train back to Pennsylvania.

With all my friends gone and Jolie at Dr. Reeve's house, the apartment seemed especially quiet. The phone rang and startled me.

"Hey," Anthony said. "*When Harry Met Sally* is on TV. Want to watch it together?"

"Sure." I grabbed the remote and cradled the phone in my neck. "What channel?"

There was a knock at the door. When I opened it, Anthony was smiling.

"What? I thought we were going to watch it while on the phone..."

"Where's the fun in that?" Anthony handed me a white pastry box.

We sat down on the couch with our legs propped on the coffee table and ate crumb cake. As friends turned into lovers on the TV screen in front of us, I wanted to finally tell him how I felt, but I couldn't find the courage.

"What?" Anthony asked.

Just say it. But I couldn't. I looked out the window at the river. "Does it get any easier?" I asked him. "The pain, the grief?"

Anthony thought for a long time. "Sometimes. But mostly it's just different."

I nodded, still looking out at the rocky waves of the Hudson. "In Pennsylvania, I lived near the Delaware River," I said. "That river was so calm. Peaceful." *Like my life was.* "And this river is so turbulent." *Like my life here is.*

Anthony was looking out to the Hudson. He craned his neck to the left, getting a glimpse of the Statue of Liberty in the distance.

As I looked out to the proud face of Lady Liberty, thrusting her flaming torch into the sky, I realized something. The Statue of Liberty, the universal symbol of freedom, was perched on a small twelve-acre island in the middle of the rocky, turbulent

Hudson River. And suddenly it occurred to me: maybe that's because the road to freedom is never a calm journey. Maybe you have to battle the currents to reach the ultimate goal. Freedom from the grief. Freedom from the mystery. Freedom from the truth.

I had spent three months looking out at the crashing waters but never seeing the opportunity.

I got up from the couch and raced toward my room.

"Where are you going?" Anthony called after me.

"Here, help me." I thrust some of the diaries into his hands. "Follow me."

I couldn't wait for the elevator. I took the four flights of steps down at lightning pace and raced out the door and down toward the park. I crossed the bike path and the stretches of snow-covered lawn and reached the edge of the river.

"Maybe we should have put on coats?" Anthony laughed.

I looked into Anthony's soft brown eyes. "Do you know that one day I looked under my mom's bed and found three milk jugs filled with coins? When I asked her what they were, she said she had been secretly saving spare change so I could get a really nice prom dress." My eyes welled up. "And when my dad's mom died, my mom went out and secretly took German cooking classes so she could make all the meals my dad thought he'd never taste again. And she was a really great artist and art historian, but she gave up her career to be a mom." I swallowed hard. "That was who my mom was. These—" I lifted the diaries off my chest. "These stories are not how I knew her. They aren't who my mother was to me."

I stepped to the railing along the river, lifted the stack of notebooks into the air, and flung them toward the dark water. The pages fluttered in the wind and the water splashed over the inked words. They didn't sink at first but floated with the breeze.

Anthony handed me the remaining books, and with vigor I propelled the books into the air, watching them flap violently, crash, and float.

I was flooded with such a sense of renewal I looked up toward the darkening sky and yelled at the top of my lungs, *"I FORGIVE YOU!"*

Anthony threw his head back and screamed, "FREEDOM!"

Then I started shouting the word *freedom* too. Together we were lunatics but with only each other for an audience. We danced around on the snowy grass, singing and laughing, until the sun had completely set and we were all at once in complete darkness.

I reached over and took Anthony's hand and we walked back toward the apartment.

"You know," I said, trying to figure out how I could possibly thank him for being there for me. "I'm sorry about how I've acted. Things between us . . ."

"Oh, come on, Em." He stopped walking and looked me in the eyes. His own were dark and shiny. "You know how I feel about you," he muttered.

"I do?"

He stepped closer and whispered, "When you're around, music plays in my head."

My eyes welled. "Music," I repeated softly.

"Well, you know." He grinned. "It's the *Jaws* theme. Da dum. Da dum." He jabbed me in the stomach.

I laughed.

He grabbed the zipper of my jacket and pulled me toward him.

Then he kissed me.

ACKNOWLEDGMENTS

THIS BOOK marks a new journey for me, one that would not have been possible without my wonderful agent, Tricia Davey. Thank you for picking my book out of the slush and giving it a chance. Thank you for your friendship and commitment to finding me the perfect home at Razorbill. Thank you to my extraordinary editor, Lexa Hillyer. Without your insight and talent, this story would have lacked so much heart. Thanks for your direction, your dedication, and your patience. Thank you to Carol and Abby Crawford, the earliest readers. Your feedback was instrumental in getting me to the next step.

The foundation of this story is about family, and I'm so blessed to be surrounded by a close-knit family and circle of friends. To my parents, Tom and MaryAnn Lovelidge: thanks, Dad, for teaching me to dream big and want more. Thanks, Mom, for teaching me to work hard, set goals, and manage both career and family. Thanks to both of you for encouraging me to pursue this dream. Thank you to my in-laws, Ron and Kay Jabaley: thank you for your enthusiasm, pride, and constant help with the kids. Thanks to my brother, T.J., for your interest and input. To my very best friends and sisters, Jackie and Kristen: life without you guys is simply unimaginable. Thanks for always listening and offering your words of wisdom. Thanks for supporting this book as well as everything in my life.

But mostly, I thank Chris. Thanks for believing in me all the way. My journey started the day you handed me a laptop and said, *I know you can do it.*